"Francis Ray creates characters that we all love to read about."

—Eric Jerome Dickey

Praise for Francis Ray's novels

ONLY HERS

"Ms. Ray continues to cut a swath across the lustrous fabric of romance history with *Only Hers*. Her inimitable style, irresistible humor, and extraordinary talent grace the pages of her books with the delicious tenacity of chocolate fudge swirls on French vanilla ice cream! She is one of the few authors who never disappoint their readers." —*Romantic Times BOOKreviews*

ONE NIGHT WITH YOU

"Master craftswoman that she is, Francis Ray is gifted at creating heart-warming love scenes that never leave you hanging." —*Romance in Color*

"Ruth Grayson is a force to be reckoned with as she sets her matchmaking sights on Faith's brother, since there is no such thing as happily single in Ruth's world. The steam the lovers create is a pleasure to behold. Ray never disappoints!"

—*Romantic Times BOOKreviews*

NOBODY BUT YOU

"A story that tugs at the heartstrings."

—*Romantic Times BOOKreviews*

MORE...

"Not only does Francis Ray rock in this book, but you also see a whole different side of racing that will keep you on the edge of your seat."   —*Night Owl Romance*

"A wonderful read."   —*Fresh Fiction*

"Fast and fun and full of emotional thrills and sexy chills. Everything a racing romance should be!"
                —Roxanne St. Claire

UNTIL THERE WAS YOU

"Ms. Ray has given us a great novel again. Did we expect anything less than the best?"
                —*Romantic Times BOOKreviews* (4 stars)

"Crisp style, realistic dialogue, likable characters, and [a] fast pace."   —*Library Journal*

THE WAY YOU LOVE ME

"A romance that will have readers speed-reading to the next tension-filled scene, if not the climax."
                —*Fresh Fiction*

"Fans of Ray's Grayson and Falcon families will be thrilled with the first installment in the new Grayson Friends series. And this is done very well...told with such grace and affection that this novel is a treat to read."   —*Romantic Times BOOKreviews* (4 stars)

IRRESISTIBLE YOU

"A pleasurable story . . . a well-developed story and continuous plot."
                              —*Romantic Times BOOKreviews*

"Like the previous titles in this series, *Irresistible You* is another winner...Witty and charming . . . Author Francis Ray has a true gift for drawing the reader in and never letting them go."
                              —*Multicultural Romance Writers*

DREAMING OF YOU

"A great read from beginning to end, it's even excellent for an immediate re-read."
                              —*Romantic Times BOOKreviews*

"An immensely likable heroine, a sexy man with a heart of gold, and touches of glitz and color, [this] is as unapologetically escapist as Cinderella. Lots of fun."
                              —*BookPage*

YOU AND NO OTHER

"The warmth and sincerity of the Graysons bring another book to life…delightfully realistic."

—*Romantic Times*

"Astonishing sequel…the best romance of the new year…the Graysons are sure to leave a smile on your face and a longing in your heart for their next story."

—*ARomanceReview.com*

SOMEONE TO LOVE ME

"The plot moves quickly, and the characters are interesting."

—*Romantic Times*

"The characters give as good as they get, and their romance is very believable."

—*All About Romance*

BREAK EVERY RULE

"Francis Ray is a literary chanteuse, crooning the most sensual romantic fiction melodies in a compelling performance of skill and talent that culminates in another solid gold hit!"

—*Romantic Times*

Heart of
the Falcon

FRANCIS RAY

St. Martin's Paperbacks

This is a work of fiction. All of the characters, organizations, and events portrayed in this novel are either products of the author's imagination or are used fictitiously.

HEART OF THE FALCON

Copyright © 1998 by Francis Ray.

Cover photograph © Shirley Green

All rights reserved.

For information address St. Martin's Press, 175 Fifth Avenue, New York, NY 10010.

ISBN: 978-0-312-36510-3

Printed in the United States of America

ARABESQUE BOOKS edition / August 2004
St. Martin's Paperbacks edition / December 2010

St. Martin's Paperbacks are published by St. Martin's Press, 175 Fifth Avenue, New York, NY 10010.

10 9 8 7 6 5 4 3 2 1

To Monica Harris, my extraordinary editor who has extraordinary patience. Thank you.

Special thanks to Nina Yancy and Alda Pool.
They know the reasons.

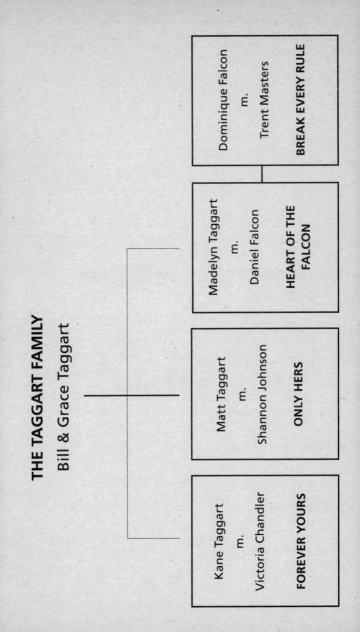

THE TAGGART FAMILY
Bill & Grace Taggart

Kane Taggart
m.
Victoria Chandler

FOREVER YOURS

Matt Taggart
m.
Shannon Johnson

ONLY HERS

Madelyn Taggart
m.
Daniel Falcon

HEART OF THE FALCON

Dominique Falcon
m.
Trent Masters

BREAK EVERY RULE

Chapter 1

Madelyn "Addie" Taggart awoke by slow degrees, turning from her left side to her back, then stretching languidly on the plush comfort of the king-sized bed. Slim arms circled her tousled head of shoulder-length black curls and rested on her pillow.

Slowly thick lashes lifted to reveal eyes the color of rich, dark chocolate. Leisurely she scanned her luxurious hotel suite. She was as impressed with her surroundings as she had been when she checked into the Hilton Palacio del Rio in downtown San Antonio yesterday afternoon.

Muted shades of beige and off-white suited the restful setting. Not one piece of carbon-copy furniture, assembly-line lamp, or misshapen, flimsy drapery marred the perfection of the room. The richness of cherry wood gleamed throughout. The lamps were heavy and brass. The draperies hung perfectly and closed snugly. And it was all hers for an entire weekend.

A smile lit her caramel-colored face. Life was good.

At times during the past three years, she hadn't been so sure. Working as a production engineer for Sinclair Petroleum Company had been the ultimate test of her professionalism and her determination to succeed.

She had done it though. She hadn't let the gray-haired critics on the job intimidate her, or the good-old-boy system discourage her. She had taken whatever they had given her with a smile on her face and taunted them to bring on more. They hadn't known she had cried herself to sleep more than one night. Not even her close-knit family had known how difficult it was for her.

There were countless times she had wanted to call them or simply quit, but something within her, whether pride or stubbornness or anger, hadn't allowed her to do either. Her parents had always taught her life was what you made it. You took the good with the bad and succeeded in spite of everything and everyone.

Those words had sounded fine through high school and college with her family standing behind her. But on her own in a large corporation, they were scary as hell until she remembered the odds her older brothers, Kane and Matt, had to overcome to succeed.

Being a woman wouldn't lessen her brothers' or her parents' expectations. God had given her intelligence, but she had to have the faith and the backbone to use it. However, it had taken a while for her to reach that realization.

She had thought she had been prepared for the cutthroat, dog-eat-dog world of business since she had done an internship at another large petroleum firm in Dallas. She had been wrong.

Then, she hadn't been a threat to anyone. She had been the baby sister of Kane and Matt Taggart, both respected men of some influence and wealth. She hadn't traded on her brothers' names to get the job, but the first week Kane and Matt had just happened to drop by to take her out to lunch.

Separately Kane and Matt could be intimidating; together they were awesome. Both understood being a minority and female; some narrow-minded people put limits on her as soon as they saw her gender and her race.

She had known such people existed—she just hadn't known how overtly subtle and demeaning being treated like a nonentity could be. She soon found out, but she also discovered she had whatever it took to show the intolerant skeptics she wasn't going anyplace. The lesson hadn't been an easy one, but she had learned—and not once had she run crying to her family.

Her brothers' tendency to watch over her was one reason she had chosen to relocate to Houston when she graduated summa cum laude from Texas A&M University. Kane had expected her to come to work for him at his cosmetics firm, Cinnamon. But developing products to help some woman's lipstick stay on longer wasn't what she had gone to school five long years for. Actually the research was too tame.

She liked something a little more dicey. Like designing the pipelines to draw oil and gas out of new wells at different pressures and depths. Accountability was high. A mistake could cost millions and your job. With her company finding and developing new oil and gas fields, she was never idle.

Oil and gas, once the boon of the Texas economy, became the bane in the eighties. The nineties had heralded a comeback. The industry was coming on strong. Energy was back, and Madelyn was doing her part to see that it stayed that way.

Madelyn's smile widened as she glanced around the spacious hotel suite again. She had done well for herself in the three years she'd been at Sinclair. Too well to suit some.

Laughter bounced off the ivory-colored walls as she remembered the shocked expression of her immediate supervisor when she was named Employee of the Month. She had been almost as shocked.

Only people in management nominated employees, and she knew he'd eat dirt before he'd do that. Even saying her last name seemed to cause Carruthers difficulty. She always got the impression he wanted to substitute the *T* for an *M*.

So naturally when she accepted the plaque and the expense-paid weekend to San Antonio, she'd given him her brightest smile. His mouth had been drawn so tight, he'd looked as if he'd been eating alum.

After accepting the presentation, she had learned his immediate superior, Howard Sampson, had submitted her name. Two months earlier she had been temporarily assigned to Sampson's team to help on a systems-analysis report.

Sampson was a hard taskmaster, but he didn't care about color or gender. He cared about results. He often commented he got his gray hairs the old-fashioned way—he earned them. She had enjoyed every minute working with him and had dreaded going back to work under Carruthers. Now she didn't have to.

Once she returned to Houston, she was being permanently transferred to Sampson's department. Best of all, she had done it all by herself, without the help of her brothers.

She thought of the bouquet of roses from her parents, the silk nightshirt from Kane and his wife, Victoria, and the ten-pound box of her favorite chocolates from Matt and his wife, Shannon, that had arrived the day after she phoned them with the news. Her family might not have helped, but they certainly were proud of her.

Life was good, and on this sunny Saturday morning in February, she was going to sample some of it.

Throwing back the covers, she bounded out of bed and headed for the shower.

There was so much going on around her, Madelyn couldn't take it all in. Her morning had been a whirl-wind of sights, sounds, and colors. She was turning her body into a pretzel, trying to make sure she didn't miss one nuance of San Antonio's colorful history with its diverse people.

San Antonio was doing its best to accommodate her. The city was in the midst of the stock show and rodeo. The area was crowded with jovial people in western and native garb outside the coliseum, intent on having a good time and eating as much high-cholesterol food as they could. With ethnic foods from Mexico, Germany, Czechoslovakia, and China, they weren't going to go away disappointed.

It had taken the rumbling of her stomach to remind Madelyn of the passing of time. The tempting aroma of sausages-on-the-stick grilling over a mesquite fire drew her gaze. With determination, she continued. She had gorged herself at the hotel's scrumptious breakfast buf-fet, and she had promised herself at the time that she'd eat a nice, sensible lunch. Sensible meant low-cal and low-fat.

Out of the corner of her eye, she saw a vendor spray-ing whipped cream over a funnel cake heavily layered with powdered sugar, then spooning on lush, ripe straw-berries. Her tongue circled her lips.

She might be having a sensible lunch, but she knew exactly what she was having for dessert. Looking around to note the spot where the booth was located, she contin-ued making her way through the crowd toward her hotel.

A short distance away on a tree-lined street, she noticed the sky had become cloudier. Hoping the rain showers forecasted for the afternoon would hold off until she reached her hotel, she grimaced and increased her pace. Each hurried step carried her farther from the crowd and the distinctive mariachi music of the strolling Mexican street band.

She cast another belligerent look at the rolling, dark gray clouds. Maybe she'd have to substitute strawberry-topped cheesecake for her funnel cake. She hoped not. Not that she wouldn't enjoy both; she just didn't like the idea of the rain keeping her inside. Spending an afternoon alone in her hotel room wasn't her idea of fun. And that wasn't the worst of it.

She could just imagine the thoughts of some of her friends and coworkers when they asked about her trip, and she had to tell them she spent most of it in her hotel room by herself.

A few might not be bold enough to say it, but Madelyn knew that every one of them would be thinking being cooped up in a hotel room on a rainy day wouldn't have been a hardship if she had brought a man with her.

But Madelyn didn't have a man.

She watched the laughing young couple in front of her—with four fingers of their hands tucked in the back pocket of the other's jeans, their hips brushing with each step—and admitted that finding someone special to love would be wonderful. The problem was her demanding job left little time for a social life. The situation was only going to get worse.

Sometimes she didn't leave work until well after seven in the evening. If she and her coworkers weren't too tired, those who didn't have family, to go home to would meet someplace for dinner. Since there was no one special in her life, she always went with them. In college she had gotten into the habit of going out in groups and saw no reason to change. So far she hadn't seen one man she wanted all to herself.

Well, she had seen him. She just hadn't met him.

Until a couple of years ago when she had seen a photograph of Daniel Falcon with her brother, Matt, she hadn't known Daniel existed. Since then she hadn't been able to forget him.

Daniel's eyes had captured her first. Dark, passionate, piercing . . . challenging. Then she had let her own eyes roam over his strong features shaped by his African-American mother and Native American father, shaped by time, shaped by life. It had been an eyeful.

Daniel Falcon was jaw-dropping handsome. She had seen handsome men before, had grown up with two men she considered unbeatable . . . until she saw Daniel Falcon's photograph. She couldn't explain the wild cadence of her heart then any more than she could now just at the thought of him.

The problem was since the corporate headquarters of Falcon Industries was located in Denver, and he was from Boston, she wasn't likely to meet him. She had looked forward to finally meeting him at Matt and Shannon's wedding since Daniel had worked a miracle in securing the ballroom for the reception, but he had been a no-show at the last minute. The thought that she might never meet him always saddened her.

Daniel Falcon had touched her in ways no other man had, and he had yet to touch her or she him.

Lost in thought, she didn't feel the first drops of rain. The sound of people shrieking was her first indication that something was wrong. In a second she realized the promise of rain had become a reality while she was daydreaming of Daniel Falcon.

Holding her tiny purse over her head, Madelyn sprinted for cover. Unfortunately other people had the same idea and had been faster to react. In less than a minute, her midcalf, gauzy white cotton sundress was soaked. With each running step, her white leather sandals slapped noisily against the concrete.

Realizing she'd have to find a place to wait out the rain or a taxi, she paused beneath the dubious covering of a palm tree to get her bearings. Directly across the street the deep burgundy awning of a stately hotel nestled between a travel agency and a French restaurant caught her attention.

Taking only a moment to check the traffic, Madelyn made a run for it against the traffic light. Surely in a tourist city, the hotel staff wouldn't begrudge offering her sanctuary.

The elderly doorman in a heavy black rain slicker and black cap circled at the crown in gold braid didn't bat an eyelash when he held open the heavy glass and gold chrome door for her. Flashing him a smile of thanks, she entered absently, noting the feeling of opulence and spaciousness of the lobby. Getting dry was uppermost in her mind. Luckily she spotted a bellman almost immediately.

"Where's the rest room?"

"To the left of the bank of elevators around from the restaurant," he told her, his dark eyes running over her in one encompassing sweep.

Madelyn glanced down and flushed. The off-the-shoulder dress was plastered to the front of her body. The lacy bra was no match against the rain and the frigid temperature of the hotel. Dusky nipples thrust brazenly against the fabric.

Flushing again, Madelyn headed in the direction the bellman had indicated. Head bent, shoulders hunched forward in an attempt to conceal her predicament, she hurried around the indicated corner and ran into something solid and immovable.

She heard a soft grunt, felt herself falling backward, and instinctively reached out in a frantic attempt to keep herself upright. A steel bar clamped around her waist. The spark of awareness stunned her as much as being anchored against something equally unyielding and hard.

Startled and confused she gasped, her eyes widening. Staring down at her were a pair of mesmerizing black eyes she recognized instantly.

Madelyn blinked, then blinked again. Had she somehow conjured up Daniel Falcon? The heat and solidness of muscled flesh beneath her splayed fingers told her this was a flesh-and-blood man. Her hands, pushing against an impressively wide chest to break the enforced closeness, stilled.

Her searching gaze quickly cataloged thick black hair lightly streaked with silver secured at the base of his neck, heavy black brows, chiseled cheekbones, strong nose, and the sensuous lips of the man holding her. They comprised an incredibly handsome face. The photograph hadn't captured the essence or the sensuous vitality of the man.

She wasn't sure anything could.

"Daniel." His name came out in a throaty whisper of awe.

From somewhere off to her right came an amused bark of laughter. "Mi amigo, is there not one beautiful woman in Texas you do not know?"

Madelyn heard the deeply accented voice, but she was unable to look away from Daniel's compelling features. After thinking and speculating about him for so long, she was finally meeting the legendary Daniel Falcon.

Midnight-black eyes were studying her just as intently. "Apparently I missed one, Carlos."

Instead of the Bostonian accent she expected, his voice was dipped in velvet and laced with infinite possibilities, all of them dangerous. Uncharacteristically she responded to the danger. "Only one. You must have gotten a late start this morning."

Deep dimples winked mischievously in his bronzed face. "Old age will do that to you," Daniel returned easily.

She burst out laughing. He was only thirty-three. Daniel's laughter joined in. She felt the deep, smooth sound all the way to her toes. Definitely dangerous.

"What's going on here?"

Jerking her head around sharply, Madelyn saw a beautiful young black .woman, her pouting red lips pressed together in disapproval, her dark eyes snapping angrily. It didn't take Madelyn longer than her next breath to guess the reason.

Daniel Falcon.

According to her brothers, women stuck to Daniel like cockleburs—that is, when they could catch him. Why shouldn't they? Besides being gorgeous and having enough sex appeal and charisma for ten men, he was a very successful and influential businessman. Madelyn could just imagine the arduous task of keeping other woman at bay while attempting to keep Daniel's attention.

She almost felt sorry for the irate woman. "Please put me down," Madelyn instructed.

"If you insist," Daniel said, a note of regret in his voice. Gently he set Madelyn on her feet. Immediately she regretted the loss of his warmth and muscled hardness and wanted to return to his arms. The unexpected yearning astonished as much as shocked her. Hastily she stepped away.

The woman gasped.

Carlos whistled.

Madelyn cringed. In Daniel's embrace she had forgotten her revealing wet dress. Embarrassed, Madelyn crossed her arms across her chest and took a sidestep toward the refuge of the rest room.

She had chosen the dress and several like it because they were light and airy, the full skirt making it unnecessary to wear a half-slip. Now, ironically, the same reasons she liked the dresses were now putting her on display.

Heat flushed her face again. She took another step.

A man's tan jacket settled around her shoulders and stopped at her knees. She glanced around to see Daniel, his dimples winking at her again.

"I always wanted to rescue a damsel in distress," he explained, a grin tugging the corners of his sexy mouth.

If she hadn't already been halfway infatuated with the man, his gallant gesture would have certainly started her on the road. "Thank you." She drew the coat tighter around her shoulders, wondering if there was a female alive who could resist his smile or those dimples.

"She's dripping all over the floor and getting your coat wet," the woman accused. "It's a Versace."

"Then, Lydia, I'm sure you'll excuse us and understand why I'm taking her to her room." Daniel's large hand on Madelyn's shoulder, he urged her toward the elevator several feet away.

"But you were going out to lunch with us," Lydia protested loudly.

"I already told you I had other plans," Daniel replied,

pushing the button for the elevator. "Give your father my best. We'll talk later, Carlos." The elevator pinged open, and Daniel hastened Madelyn in. The door closed on Lydia's angry face. A silent Carlos stood by her side.

"Which floor?"

"I'm not staying here," she confessed, pulling the jacket closer to her body. "I came in only to get out of the rain and dry off a little."

Incredible black eyes studied her for a moment, then he turned toward the panel. A lean brown finger punched seventeen.

"What are you doing?" Madelyn exclaimed, her anxious gaze going from Daniel to the panel clicking off the floors.

"You may be out of that rain, but you have yet to achieve your second goal." Folding his arms, he leaned against the highly polished paneled wall. "From your reaction downstairs and the way you're clutching my coat, you now have a bigger problem."

Madelyn glanced at a dangerously attractive Daniel Falcon, a certified stealer of women's hearts and common sense, then away. "I'm not going to your hotel room."

The elevator door slid open smoothly on seventeen. Madelyn remained unmoved.

Daniel pushed the button to keep the door open. "Whatever you've heard about me, did anyone ever say I took advantage of women?" he asked, his voice infinitely patient.

Her head came around to face him. "How do you know we haven't met?"

"Some women you don't forget."

A tiny shiver of pleasure worked its way down her spine. She shifted uneasily under his intent regard. "The woman downstairs seemed upset."

"Not my doing, I assure you. Now do we get off, or do we go back downstairs and I call you a cab?"

Nervously she chewed on her lower lip. "I don't suppose I could keep your coat, could I?"

"You can keep the coat until you're ready to give it up. I wouldn't want you to think you needed rescuing from me as well," he told her with the same patience he had displayed earlier.

It wasn't fear she was feeling, but something totally different and new. Her problem. Her brothers trusted this man. He wasn't about to try and take advantage of her or any other woman. He didn't have to. Women fought for the chance to get his attention and be in his bed. The angry woman downstairs was a case in point.

Madelyn shivered again from the cold, from something she wasn't ready to examine too closely. One thing she couldn't ignore was the wet dress clinging to her body like a second skin.

Water ran in silent rivulets from her hair down the sides of her face. More water dripped from the hem of her dress to the carpeted floor. Irresistible she was not. She stepped off the elevator.

Lightly grasping her elbow through his coat, Daniel led her down the wide, carpeted hallway to his room. Opening the door with his plastic key, he stepped back.

Swallowing, Madelyn slowly entered. One step inside, she knew her room was nothing compared to Daniel's suite. Her feet sank into lush white carpet. Chinese art graced the walls, and art deco pieces sat on the intricately carved entry table.

Wide-eyed, she stared up into Daniel's bronzed face. "I can't."

Black brows drew together. "I thought we had settled that you were safe."

She shook her head, then stopped and flushed again

as water sprayed the front of his cream-colored shirt. "It's not that. I'll mess up the place."

Relief washed over his handsome face. "I'll leave a generous tip for the maid. Come on, let's get you into something dry."

Madelyn was so shocked by what he had said that she didn't resist the strong hand propelling her past the spacious living room with a dining table seating eight into a bedroom that screamed luxury and comfort.

"There's a bathrobe on the door. Do you want coffee, tea, or chocolate?"

Trembling fingers clutched his coat. "Chocolate."

Nodding, he gently but firmly urged her inside the bathroom. "I think you'll find everything you need." Smiling, he closed the door.

For a long moment Madelyn simply stared at the door. Trusting Daniel was one thing—taking off her clothes in his bathroom was another. Swallowing nervously, she glanced around and gasped at her reflection in the immense mirror.

She had seen drowned rats who looked better. Rain had taken the curls from her hair, the light makeup from her face.

It didn't take much to remember the well turned out and beautiful Lydia from downstairs and her elegance in a bright yellow silk sheath. Of the two of them, Madelyn had to admit the other woman would be chosen hands down. Daniel was only being nice. The same way he had been nice to her sister-in-law when she had needed rescuing.

Shannon had told Madelyn on more than one occasion how protective and solicitous of her Daniel had been when they first met. At the time Shannon had been in love with Madelyn's stubborn, hardheaded brother, and he had been fighting it all the way.

Matt had tried to deny his feelings for Shannon, but that hadn't stopped him from being intensely jealous of Daniel. After Matt came to his senses, he realized all Daniel had offered Shannon was friendship when she had needed it the most.

Madelyn knew when she fell in love, she'd be more like Kane. From the first moment her oldest brother had beheld Victoria, he'd known she would be important in his life. Their first kiss sealed their fate. Falling in love for Madelyn would be just as simple and satisfying.

A knock sounded on the bathroom door. "Someone's here to pick up your things."

"Just a minute," she called. She was a grown woman, for goodness' sake. Going back downstairs and waiting for a taxi, dripping water all the way, was idiotic when she didn't have to. Daniel was an honorable man.

Taking off the coat, she reached for the elastic shoulders of the white dress. Quickly pulling her arms free, she pushed the clinging dress down over her legs and stepped out. Making sure she didn't look in the mirror again, she pulled on the robe and tied it securely around her waist.

Cracking the door slightly, she held out the dress wrapped in a towel. Seeing his large hands close around the bundle almost had her snatching it back. Instead she closed the door. Some of her friends would laugh themselves silly if they knew how nervous she was.

Daniel wasn't going to see any more of her now than he had before. In fact, he was going to see less. It was just the idea that he knew she was taking off her dress that had her so jittery.

Moments later another knock sounded on the door. "Was that all you wanted to send?"

A wave of heat swept from her breasts to her cheeks. "Yes," she said crisply.

His answering chuckle was part teasing, part sinful, and wholly intriguing. "Just checking. Hurry up or your chocolate will be cold."

The scoundrel! Madelyn thought, but she was smiling. She glanced into the mirror, and her heart sank. She looked like a lost waif, a very wet lost waif.

Why couldn't she have met Daniel when she was dry and had a smidgen of makeup on? She might not want her name added to his long list of past lady friends, but that didn't mean she didn't want him to find her attractive.

Fat chance she had of that happening now. Taking a towel from the roll on the marbled vanity, she mopped up the water from the floor.

Chapter 2

She looked adorable standing in the door of his bedroom in the oversized white bathrobe. Adorable wasn't a word Daniel equated with women in his life, but it seemed to fit the hesitant woman staring at him with huge chocolate eyes.

"I was beginning to think I'd have to drink all this chocolate by myself," Daniel said, hoping to ease some of her obvious tension.

"I thought about letting you," came the soft reply.

Daniel smiled. He had been doing that a lot since the woman now chewing on her bottom lip had literally fallen into his arms. "I'm glad you didn't. Have a seat and I'll pour."

Clutching the neck of the robe, she crossed the room. Toenails painted a deep burgundy emerged from beneath the dragging hem with each step. Gracefully she sank into one of the four easy chairs positioned around the coffee table.

"Why don't you put your feet up?" he asked her, pouring her chocolate and handing it to her.

"This is fine, thank you." The cup and saucer rattled slightly in her hands. "How long will it be before my dress is ready?"

"Soon." He took a seat next to her. Obviously she wasn't used to sitting around in a robe in front of a man. On one hand he was pleased; on the other he was hoping to change that. "I told them to put a rush on it."

A shy smile flickered across her beautiful face. "Thank you. You've been very kind."

"I try to take care of things that are important to me."

Her smile slipped a notch. "Octavia was certainly right about you being the silver-tongued devil."

He jerked upright in his chair. "Octavia. Octavia Ralston, Matt Taggart's housekeeper?"

"The one and only."

"You aren't one of her granddaughters or some-thing, are you?" he asked. *Please, don't let her say yes,* he thought fervently.

"No. Why?"

Relieved, he settled back in his chair. "Just check-ing. Is that who you heard about me from?"

For a few moments she stared into her cup, then lifted her head turbaned in a white bath towel. "Actually I've heard about you from a number of people."

"Such as?" Daniel questioned, uneasiness creeping back over him.

"First from Shannon—then of course Matt had to put in his two cents' worth. Kane said very little, but Victoria added a few points." She sipped her chocolate. "Cleve was almost as closemouthed as Kane, but Octa-via talked enough for all of them."

"Who are you?"

"Can't you guess?" she asked, setting her cup aside.

He studied her beautiful caramel-colored face again, the winged brows, the lush lashes, the supple lips, the sparkles in the deep eyes a man could get lost gazing into. More than that, he recalled what she had said. The

Taggarts weren't given to gossip; neither were Cleve or Octavia.

That left one damning and unwanted answer. "You can't be Kane and Matt's little sister."

She grinned impishly at him. "And why not?"

"Because little sisters don't look like you!" he said almost accusingly. The moment the words were out of his mouth, he thought of Dominique. His wandering younger sister created a minor stir wherever she went. Presently she was in Paris doing a photo shoot—only this time she was behind the camera instead of in front of it.

Daniel's guest laughed, a full, throaty sound that delighted and annoyed him at the same time because he knew he wasn't going to hear it while she was lying next to him in bed. "Oh, Daniel, I believe you've given me a compliment. But little sisters do grow up."

His hot gaze raked her body again. He remembered the lushness of her breasts—the soft curves of her body that the wet, clinging dress made impossible to ignore—and silently groaned. That was putting it mildly.

She held out her hand. "Madelyn June Taggart."

Daniel rose to take her small hand in his, noting the fine bone structure, the softness, the unexpected jolt of awareness. "I thought they said your name was Addie."

Madelyn made a face. "As a child I had difficulty pronouncing my name and left off the *M* and the last syllable. I refused to answer to anything but the mangled form of my name, Addie. Since graduation from college, I've refused to answer to anything except my given name."

A slight smile tilted the corner of his mouth. "Stubborn just like your brothers, huh?"

"I choose to see it as determined."

His expression became grim. "When I asked Matt about you, he said they were still trying to get your teeth straight."

Pulling her hand free, she showed him perfect white teeth.

Both hands on his hips, Daniel scowled. "He really had me going."

"You and every male over the age of eighteen. What is it they say about rogues and rakes making poor husbands? They make even worse older brothers." Wrinkling her nose, she pulled her feet under her.

Daniel saw a flash of smooth brown leg and seriously thought of giving Matt that broken nose they always joked about.

"He probably told you I was nearsighted, kept my head buried in a book, and was so shy I seldom went out in public." Madelyn folded her arms. "Kane's not as bad, but they're both overprotective."

Daniel finally reclaimed his seat. "That's like saying a hurricane is a strong wind."

"Matt doesn't usually lay it on so thick. Your reputation must be worse than they let on or even Octavia suspects."

The words were said teasingly, but from the way she looked at him, he suspected she was half convinced he couldn't make a step without tripping over a woman. He usually didn't care what people thought of him, but the woman across from him made him think differently.

"Since the only time I met Octavia was shortly before Matt and Shannon's engagement, I don't suppose what she had to say was too complimentary," he explained.

Those perfect white teeth flashed. "Actually Octavia likes you. Matt likes you, too, as long as you're not within a hundred miles of Shannon."

"I never trespass. Matt should have remembered I have certain rules I live by. Rules I never break," Daniel said. "You have chocolate on your upper lip."

Madelyn ran a finger across the area, then flicked her tongue over her upper lip. "Did I get it?"

"Yes," Daniel said, shifting restlessly in his chair. He had rules he lived by, and he had never been tempted to break them. Until now.

He was being tempted now to get up and taste the chocolate on her lips and go from there until he intimately knew the taste and shape of every inch of her body.

"You were dealing with the old Matt," Madelyn told him. "Marriage agrees with him. I've never seen him happier."

"I hope it lasts," Daniel replied, glad they were on a subject guaranteed to cool down his blood.

Madelyn frowned. "Why shouldn't it? They both love and respect each other very much."

"Sometimes love isn't enough," he said.

Her frown deepened. "You can't mean that?"

"I do."

She shook her head. "If Matt could change, there's hope for every man. He thought love and marriage wasn't for him until he met and fell in love with Shannon." She tilted her head and openly studied him. "The same thing will happen to you. You'll probably fight harder than he did, but you'll lose."

He crossed his arms across his broad chest. "You sound like you're looking forward to my downfall."

She flushed and clasped her hands in her lap. "I-I simply meant I believe in love and think people are happier in love. Matt is proof that love can change anyone."

"Has love changed you?" Daniel asked, unfolding his

arms and leaning forward to hear her answer with more interest than he cared to admit.

Her head ducked. "I haven't found him yet."

"But you believe he's out there?"

Her head lifted. Brown eyes met his with boundless assurance. "With all my heart."

Somehow the idea of some faceless man waiting for Madelyn didn't set well with Daniel. That man would have the right to slide the thick robe off and lay claim to her silken body.

But he could never be that man.

"You're frowning. I'm sorry." She shifted uneasily in her chair. "After all you've done for me, I didn't mean to offend you."

"You didn't."

A knock sounded on the door. Grateful, he rose. It was past time to send Madelyn on her way before he did or said something they'd both regret. "It must be your dress."

Instead of a bellhop, an enraged Lydia stood in the hallway. Without a word she brushed by him as if she had every right to do so. Tight-lipped and apologetic, Carlos slowly followed.

At another time Daniel would have put a stop to Lydia's nonsense. Presently he needed a buffer.

"Do come in," he drawled and closed the door.

"Just as I thought," Lydia snapped. "Why isn't she in her room?"

Large brown eyes sought Daniel's. Madelyn's delicate hand went to the collar of her robe. Daniel might need a buffer between him and Madelyn, but he'd be damned if he'd stand by and see her embarrassed.

"I wasn't aware that either I or my guest had to give you an explanation for our actions." Stepping around the other woman, he went to stand by Madelyn.

"How heroic, Daniel. Apparently you didn't waste any time getting to know each other better," Lydia said snidely, glaring at Madelyn.

"Not as much as we would have liked before you arrived," Madelyn said, surprising herself by the loaded innuendo. Her hand left the collar of the robe to rest negligently in her lap.

Something about the haughty arrogance of the woman grated on Madelyn's nerves. She didn't dare let herself think it was because Lydia's presence made Madelyn feel even more drab and unattractive in front of Daniel.

Daniel's head jerked toward the breathy sound of Madelyn's voice. He blinked in amazement, then grinned. Perhaps she wasn't the innocent he thought. One thing he was sure of was that being around two strong-willed, no-crap-taking men had apparently rubbed off on their little sister.

Carlos stopped pretending to study the watercolor landscape and instead studied Madelyn.

Lydia's scarlet lips clamped tightly at seeing both men's attention shift to another woman. Perfectly manicured nails, the same bright red as her lips, flexed in agitation on the gold chain of her handbag.

"Daniel and I were just having some chocolate, would you like to join us?" Madelyn asked, uncurling from the chair and reaching for the pot.

"I don't want any chocolate," Lydia snapped.

Madelyn straightened. "So, Lydia, what exactly is it you want?"

The woman turned toward Daniel, her face unexpectedly softening. "So you've been talking about me."

"Sorry to disappoint you, Lydia, but your name never came up," Daniel answered truthfully.

A frown marred the woman's beautiful face. "But how did she know my name?"

"I have a knack for remembering names. Yours and Carlos's were mentioned downstairs," Madelyn told her.

"And what is yours?" Lydia flung.

Madelyn pushed to her feet. This waspish woman would never get a man like Daniel. She probably didn't even notice Carlos's longing looks at her. He was a good-looking guy with warm brown eyes.

"Madelyn Taggart." This time she didn't offer her hand. She knew it would be ignored.

Lydia's expression went from sneering to speculative. "You're related to Matt and Kane Taggart?"

Madelyn hadn't expected the woman to know her brothers. A moment of uneasiness swept through her. If either found out she was in Daniel's room in a bathrobe, she was in for a hard time—and Daniel was looking at a possible trip to the emergency room. "Do you know them?"

Lydia smiled with pure malice. "No, but I have heard of them. They're Daniel's friends, aren't they?"

Not knowing where the conversation was leading, Madelyn said, "Yes."

Lydia laughed. The harsh crackling sound coming from the mouth of such a beautiful woman was unnerving.

Still smiling, Lydia faced Daniel. "You didn't know who she was in the lobby, did you?" She continued as if she didn't expect an answer. "Of course not, or you wouldn't have rushed her up here." Laughter erupted again. "Now you will know how it feels."

Continuing to smile, she turned to Madelyn. "My family has controlling interest in this hotel. If there is anything you require, please don't hesitate to ask. I'll leave word at the desk."

Madelyn couldn't understand the sudden change in the woman. "Thank you, but that won't be necessary."

"I think it might be. He hasn't told you about his little code, has he?"

"Lydia, it's time we left. Your father and the others will be waiting for us at the restaurant," Carlos suggested, gently grasping her elbow.

Black eyes flashed angrily. Lydia brushed off his hold. "Since he hasn't told you, I will. Daniel has a thing about not becoming involved with relatives of his friends. So your little scheme downstairs won't work."

The unmitigated gall of the woman! If Madelyn knew how to work her neck, this was one time she'd do it and give two snaps to boot. "Unlike some women, I don't have to resort to subterfuge to catch a man."

Lydia gasped at the implication. "You'd have to do something. You look like a skinny, drowned chicken."

"Now wai—"

"Lydia."

The woman whirled toward Daniel, and Madelyn had to give her points for courage. If he had called her name in that same cold voice, she would have been running in the opposite direction.

"I don't care who owns this hotel," he continued just as coldly. "This is my room, and I want you out of here."

Outrage marred Lydia's perfect features. "You can't throw me out of my father's hotel."

"He'd do it for me, if he were here."

"I'm not go—" She gasped and jumped back as Daniel took a step toward her. Her eyes became malevolent. "How dare you treat me like this!"

"You brought it on yourself. Now leave," Daniel said flatly.

"I'll leave, and I'll make sure everyone at lunch knows what went on up here!"

In two steps he towered over her. "Say one word that might embarrass Madelyn or her family, and I'll make sure you regret it for the rest of your unhappy life."

Lydia staggered back, her hand going to the heavy gold necklace at her throat. "Carlos, do something. Carlos?"

"I am. I'm doing something I should have done long ago." He turned to Madelyn. "Goodbye. I wish we could have met under different circumstances," then to Daniel, "I'll see you later." Opening the door, he was gone.

"Carlos," Lydia screamed, but he kept going.

"If I were you, Lydia, I'd run after Carlos and try to get him to forgive you," Daniel said. "Although personally I think he's finally realized you're not worth the effort."

Lydia looked at Daniel with heartless eyes. "One day I'll make you pay for this."

"You're welcome to try, but make your first shot count because you won't get another one—and then it will be my turn," Daniel finished with deadly promise.

The woman shivered, her hand once again clutching her throat. Turning, she fled and almost ran into the bellhop who carried Madelyn's dress. The young man's questioning gaze went from the escaping Lydia back to them.

Daniel took the dress enclosed in clear plastic wrap in one hand, tipped the man with the other, and closed the door. "Your dress. Looks like they did a pretty good job."

"I thought Kane was joking, but he wasn't," Madelyn said, staring at Daniel.

"Joking about what?" Daniel asked, inwardly preparing himself for her censure. He could be a ruthless bastard. No one knew that more than he, but he usually managed to control it better.

"He said the emblem on your plane of a falcon with claws outstretched was a warning to anyone who crosses you. He said when you go after someone, you go for blood."

Daniel never wanted to see fear or revulsion in this woman's eyes when she looked at him. "You have nothing to fear from me, Madelyn."

"Afraid of you?" she scoffed and rolled her brown eyes. "Apparently you've never seen Kane or Matt on a roll. I have. They're no harder than they have to be. Neither are you. But like Kane, you don't like repeating yourself or having your authority questioned."

Daniel studied her with renewed interest. "You're full of surprises."

"Just being realistic," Madelyn said, taking the dress from his hands. "Matt and Kane might like you, but they wouldn't like hearing I was in your room in a bathrobe."

The corner of his mouth kicked up in a half smile. "The same thought crossed my mind."

"You're pretty good at rescuing women, Daniel." She smiled up at him with all the warmth he wanted and could never have.

Daniel's face settled into grim lines "I'm a rogue, and innocents like you shouldn't forget it."

Her smile faded as he knew it would. "I'll go change and get out of your way. I'm sure you must have a lot to do."

"I've already done it." At her puzzled look, he continued. "Seen my bootmaker. My mold was damaged, and I had to come down and have it redone."

Frowning, she shook her head in disbelief. "You came from Denver to be fitted for a pair of boots?"

"I'm particular about what I put on my feet. A bad pair of boots—"

"Can ruin your feet," she finished. "I know that, but it's still hard to imagine someone coming all this way for boots."

"If you want something badly enough, too far or too much doesn't enter into it."

The way he said the words had Madelyn clutching the dress closer to her. No woman would be safe if he decided to come after her. The idea was fascinating and frightening.

"I'll be out in a minute." Whirling, she hurried to the bathroom, her heart racing. She was imagining things. Daniel had no special interest in her. Hadn't Lydia made it perfectly clear he didn't become involved with relatives of friends?

But what if Lydia didn't know what she was talking about? What if Daniel handed her that line to get her out of his face?

Madelyn lifted her face to the mirror. There was only one reason she was asking herself all those questions. She wanted Daniel to look at her and see a desirable woman, not the little sister of his friends. She wanted a man who, rumor had it, had no heart. Heaven help her.

"I'm lost."

Several minutes later Madelyn emerged from Daniel's bathroom. She felt more in control of the situation now that she was in her own clothes, her hair was dry, and she had on her lipstick.

She made a face. Maybe she had been too hasty in her thoughts on the unimportance of lasting lip color.

"Something wrong?"

Her head jerked around to see Daniel rising from

the chair . . . all six-feet-plus of him. She might have been too nervous to appreciate the sheer male beauty of the man when she was in his bathrobe, but she wasn't now.

He exuded a raw magnetism that was disquieting. Those midnight-black eyes were as sharp as talons. The intelligence in them shone just as brightly and kept her from bolting back into the bathroom.

"You've changed."

"There's another bathroom off the dining area," he explained.

Jeans suited the muscled hardness of his long legs. The white shirt complemented his dark, good looks. He looked sinful and forbidden, and much too tempting.

She moistened her lips. "Well, I guess I better be going."

"What are your plans?"

Madelyn glanced toward the windows before answering. The draperies were partially drawn. She couldn't tell if it was still raining, but the sky didn't look so gloomy and dark.

"They were for a sensible lunch and strawberry-topped cheesecake, but if the weather cooperates, I think it'll be Tex-Mex food with salsa that will take the skin off the roof of my mouth followed by a funnel cake loaded down with strawberries and whipped cream."

"Care for some company?"

There was no way for her to hide her shock. "You?"

"I know this little restaurant that sounds exactly like what you're looking for," he told her.

Briefly she thought of what Lydia had said, then pushed it to the back of her mind. She'd never know if she didn't try.

"After I go back to my hotel room to change, you're on."

Chapter 3

Cafe Mexicana was everything Daniel promised. The freshly prepared food was delicious. From where their table was located, Madelyn could see an elderly man in the back making tortillas.

She and Daniel had stuffed themselves on salsa and chips, refried beans, Spanish rice, enchiladas, and fajitas. By the time they left the restaurant, Madelyn was sure she had gained two pounds.

"Daniel, you're a mean man," she groaned.

"What did I do?"

"Condemned me to rethink my position against eating sprouts and granola bars for lunch."

"We'll walk it off."

"Walk? I'm not sure I can go another ten feet."

Laughing he slung his arm companionably around her shoulders. She tried to ignore the tingling sensation winging its way down her spine. "Then how about riding?"

At her puzzled stare, he pointed toward a river taxi gliding by. "How about it?"

She smiled despite her rapidly beating heart. "You're forgiven."

It was a short walk from the bank to their point of

embarkment. The rain must have kept most people in-
doors because they were able to board the colorful red
and orange boat within minutes of their arrival.

Gratefully Madelyn climbed aboard and sank down
into one of the cushioned seats. Lush vegetation and
palms lined the bank along with sidewalk cafes, shops,
galleries, hotels, restaurants, and clubs.

"Feeling better?" Daniel asked, settling his black
Stetson more securely on his head as the boat picked
up speed down the canal of the San Antonio River.

"Yes, thank you. I shouldn't have eaten so much.
First breakfast, then just now." She leaned back against
the railing. "The only excuse is that I don't have time
for good meals at home."

"Where's home?"

"Houston. I work for Sinclair Petroleum Company
as a production engineer."

Daniel's broad shoulders tensed. He stared down
at her. "You work for an oil company in Houston?"

"Yes. I have for three years." She frowned. "You
have something against Houston or the oil industry?"

Facing straight ahead, he leaned back and propped
his arms over the railing. "Neither. I was just surprised
you weren't living in Dallas or Fort Worth. I seem to
remember Kane mentioning he wanted you to work for
him."

She relaxed again, enjoying the ride through the
Rivercenter. "I know, but I wanted to be on my own.
Houston is close enough for us to visit, but far enough
away where they can't try and run my life."

"Or screen your dates?"

She gave him a sharp look of disappointment. "Actually I was thinking more of interfering with my job.
As for the dates, if a man can be intimidated by my
brothers, he's not the man for me."

Daniel's disturbing gaze found her again. "You're quite a woman."

Madelyn flushed with pleasure. "Glad you approve."

"Oh, I approve. Kane and Matt must be very proud of their little sister."

The softly spoken words touched and saddened her. He still thought of her as the little sister of his friends. If she wanted more, that was her problem.

Gathering her slipping composure, she lifted her face to the bright rays of the sun for a minute. "I'm glad you suggested this. I didn't get a chance when I came on a field trip in high school."

"Came to see the Alamo, I'll bet." Daniel shifted slightly and stretched his long legs out in front of him. His red lizard boots were polished to a rich sheen.

She nodded, trying to concentrate on the peaceful ride through the Rivercenter instead of the hard length of Daniel's muscular thigh pressed against hers. "The Alamo and the state capital in Austin are practically unwritten requirements to graduate from a high school in Texas."

"Why didn't you get a chance to go on the river taxi?"

Madelyn shifted uneasily before answering. "Things just didn't work out."

"Did it rain then?"

"No."

"Are you going to tell me why, or do I keep on guessing?" he asked mildly.

Unsteady fingers plucked at the hem of the shorts she had changed into at her hotel before finally meeting Daniel's enigmatic eyes. "One of our chaperons was a really nice man. He thought, along with the history, we should experience some of the unique flavor of San Antonio.

"He talked the teachers into letting some of us take

a river taxi ride. It quickly became a couples thing, and since I didn't have anyone to go with, I stayed in the hotel room with some of the other girls and we ordered pizza instead," she explained, the occasion indelible because her date had dumped her for another girl.

Daniel pulled up his legs and gave her his full attention. "Are you telling me in high school you didn't have a boyfriend?"

"I had them. I just wasn't able to keep them," she said, glancing away. Her inability to keep a boyfriend wasn't something she wanted to discuss with a man like Daniel Falcon.

"Kane and Matt the problem?"

"Partly." She studied the shops lining the walkway. "There's a T-shirt shop. I promised to bring the twins one."

He frowned down at her. "The twins? Kane and Victoria's children?"

"Yes. You should have seen them at Matt and Shannon's wedding. They were adorable. We were all disappointed you couldn't come."

"Something came up," he said, his voice remote. He stood as the boat docked. "We can get off here."

Madelyn allowed him to assist her off the boat, but didn't speak until they were in front of the shop. She extended her hand, hoping her smile didn't appear as forced as it felt. "Thank you for lunch and the taxi ride."

He stared at her hand, then lifted a dark brow. "You wouldn't be trying to get rid of me, would you?"

"I'm sure you hadn't planned on doing touristy things with the little sister of your friends," she told him, her hand wavering.

"Nope." He gathered her smaller hand in his. "I had planned on a boring lunch with some business associates. This is much better."

Madelyn fought to sound normal when her insides were shivery. "Are you sure?"

"Didn't someone mention I never do anything I don't want to?" he questioned mildly.

A smile and a tiny ray of hope lit her face. "I believe it came up once or twice."

"Well, then."

"All right, but remember, you asked for it."

The afternoon turned into evening and evening turned into night. Madelyn couldn't remember ever having so much fun. Somehow the tenseness between them seemed to leave as they tried to pick out the right T-shirts for the twins. They finally settled on one with SAN ANTONIO emblazoned in bright colors on a white background.

Continuing down the sidewalk, they passed a shop and saw a piñata. Madelyn mentioned the twins' birthday was coming up and how much fun a piñata would be for each of them. Off they went to the Market Square. Daniel was as finicky as she was in finding one with the right colors and shape.

After wandering down the aisles, they finally found two donkeys that were exactly what they had been searching for. Against her protests, Daniel paid for the piñatas.

After depositing everything at her hotel, they were off again, ending up at the street fair surrounding the coliseum. Passing the funnel cake concession, Daniel had asked if she wanted one. She had punched him playfully on the shoulder.

Seemingly without a moment's hesitation, he draped his arm around her shoulders again and they continued down the aisle. Her heart beat faster, her skin tingled.

They were strolling past the game booths when Madelyn stopped and watched an excited teenage girl clutch an enormous lion the young boy with her had just won for her. Both of them had to carry the toy as they walked away.

Madelyn watched them fondly. "I've always wanted someone to win one of those animals for me—one so big it would be hard to drag home."

"Your boyfriends didn't seem to be around when it counted."

She grimaced. "One did win me a four-foot fuzzy green snake at the State Fair of Texas in Dallas when I was sixteen."

"I think I can do better than that."

"Daniel, I wasn't hinting."

"I know. That's why I'm going to win you one." Taking her arm, he steered them through the crowd toward the counter.

Before they were halfway there, the sharp-eyed booth huckster saw them approaching and began his pitch about how easy it was to win the young woman the stuffed animal of her choice from the top two rows. All the strong man had to do was completely shoot out the red bull's-eye on the target in twenty pellet shots.

Taking out his wallet, Daniel turned to Madelyn. "How many?"

"Two dollars for twenty shots," replied the worker, placing a pellet gun on the scarred wooden counter.

Daniel didn't take his eyes from Madelyn. "I was asking you how many stuffed animals you wanted."

She barely kept her mouth from sagging. Not for a moment did she think he was bragging. He was utterly confident in his ability to do anything he set his mind to. It was an awesome realization.

Although shredded target centers hung from one end of the booth to the other, she didn't doubt the difficulty of accomplishing such a task. Each time a pellet struck the target, the paper would fan backward, making it more difficult to hit the red center with the next shot.

Madelyn glanced at Daniel, noting his patience, his confidence. She was just as confident in him. She switched her attention to the display of elephants, lions, and bears. There wasn't a green snake in sight.

"The brown teddy bear."

"That's on the bottom row. You'll have to hit five in a row. No misses," the man said.

"Dan—"

"Line them up," Daniel said, cutting her off.

"Ten dollars."

Daniel handed the man a ten-dollar bill. Only then did the attendant move to set up the targets, then he placed four other pellet guns beside the first.

"Remember if you miss one, you'll have to start all over again," the attendant reminded him.

"He won't miss," Madelyn said, her arms folded across her chest. She glared at the man behind the counter.

Daniel winked at her, then picked up the gun. Her confidence in him shouldn't have made him feel a foot taller, but it did. If he didn't watch himself, Madelyn could become more of a problem.

He should have left her hours ago, but there was something about her smile that was irresistible and made him want to keep her smiling. He had come to San Antonio to donate funds and finalize plans for a work-study program to be overseen by Carlos for Hispanic, Native American, and African-American high school students—not fool around with a woman. Yet here he was, trying to win her a darn teddy bear whose fur would probably fall out in six weeks.

Hoisting the gun upward, Daniel sighted down the

barrel and began pulling the trigger. Paper popped and danced as the small black pellets tore into the red circle. Picking up another gun, he began firing again. He continued until the last gun was empty.

Madelyn's slim fingers closed around his arm as the attendant slowly removed the clothespins holding the targets. By the time the grim-faced man laid the last tattered remains in front of Madelyn and Daniel, a crowd had formed to see the results.

Madelyn squealed like a schoolgirl. In each one the red circle was completely obliterated. "You did it! You did it! We won! We won!"

She threw her arms around Daniel's neck, intending to kiss him on the cheek. His head turned. Their lips met, clung.

Fire swept through her. Need warred with common sense. Move closer or pull back?

Every instinct in Daniel shouted for him to push her away. He couldn't. Her lips were too soft, too sweet and alluring. He knew he was headed for disaster, but he was powerless to keep from pulling her into his arms and deepening the kiss.

It was the best and worst decision of his life. Her body seemed to melt into his, offering herself to him without reservation, without coyness. Daniel accepted the gift with reverence, with barely leashed desire.

"Way to go, man."

"Wow!"

"See what winning can do for you men? There's nothing like a grateful, happy woman. Who's gonna be the next man to step up and play?"

The loud voices snapped Daniel back to awareness of where he was and what he was doing. Abruptly he lifted his head. Looking into Madelyn's dazed, desire-filled eyes, he wanted nothing more than to take her someplace and make love to her.

None too gently, Daniel pulled Madelyn's arms from around his neck and set her away from him. The look of rejection on her beautiful face tore at him and almost had him pulling her back into his arms. Almost.

He faced the grinning attendant. "I believe you owe the lady a teddy bear."

"Don't you want to win the mate and make her twice as happy?" the carnival worker questioned slyly. "It would be a shame to separate them since they're the only bears I have."

"Some of us don't need mates," Daniel snapped.

The man quickly rushed to pick up the bear and set it on the counter. "Whatever you say, mister."

Feeling irritable, Daniel handed the stuffed animal to Madelyn. "Here you go."

"Thank you." Her fingers sank into the soft brown fur. Glassy black eyes stared up at her. She glanced at the other teddy bear behind the counter and bit her lip. Although she knew the man was trying to con them, she still wasn't immune to his suggestion. She looked at Daniel.

"If you want the other one, I'll win it for you but not because of what he said," Daniel told her tightly. "It's silly to think of a stuffed animal needing a mate when most people can't find and don't want or need one."

Madelyn's fingers tightened. Her happiness of moments ago disappeared. He was upset with her. She shouldn't have kissed him. "No thank you," she replied politely.

His jaw clenched. "If there's nothing else you want to see, I think I should take you back to your hotel."

Madelyn swallowed the lump in her throat. "No, I'm ready to leave."

Taking the animal from her, Daniel started from the area. Fighting tears, Madelyn followed. By the time they reached the door of her hotel room, Madelyn's nerves were ragged. Daniel hadn't said one word since they left the street fair.

She had barely opened the door before he stepped past her to place the animal in her room. "Good night. Have a safe trip home."

"Daniel," she said as he stepped back into the hallway. The expressionless face that turned toward her wasn't reassuring. It certainly didn't invite conversation.

"Yes?" The word was clipped.

She clutched her purse in her hand, gathering her courage. "Tell me one thing. Are you leaving me at the door because I'm Matt and Kane's sister or because I'm a lousy kisser?"

Heat flared in his slumberous eyes, then centered on her lips. Her body quickened.

Slowly his gaze lifted. "I'm not one for long-term relationships."

Madelyn took her courage in both hands. "I don't remember asking you for one."

He smiled sadly. "Everything about you asks for one. You're not the kind of woman to go from one affair to the next. I'm not the kind of man who offers a woman anything else."

"Would we be having this conversation if I weren't who I am?" She knew she was pushing it, but when you were hurting inside, you'd fight for survival at all cost . . . including laying your pride on the line.

"Good night, Madelyn."

Her throat stung. "Thank you for the stuffed animal. I had a won—" She swallowed. "Good night."

"Don't do this to either of us."

She gazed at him with mute eyes, then swallowed again.

"If I give you what you're asking for, neither one of us is going to be able to look the other in the eye in the morning."

He couldn't have said it any plainer. She could have him for the night, but only the night. She wasn't that courageous or that stupid. "I'll be sure and tell the family I met you."

Blunt-tipped fingers touched the brim of his black Stetson. Turning, he walked down the hall toward the elevators.

With each step, she felt the tightness in her throat grow more unbearable. Swallowing did little good. Just before the hallway ended, he stopped and glanced over his shoulder.

"Close the door and go inside," he ordered.

She bit her lip.

"You aren't a little girl any longer. Don't ask for something you can't handle."

Nothing he could have said would have worked any better. Stepping back, she closed the door. Pressing her back against the smooth wood, she stared at her teddy bear.

It occurred to her as tears rolled down her cheek that for the second time in her life, she had been left alone in her hotel room in San Antonio because she didn't believe in casual sex. The other time it hadn't mattered—this time she was afraid it mattered too much.

Daniel's tense shoulders slumped. Who would have ever thought he'd have trouble keeping his hands off a wide-eyed woman like Madelyn Taggart.

She called to him in ways he had never experienced

before. Her smile charmed. Her laugh invited him to join in. Her voice stroked him. Her touch fired his blood.

Madelyn Taggart wasn't for him. So why was walking away one of the most difficult things he had ever done in his life?

The answering machine was blinking in Madelyn's bedroom when she arrived home Sunday afternoon. She wasn't naive enough to think it was Daniel calling. He didn't have her phone number. That he hadn't asked for her unlisted number even before the kiss continued to bother her. She couldn't help feeling as if she had failed to interest him as a potential friend as well as a woman.

After hauling in her luggage, the gifts for the twins, and the teddy bear, she punched the recall button. As the messages played, there were no surprises.

Her parents wanted her to call when she arrived home. The same instructions from Kane and Matt . . . only their wives had made the phone calls. The fourth message was from Jeremiah Gant. His irritatingly cocky voice made the same request.

Madelyn screwed up her face. If he asked her out again, she was going to scream. He was a successful accountant who attended her church, but he was also full of himself. He couldn't seem to understand why she and every other woman wasn't beating his door down.

The next caller had her smiling again. Sid Wright, her neighbor from two doors down in her apartment complex, wanted to remind her that they had tickets to the Houston Grand Opera to see *Carmen* the next night. Going out with Sid wasn't dating. His girlfriend, Gloria, was an international flight attendant and was gone a great deal.

Picking up the phone, Madelyn began returning the

calls. She put off the most difficult call . . . Kane . . . to last. Somehow he always knew when things were bothering her. Casually mentioning she had met Daniel Falcon to her parents had elicited only mild interest. Her oldest brother would be another story.

"What was he doing in San Antonio?" asked Kane.

"Getting a new mold made for his boots."

Kane chuckled. "He likes the finer things in life, but flying over nine hundred miles is reaching even for Daniel. There had to be another reason."

Madelyn glanced at the teddy bear. "If there was, he didn't confide in me."

"Don't feel bad. He confides in few people," Kane said. "I didn't know until I heard the news this morning that his company is moving from Denver to Houston."

"Houston?" she almost shouted.

"I take it he didn't tell you."

Madelyn's misery increased on recalling his unease when she told him she lived in Houston. He probably thought she would be one of those women chasing after him. Kissing him had only confirmed his speculations.

"N-No, he didn't."

"Sounds like the Daniel I know. Can't blame him though. Looks like the oil and gas industry is about to go boom again, and he's going to be a big part of it. Letting the competition know your plans would be business suicide."

"Yes."

"Looks like you'll be seeing him again then."

Madelyn chewed on her lip. "I doubt it. He's a busy man."

"You're both in Houston. Both in the petroleum business. You'll see him from time to time."

She managed a shaky laugh. "The underlings don't often mingle with the top brass."

Kane snorted. "Daniel's not the type to judge a person by their job description or their salary. You'll see him again."

Madelyn was unsure if she was feeling better or worse when she hung up the phone five minutes later.

Daniel was coming to Houston.

Heaven help her.

Chapter 4

Heaven might help her, but the news media wouldn't.

Daniel Falcon hit Houston with a media blitz that was unprecedented in recent history. Everyone wanted to interview him, see him, press flesh with him. The mayor and the city council members loved anyone who was legally bringing millions of taxable dollars into the city.

He was an instant hit.

Not since the Houston Rockets won the NBA title had the media covered an event so thoroughly. Only now one man held center court, and he did it brilliantly.

The camera loved him. He didn't have a bad angle to photograph or film. The press and citizens of Houston couldn't seem to get enough of his effortless charm or his exotic male beauty.

Friday afternoon at Special Occasions Beauty Shop proved no exception. The moment his smiling, handsome face appeared on the TV screen, everyone paused to watch, listen, and speculate.

"Now that's what I call one fine man."

"Look at those big hands. I bet that man could do a lot of damage."

"Hands nothing," shouted a dyed redhead getting a wave. "I wanna see the feet to see if he's gonna go the distance."

Special Occasion Beauty Shop erupted into bawdy laughter, foot stomping, and finger snaps. The wide open elongated room, done in purple and white, and filled with a profusion of cascading ivy and lush tropical plants, invited conversation and interaction between its clients—which they took full advantage of.

Refusing to join in, Madelyn hid her face behind a copy of *Our Texas* magazine. Scrunching down farther in her overstuffed purple floral chair, she wished she were still under the dryer.

Daniel Falcon had struck again—this time on a live broadcast with the local TV station. It was almost impossible to turn on the TV news or read the paper without seeing his face. Although she admired him and his accomplishments, she just wished seeing him didn't remind her of how little she had impressed him.

Not one time had he mentioned to her his plans to relocate Falcon Industries. Yet he was telling the interviewer the move had been planned for months. Add to that his plans to pitch his considerable wealth into finding the next mega oil fields, and she felt almost betrayed.

He could have said something, given her a hint. He hadn't. His silence couldn't have made it clearer that he didn't trust her or expect her to be a part of his life when he reached Houston.

Although she tried to concentrate on the editorial by General Berry in the magazine, it was impossible. The announcer's words drew her like the proverbial magnet. In almost reverent tones she described Daniel as brilliant, intelligent, and charismatic. Madelyn noted she left out ruthless in getting what he wanted. The reporter last night on the ten o'clock news hadn't, but the newscaster had been a male.

Mr. Falcon has an uncanny knack for tapping into the next big-money venture before it hits big. His record as an industry forecaster and trendsetter is unprecedented in the business world. If anyone doubted that after a decade of lean years for the energy industry that energy would be back, then I suggest you look at Daniel Falcon.

I know this reporter will be watching closely. This is Erica Stone reporting live from the temporary headquarters of Falcon Industries in downtown Houston. Back to you in the studio, Elvin.

"Somebody give Erica a bib, I think the woman is drooling."

"I bet she won't be back in the studio for a while."

"You think he likes 'em chesty?"

"He's a man, isn't he?"

"My man says more than a mouthful is a waste."

"That's because you're still wearing double-A's."

More laughter, including the teased woman wearing double-A's.

Surreptitiously Madelyn glanced down. She was all right in that area. But it wasn't likely that Daniel had any interest in finding out. He had been in Houston two weeks, and he had yet to contact her.

She snorted. As if he'd take the time. He was too busy giving interviews and grinning at chesty females like Erica Stone, who probably wore a push-up bra.

Instantly Madelyn was ashamed of herself. It wasn't like her to be waspish or vindictive. Daniel had her as

confused and off kilter as she had ever been. She didn't
know what to think of him, and apparently she wasn't
alone.

It was a testament to his craftiness that he had virtu-
ally snuck into the oil and gas industry unnoticed. The
same day he broke ground for his five-acre business
development, he announced his purchase of Slate Oil
Company, stunning people again. Slate Oil had been
family owned for over seventy-five years and no one
expected George Slate to sell a company his grandfather
started despite its financial woes.

George Slate couldn't be reached for comment, and
Daniel Falcon wore his perpetual smile just before saying, "No comment."

"Madelyn, I'm ready for you."

Madelyn almost leaped into the black leather chair.
In thirty minutes she'd be out of here and on her way
home. Tomorrow she planned a quiet day at home, and
she wouldn't have to listen to one person comment
about Daniel. Her relief was short-lived.

"You work for Sinclair Petroleum Company, don't
you?" questioned the beautician blow-drying Madelyn's black hair.

Beneath her pink blouse, she rolled tense shoulders.
"Yes."

"Any chance you might meet that good-looking
hunk?" Stephanie asked, her speculative gaze meeting
Madelyn's in the oval mirror in front of them.

"I doubt it. We move in different circles."

Sectioning Madelyn's hair Stephanie picked up the
curling iron, expertly curled the black strands, then replaced the iron in its stand. "Too bad, I'd love to get my
hands in his hair."

The beautician beside Stephanie snorted. "That's not
all you want to get your hands into."

Stephanie, who was gregarious and easygoing, threw out one slim hip in exaggeration and struck a pose with the rattail black comb in her right hand. "I never said I'd stop there, now did I?"

The women hooted. Madelyn made herself smile. Stephanie had more men friends than she knew what to do with. There wasn't a doubt in Madelyn's mind that the other woman knew exactly what to do with Daniel if she got her hands on him.

Refusing to give in to self-pity or cattiness, Madelyn said in all truthfulness, "I'm not sure a man like Daniel Falcon would want to get in your long line."

Stephanie grinned and leaned down. "I'd let him go to the front."

"You and half the women in Houston," said the attractive woman who was sitting in the chair next to Madelyn, getting her hair braided. "A lot of them are rich, society women. Women who work for a paycheck don't have a chance."

"You think the brother is a snob?" asked the redhead from across the room.

"Whether he's a snob or not, how are you going to stand out among all the women trying to get a piece of him?" she asked. "When you've been used to the best, why settle for less?"

"Daniel's not like that," Madelyn said before she could stop herself.

Twenty-one pairs of eyes converged on her. Including women under the dryer.

Stephanie whirled Madelyn around in the chair so fast she had to clutch the armrests to keep from falling. "Daniel? I thought you didn't know the dude."

Madelyn fought the vision of leaving the beauty shop with her hair half done. "I said we move in different circles."

"So do you know the man or not?" asked the talkative redhead.

"We met briefly in San Antonio," Madelyn admitted reluctantly, because she knew what was coming next.

"When you were on that weekend trip by yourself? You mean you let a fine-looking, rich man like that get away from you?" Stephanie questioned as if Madelyn had done the unforgivable.

Glancing around the shop, she wasn't sure she hadn't. Some of the faces wore surprise that they had met someone who had met Daniel, others were openly appraising. "We just didn't hit it off."

The look of sympathy that crossed her beautician's pretty face was unmistakable. "Probably a snob, like Eula thought. You're better off without him."

There was a distinct quietness in the shop before the conversation turned to the day's soaps. Madelyn stared straight ahead. Now the entire beauty shop knew Daniel Falcon had found her lacking. For a man she had never met until two weeks ago, he had certainly screwed up her life.

The phone was ringing when Madelyn opened her apartment door. Rushing to pick up the receiver, she answered breathlessly, "Hello."

"Hi, sis. Caught you coming in, huh?"

Madelyn smiled at the sound of Kane's voice and perched her hip on the arm of the sofa. "Just walked in from the beauty shop. How're Victoria and the twins?"

"Fine. I'm a lucky man." The pride and love in his deep voice was unmistakable.

"So are they. You're the best." She tossed her purse and keys on the cushion beside her.

Kane laughed, a rich, booming sound. "As long as

you think that, I know some man hasn't stolen your heart."

She bit her lip. She wasn't so sure about that sometimes, but she wasn't about to discuss her feelings with Kane. He was too perceptive, and Daniel was too close a friend. "I'm too busy for that."

"At twenty-four you're also too young and naive. A lot of men out there can't be trusted. I almost asked Daniel to look out for you when he called."

"What!" she shouted jumping to her feet. "Tell me you're only teasing."

"Calm down," Kane said. "I know how you value your independence."

She bit her lip again. "Why did he call?"

"He wanted my input on some names he was given to head a work-study program for the minority youth in Houston."

Madelyn frowned and slowly sat back down. "I haven't heard anything about such a program."

"You won't," Kane told her. "He insists on total anonymity so he can pick the men and have full control. He wants the money going to the kids and not to bureaucratic red tape. He was in San Antonio finalizing a similar program. The Dallas/Fort Worth area is next, then Austin."

Madelyn fleetingly wondered if the boot mold was just a ruse, then another thought struck. "That will cost hundreds of thousands of dollars."

"I know. He had the same programs in Denver while he was there," Kane told her. "He feels as strongly as I do about helping to put something back into the community and state that has given him so much."

"He really isn't as ruthless as he pretends," Madelyn said, her voice soft.

Kane snorted. "Until you cross him, then watch out. But he protects his own. I respect him."

"He thinks highly of you and Matt, too."

"He's a good friend to both of us. Well, take care of yourself."

"I will, and thanks for not telling Daniel to check on me," she said.

"You're welcome. Just don't make me regret it. Bye."

"I won't. Bye," Madelyn said and hung up the phone. So Daniel had a soft side. He called to her on so many levels. Now she had added another one. Growing up she'd always known she'd choose a man like her brothers: tough, aggressive, intelligent, but always aware of those weaker individuals who needed your help.

Picking up her things, she wondered why Daniel wanted her to think he was so ruthless—and more importantly, would she ever see him again to learn the answer.

Daniel Falcon tried to sit patiently while the long-winded gentleman at the podium extolled the return of the oil and gas industry. It was difficult. Especially when he wanted to get up again and see if he had actually seen Madelyn Taggart in the audience or just imagined her.

It wouldn't be the first time since he had arrived in Houston three weeks ago. He had almost spoken to one young woman. She had laughed just before he reached out to touch her. Instantly he'd realized his mistake. The laugh was pleasant enough—it just didn't make his heart beat faster or his blood run hotter.

Madelyn and her laugh had done both. Too well.

He should forget her, but somehow he couldn't. She had appeared so lost and alone standing in her hotel room doorway in San Antonio. He didn't regret walking away—he regretted that she didn't understand why he had to.

Judson Howell, the man at the podium, took a sip of water, shuffled his notes, and was off again. The man seated beside Daniel sighed.

Daniel studied the tip of his Bally loafers, then crossed one leg over the other. While doing so he barely refrained from glancing at the eighteen-karat gold and stainless steel Cartier watch on his wrist.

Now wasn't the time to appear impatient. Being asked, even at the last minute, to speak at the annual Cambridge Energy Research Associates meeting being held in Houston was a coup. Cambridge was a leading industrial consulting firm, and being on their agenda meant Daniel's foray into the energy business was being taken seriously.

It had better. He didn't do anything by halves.

Perhaps that's why he couldn't forget how badly things had ended between he and Madelyn. Kissing her hadn't been wise. The taste of her lips still haunted him. Sometimes he'd catch himself running his tongue over his lips to see if he could find a trace of her sweetness still there.

Knowing the idea was crazy hadn't helped him stop. With one erotically charged kiss, she had done more to upset his plans to remain emotionally uninvolved than any woman before her.

The polite smattering of applause alerted Daniel that the gray-haired gentleman had finally wound down. Straightening, Daniel added his own applause, then listened to the moderator introduce him as their "special, unannounced guest."

Daniel stood while the applause was still being given. Sharp black eyes searched the luncheon crowd of over five hundred with an intensity and concentration that his employees had learned to dread. Fortunately the people in the audience didn't know that. Unfortunately he didn't see the one person he had been looking for.

As soon as the applause began to dim down, he began speaking. His strong compelling voice reached to the back of the room as clearly and as easily as if he were speaking to each person directly. Placing one manicured hand on the podium, he spoke to the people as if he had always known them.

A quietness settled around the room as people stopped whispering at the tables, stopped trying to get one more bite of carrot cake, stopped clinking their spoons against the sides of their cups or glasses to stir sweetener into their coffee or tea. Daniel Falcon had them in the palm of his capable hand.

"Worldwide the demand, the need, for oil and gas is growing. We are in a position to meet that need. The profit potentials are staggering. You are to be commended for your faith, courage, and fortitude in standing firm in your belief when others loudly proclaimed the doom of the oil and gas industry. I salute you and welcome the opportunity to work alongside you in the coming years. Energy is back. Thank you."

The applause was thunderous. Before he could reach his seat, the ten men and women on the stage with him were there to shake his hand.

Daniel accepted their praise and congratulations with true appreciation. Working with friends was infinitely preferable to being in the midst of enemies. With a final handshake to the elderly speaker before him, Daniel headed for his seat. Something made him glance at the audience again.

This time he spotted her immediately. She sat near the back of the large ballroom. Dressed in a champagne-colored double-breasted suit with a portrait collar, she appeared to stiffen, then she glanced away.

His teeth clenched, Daniel continued to his seat. He had paused only a few seconds, but it was enough to tell him there was still something unfinished between them.

Thankfully the speaker after Daniel was short and to the point. With a fond farewell, the moderator adjourned the meeting and said he hoped to see everyone that night at the Petroleum Ball.

Daniel was out of his chair in an instant. His gaze locked on Madelyn until someone moved into his line of vision. Afterward he never stood a chance of catching her. People crowded around him, wanting to shake his hand, wanting to congratulate him.

With a patience he was far from feeling, he smiled and thanked them. Thirty minutes later when he finally left the raised platform, Madelyn's table was empty.

He should let it go at that and count it as a narrow escape. What was he going to say to her anyway? He honestly didn't know. All he knew was that once he saw her, he had to see her again.

Madelyn was shaking as she stepped into the glittering ballroom that night. The immense room where they had eaten lunch had been transformed. Fifty-foot oil derricks were scattered throughout with the name of the most famous oil and gas strikes in Texas emblazoned on them.

On each side of the long tables laden with everything from succulent roast beef to poached salmon were nine-foot trees glittering with tiny white lights. Round, linen-draped tables, each with a stunning floral centerpiece in cylindrical crystal vases, were in a semicircle, leaving the middle open for dancing, milling around, and the all-important networking.

Walking farther inside, Madelyn searched the crowd for one person: Daniel Falcon.

Seeing Daniel on the podium at lunch had been a complete surprise. She, like everyone in the room, had been entranced by his voice. He was as dynamic as she remembered. When he had stopped on the stage and looked at her, every nerve cell in her body went on full alert.

She had remained at her table a full five minutes after everyone left, hoping he might come over and say hello. She left when it became obvious some of the people in the room were reluctant to let him go.

She had gone home and immediately started looking through her closet for a dress to wear to the Petroleum Ball. Before seeing Daniel, she hadn't planned on attending. Afterward she couldn't think of anything else.

All her mental anguish had been forgotten as she pulled a long, black crepe creation from her closet. Daring, sleek and sophisticated, the gown fit lovingly over her breasts, leaving one shoulder completely bare before skimming down to her narrow waist to flare from the knees down.

The other women would probably be wearing sequins and glitter. She'd rely on simplicity to capture Daniel's interest. She could no longer deny she wanted his attention and much more. The woman in the beauty shop was right . . . flash and dash wasn't going to do.

"You wanna dance?"

A man's voice jerked her around. In front of her was a man in his midtwenties, blatantly staring at her breasts. Besides bad manners, his cologne made her head ache. The jacket of his black tuxedo hung on thin shoulders. "No, thank you."

"Are you waiting for someone?" he persisted, giving her another once-over.

"Yes," she answered without a moment's hesitation.

"If he doesn't show up, I may still be available." Snickering at his own humor, he moved farther into the room and asked another woman to dance. He must have received a similar answer because he walked away.

"Madelyn, glad you decided to come after all."

Glancing around she saw her boss, Howard Sampson. Robust and balding, he smiled down at her. Working with him on a full-time basis was everything Madelyn had thought it would be. Each day he challenged her and accepted nothing less than her best.

She smiled warmly in return. "Hello, Mr. Sampson."

"This is my wife, Jane," he said proudly of the matronly woman by his side. "Jane, Madelyn Taggart, the newest member of my team. If she can stand the heat, she might make a darn good production engineer one day," he offered in a bit of oil humor.

His wife, in understated lavender chiffon, smiled indulgently. "Don't you let him intimidate you, dear. I've known him for sixty years and been married to him for forty-three of those. His bark is worse than his bite."

Madelyn liked the gray-haired woman instantly. "I'll try to remember that."

"Do you have a seat?" asked Jane.

"No, I just arrived."

"Then come and sit with us . . . if you don't think we'd bore you to death," Mrs. Sampson said with a teasing smile.

Madelyn didn't hesitate. "I'd love to."

Later that evening Madelyn couldn't quite believe she was sitting with some of the top executives at Sinclair. She had seen more than one person from the office send envious looks her way.

One of those was her ex-boss, Robert Carruthers. He was staring so hard he bumped into another gentleman. Madelyn loved it. Sending him a little wave over her shoulder, she straightened in her seat and looked directly into Daniel Falcon's fathomless black eyes.

Once again she had that breathless feeling. He made a woman consider sitting on her hands to keep from grabbing him.

Dressed in a tailored black tux that fit his tall, muscular body to perfection, he exuded sex appeal. Madelyn didn't have to look around the table at the women to know each one of them was affected. They all might be happily married, but they weren't dead.

"I hope I'm not interrupting. I just wanted to say hello to Ms. Taggart," he said, his voice a rich mixture of velvet and sin.

She felt a ripple of excitement. Maybe, just maybe.

Then she noticed the woman next to him: glittering from the crown of her head with an overdone tiara, a clunky gemstone necklace, and drop earrings to match. Madelyn couldn't see the woman's feet, but she was sure her evening shoes were just as sparkling.

Aware of the attention around the table on her, Madelyn forced herself to smile and make the introductions. She finished by saying, "I'm sorry, I don't know your companion."

Squeezing Daniel's arm, the dark-haired woman didn't wait for him to introduce her. "You must not attend the opera. I'm Natalie Kemp."

The words were deliberately condescending. "I love the opera," Madelyn explained. "One of my fondest memories is meeting Katherine Battle after she gave an outstanding performance at the Metropolitan Opera. The acoustics are marvelous. But I'm sure you know that since all the greats have performed there."

Uncertainty touched the other woman's face. "Not yet."

"Then what might I have seen you in?" Madelyn asked pleasantly, too aware of the conversational lull around the table. She'd be nice if it killed her.

Natalie glanced nervously around the table, then at Daniel before answering, "Mercedes in *Carmen*."

"Ah, one of the gypsy women," Madelyn said, clearly astonishing the other woman with her knowledge of one of the minor roles in the opera. "Some of my friends are going tomorrow night. I'll have to tell them to look for you."

Natalie flushed.

"Come along, Madelyn, I think I've been sitting too long," Jane said and stood. "I'm not sure how long we'll be gone, so I'll say my goodbye to you now, Mr. Falcon, Ms. Kemp."

"Goodbye, Daniel, Ms. Kemp." With her hand on Jane's arm, they moved across the room.

"Don't worry, Madelyn, real men don't stay around vicious, catty women," Jane offered, accepting a flute of champagne from a white-jacketed attendant. "I'd say Ms. Kemp won't last the night."

Madelyn's hand trembled on the long stem. "I don't suppose it would do me any good to say I don't know what you're talking about."

"Please don't. I detest people who lie, and I already like you a lot."

A smile tugged the corner of Madelyn's mouth. "I like you, too."

"Good, then let's give them five more minutes and then we'll go back." Jane took a sip of wine.

"Thanks for the rescue," Madelyn replied softly.

"Women have to stick together." Jane lifted her glass in a salute. Madelyn joined her.

"Hey, this is pretty good," Jane said after downing half the contents. "I usually have only half a glass because it goes straight to my head, but since Sinclair is helping to underwrite this affair, we should do our best to have a good time."

"I agree." Madelyn drained her glass. Grinning, they placed their empty glasses on the tray of the circulating waiter and reached for full ones.

When they returned to their table several minutes later, Madelyn was feeling comfortably mellow. Her boss took one look at his wife's wide smile and decided it was time to go home.

Not wanting to stay, Madelyn followed them outside. "Good night, Mr. and Mrs. Sampson. Thanks for allowing me to sit at your table. I had a wonderful evening."

The older woman patted Madelyn's hand. "Call me Jane. We like each other, remember?"

"I remember." With a wave, Madelyn started toward the parking lot.

Mr. Sampson called after her, "You didn't valet park?"

"No, the line was too long." *And I was foolishly impatient to get inside and see if Daniel was there.*

"We'll take you to your car," Jane offered, her expression worried.

"It's all right. I'll be fine."

With a wave, she headed for the packed parking lot. When she had arrived it had been twilight, but now darkness shrouded the area away from the bright gold and chrome hotel entrance. It was just her run of bad luck that the overhead light was out on the aisle where she had parked her car.

Chastising herself for her earlier impatience, she stopped near the outer perimeter of light shining from another part of the hotel to search in her bag for her car keys. A noise behind her spun her around.

Less than seven feet away was the ill-mannered man with the horrible cologne. "Thought you were waiting for someone."

"That wasn't your concern then or now."

He shrugged and the too-large jacket almost slipped off his shoulder. "Since we're both alone, what do you say we go someplace?"

"I'm going home. Alone."

He stepped closer. "Don't play so hard to get. You and me could have a lot of fun together."

"You're pushing it." She was more angry than frightened. Men could be such egotistical jerks.

The man snorted. "Like I'm scared. What are you gonna do to me any—"

He never completed the sentence. He might have if he hadn't reached for her.

She reacted instinctively to the threat. Grabbing his hand, she used the momentum of his off-balance body to flip him over on his back. His wrist secure in her hands, she pressed her foot to his chest to keep him down.

"You were saying?" she asked mildly.

Angry curse words singed the air. However, another deeper, angrier voice had no trouble being heard.

"Shut up, you piece of trash. Count yourself lucky she got to you before I did," snarled a cold voice.

Madelyn jerked her head up and around. She'd know that voice anywhere. Daniel stood glaring down at the man who had suddenly quieted.

When Daniel looked at her, she saw black rage burning just short of control in his dark eyes. She swallowed.

"Are you all right?"

She swallowed again before she could answer. "Yes."

His gaze swept over her like silent, invisible fingers. "We'll talk about your part in this later." Taking the man's hand, he moved her aside, yanked him off the ground, then twisted his arm high up behind his back.

"Ohh! You're breaking my arm."

"Shut up and move."

The man moved.

Daniel called over his shoulder. "I'm not in a very good mood, so I suggest you follow us inside."

What did she care about his mood? He had messed up hers three weeks ago. And where was Miss Congeniality?

Picking up her purse and the scattered contents, Madelyn remembered Daniel's high-handedness in taking the man once he was down. Show-off.

Then she remembered something else: Daniel's close connection to her brothers. If they or her parents heard about this, she'd never hear the end of it.

"Daniel, wait a minute. We need to talk." Her skirt raised up over her knees, she sprinted to catch up. Her comfortable state of mellowness had lasted all of ten minutes.

Chapter 5

Madelyn couldn't believe what was happening. She had seen Kane on a tear, but he was mild compared to Daniel. She didn't blame the on-duty executive manager for looking uneasy. The chief of hotel security didn't escape his wrath, either.

Daniel's tone was scathing when he mentioned the light out in the parking lot and the stupidity of not putting on extra security people to patrol the parking lot on the night of a big event.

Both men had initially tried to defend themselves, but after Daniel got through with them, they simply listened. Madelyn didn't blame them. She wasn't about to forget his words about her part in this.

As for Jerome Turner, the man who had started all this, he remained slumped in his chair, his thin shoulders hunched forward in the ill-fitting tux. He worked in the janitorial department of one of the oil companies and had stolen the invitation out of the wastebasket. He probably hoped Daniel had forgotten him.

The thought was wasted. Every few seconds Daniel would turn those steely, black eyes of his on the man, and the tension in the room would almost sizzle.

Madelyn had thought of leaving the private office

they were quickly and quietly escorted to, but as if he had a sixth sense where she was concerned, each time she began to ease up from her chair, Daniel's attention immediately shifted to her. Considering she had to ask a favor of him, she decided after being caught for the second time, she'd stay.

"If Ms. Taggart had been harmed in any way because of your carelessness, you would have answered to me," Daniel said, his voice crackling with dark promise.

He was a magnificent warrior, she admitted reluctantly. He intimidated and commanded respect. No one in their right mind would antagonize him. She'd read that traits such as fearlessness and daring were inheritable. He'd certainly gotten his share.

"I'm sorry, Mr. Falcon," David Flowers, the executive on duty repeated, his Adam's apple bobbing up and down in his thin neck. "Maintenance is taking care of the light, and extra security is on the lot. We've pulled off some of the valet attendants to escort unescorted ladies to their cars."

"The police are on their way," offered the middle-aged security guard, his hands noticeably by his sides instead of hooked in the waist of his pants as when he had arrived. He had ripped them out two seconds after Daniel tore into him.

"Police," Jerome shouted, straightening in his chair. "Now wait a minute. Ain't no call for that. I just wanted to pick her up for a little fun."

Daniel whirled and reached for him.

"Stop him," Jerome yelled, toppling his chair backward in an attempt to get away from Daniel. It was useless. Tossing the straight-back chair to one side, Daniel kept going.

"Daniel, if you touch that man you'll end up in jail, and I thought you wanted to talk to me," Madelyn said, trying to sound calm when her entire body was shaking.

He stopped, but didn't turn. "I know where to find you." The implication was that the cowering man might not be so easy.

Both hands defensively in front of him, the young man scooted until his back hit the wall. He swallowed repeatedly. "Look, man, I'm sorry. I didn't mean no harm. I was on my way to the bus stop, saw her and thought I'd try one more time."

"Bus stop," Madelyn cried in disbelief. "You were trying to hustle me, and you didn't even have a car?"

"What's this about one more time?" Daniel asked coldly.

"I-I asked her to dance. She turned me down." He shook his head. "I didn't mean no harm. I just reached for her, and she pulled that judo crap on me."

"I thought Mr. Falcon subdued you," said the executive.

The man on the floor shot Daniel a glance before answering. "I-I forgot."

Madelyn returned the speculative looks of the hotel executive and the security guard with what she hoped was an I'm-just-a-helpless-female look. It galled her to do so. But the thought of having her name on a police report wasn't thrilling.

"Daniel, can we go now?"

With one last lethal look at the cowering man, Daniel turned. "Let's go."

"Man, please—don't send me to jail. I ain't got no record, and I'm gonna lose my job as it is," Jerome pleaded.

Daniel jerked around, his eyes as ruthless and chilling as his voice. "You should have thought of that before you tried to attack her."

"Man, I told you, I just wanted to pick her up. My partner said he came to one of these things last year and scored. He didn't have no car, either."

"And you believed him?" Madelyn asked incredulously.

"Greg's a player. Says he always scores. Said they left in her ride. I figured I could do the same. Please," Jerome cried, "I apologize. I was being cocky, but I didn't mean to scare your woman, man. I swear. My mama would take a broomstick to me."

"Your mother?" asked Madelyn softly, her curiosity growing with every word the young man spoke.

As if realizing his hope lay with Madelyn, the young man gave his full attention to her. "I live with my mother. If I didn't have to give her a hundred dollars every two weeks for rent and take out health insurance, I'd have a car—and Keisha wouldn't have kicked me to the curb."

"You might have needed the health insurance if you had touched Ms. Taggart," Daniel reminded him.

The young man began shaking. Madelyn wanted to swat Daniel. Any man who paid his mother rent money wasn't all bad. "Have you ever missed paying rent?"

His gaze touched the floor. "Once—but she had my clothes packed two days later. I had to borrow the money from my partners."

"Was Greg one of the men you borrowed money from?" she asked.

"No. He said his ex-wife was hassling him about child support. He wanted money from me," Jerome admitted.

"Greg sounds like a person I'd stay away from," she said.

"That's what my mama says."

"Then perhaps I should call her and let her know you didn't listen," Madelyn threatened.

Wide-eyed, he came off the floor. "You can't. My mama would kill me if she knew about this."

Daniel had matched movements with the man, his huge bulk defensively in front of Madelyn. Scowling at his broad back, she stepped around him. The man's fear was obvious. Somehow Madelyn knew he didn't mean "kill" literally.

"I won't, if you do some things for me." The man was bobbing his head in agreement before she finished. "Apologize to your employer, scratch Greg off as a buddy, and give your mother a hug when you get home."

He hung his head. "If I hug her, she'll know I did something wrong."

"Then you'll just have to suffer the consequences. It's better than going to jail," she told him. "In case you think about forgetting . . ." She paused, adding, "Remember this man standing by my side, because he certainly won't forget you."

"I won't forget," he promised, looking as unhappy as any teenager made to own up to his misdeeds.

Madelyn touched Daniel, felt the tenseness in his arms, and forged ahead anyway. "I believe him. There are enough young men with police records. Life for a young black man can be rough enough without that. You believe in giving young people a chance, or you wouldn't have started the work-study programs," she finished softly for his ears alone.

His surprised gaze jerked toward her.

"Please," she said. "I think he's telling the truth. I don't want to press charges."

A muscle leaped in Daniel's bronzed jaw, then he

spoke to Mr. Flowers. "If it checks out he has no prior arrest records, we won't press charges."

"Thank you. Thank you," Jerome cried.

Daniel turned cold eyes on him again. "Don't make me regret my decision."

"You won't. And, miss, I'm sorry."

"I hope you are, but another thing you can do for me is start treating women with respect," she told him.

"Come on." Daniel urged her out of the office and down the lush carpeted hallway to the immense atrium lobby. Passing the two rushing Houston policemen, they kept walking.

"You don't want to talk with them?" Madelyn questioned.

"I've ranted enough for one night," Daniel answered.

From beneath her lashes, Madelyn glanced sideways at his stern profile. "You mean you don't always have men sweating bullets."

"I'm glad you can smile about it," he said, steering her around a group of chattering people.

She heard the tightness of his voice and knew she shouldn't have teased him. He had been concerned about her safety.

"I'm all right, Daniel. I was too angry to get scared. I overreacted." Her lips twitched. "Imagine him trying to pick up someone while riding a bus." Laughter bubbled from her throat.

Daniel stopped and stared down into Madelyn's animated face. She could laugh—and he was still shaking. His rage against the hotel staff had been misplaced. He was the one really to blame.

The instant he had seen the light go out of Madelyn's dark eyes when he introduced the opera singer, his guilt had begun. The woman had meant nothing to him. Another woman who wanted to add his name to her list of lovers. He had met her at the ball and had escorted her back to her table after she had tried to insult Madelyn.

She should have saved her breath for her arias. No one got the best of the laughing woman in front of him. Not some cocky jerk trying to pick her up, and not Daniel Falcon.

He had seen her leave with the Sampsons and followed. People stopping him to speak had caused him to lose sight of her. The valet had pointed Daniel in the right direction. Hearing the man boast, then seeing him reach for her, had enraged him. He didn't know who was surprised the most—him or the man on the ground with her foot in his chest.

He shook his head. "You're something."

"Glad you noticed."

"I noticed." He started walking again. "I'd appreciate it if you wouldn't tell anyone about my involvement with the work-study program."

"I won't. Kane explained everything to me." She glanced up at him through a dark sweep of lashes. "I think it's very generous of you."

He shrugged. "Don't go picturing me any different than I am."

"Why won't you let me think anything good about you?"

"Because there isn't," he said, leading her down three marbled steps. "We'll get my car first, then I'll follow you home."

"That isn't necessary. Besides what about Miss Congen— Kemp?" Madelyn quickly corrected.

"I met her only tonight," he said, ushering her through the outside glass door held open by a uniformed attendant. "I'm not going to renew the acquaintance."

"Mr. Falcon, Mr. Flowers called and your car is

waiting." The smiling young man looked at her. "I'll be happy to escort you to your car."

"Thank—"

"That won't be necessary," Daniel said, cutting her off, then urging her to his Bentley coupe parked by the curb. He opened the door. "Get in. I'll take you to your car."

Madelyn lifted her chin. She was tired of him seeing her as his friends' helpless little sister who always needed rescuing. "I can see myself home."

"Do I call Kane or Matt first?"

Madelyn got in the car without another word. Closing the door, Daniel tipped the attendant standing a respectful distance away.

"You really aren't going to tell on me are you?" she asked, gnawing on her lower lip.

"That depends," he said, setting the car in motion.

"On what?"

He shot her a glance before turning in the direction of the parking lot, glad to see a security guard on foot patrol and the burned-out bulb replaced. "On whether you appease my appetite or not."

A soft gasp echoed in the car.

Daniel didn't know if the sound pleased or displeased him. "I didn't get a chance to eat at the banquet today or tonight. Any chance on fixing me a sandwich or something?"

Madelyn vacillated between anger and disappointment. She took both out on the French bread she was slicing on the cutting board. How could she keep letting herself in for disappointment?

Easy—she got within an inch of Daniel, and her brain shut down. Too bad his didn't do the same.

"You sure I can't help?" he offered.

She glanced up and wished she hadn't. He had made himself comfortable. His jacket was gone, his shirt unbuttoned at the collar, and the sleeves rolled back. But the worst thing he had done was to take the band from his hair.

Shannon, her sister-in-law, hadn't exaggerated when she described it as being sensual. The lustrous black hair lightly streaked with silver moved with a supple grace that was almost hypnotic.

She didn't know if the reason was because she wasn't used to seeing men with long hair, the hair itself, or because everything about Daniel seemed to make her heart beat faster.

"My beautician wanted me to tell you she wanted to get her hands on your hair," she said, thinking she'd better leave the other part out. "I told her I'd tell you if I saw you."

Pushing away from the door, he came to stand beside her. She barely kept from jumping when he touched her hair. "She did a good job with yours, but I think I'll pass."

Nodding, she went back to making the submarine sandwiches. Daniel's blunt-tipped fingers picked up an olive and popped it into his mouth.

"These will be ready in a minute." *Faster if you'd move.*

"No hurry. You're sure I can't help? Even I can slice and dice," he said.

She shook her head, piling on shredded lettuce, pickles, tomatoes, and onions. "Matt burns water. Kane is a fantastic cook."

"How about you?" he asked.

She smiled in spite of the tension. "Somewhere between Kane and Matt. I was in a lot of activities at school, and I just didn't seem to have the time. You're lucky I went to the store yesterday. Mama's care package isn't due until Friday."

Picking up the round platter of sandwiches, she placed them on the table. "Is cola all right, or do you want a beer? I mean is beer okay?"

"Alcohol has never been a problem for me, although I seldom drink." He smiled and Madelyn's heart did a little flip-flop. "Do your brothers know you drink beer?"

"It belongs to them," she told him with an answering smile.

"Then cola is fine. Matt probably keeps count."

She laughed and sat down in the chair he held for her. "You know him well, don't you?"

"He's a good friend," Daniel said, no longer smiling.

Madelyn placed her hands in her lap, her appetite gone. "So I can't be one, is that it?"

Black eyes bore into hers. "It wouldn't stop there, and we both know it."

"We could try," she offered.

His laughter was rough. "You couldn't be that naive."

"I'm not naive or afraid of what I want."

"You should be." Rising, he pushed his chair back under the table. "I'll get something on the way back home. You need to rest."

She was right behind him as he went to the door. "Stop telling me what I need. I can take care of myself."

He whirled, his eyes blazing. "Just because you put down that guy tonight doesn't mean it might not have been a different story if he had been armed or more determined."

"I've taken tae kwon do classes for four years. Any man who touches me better have his life insurance paid up."

"Is that so?"

"That's so!" She knew she had challenged the wrong man the instant the words left her mouth.

She expected him to come after her, no holds barred. She knew she wouldn't be any match for Daniel. Skill might count for a lot, but he outweighed her by a good ninety pounds. Besides, something about the way he carried himself let her know he could walk into the meanest bar in Texas and come out unscathed.

"You like challenges, do you? Let's see how you like this one." Abruptly he pulled her into his arms. His head dipped.

She closed her eyes, expecting an assault on her body. She should have known better.

The assault came, but it was against her senses. The tiny, nibbling bites on her lips—the slow, rough glide of his hot tongue against the seam of her lips—stripped her of her defenses and left her hungry.

He was feasting on her lips, and she was starving.

Her hands loosened their hold on his shirt and slid around his neck, pressing closer to his masculine strength and warmth. She wanted more. Her lips parted, trying to join their mouths.

His lips kept moving, always an instant in time ahead of hers. Frustrated, she reached up and grabbed handfuls of thick hair and kept him still. His mouth finally closed fiercely over hers. The fit was perfect, natural. Instead of assuaging the hunger as she thought, the mating of their tongues made the ache spiraling from the middle of her body intensify.

Whimpering, she pressed her body against his, trying to make the ache go away. His hands pulled her hips firmly against his blunt arousal. Air hissed over her teeth at the utterly arousing and erotic contact.

Her knees sagged. Her head fell backward.

Daniel took the opportunity to press kisses against

the slim column of her graceful neck, the rapid pulse beating at the base of her throat. Her tempting, full breasts were only a short distance away. His lips skimmed downward on her bare skin.

Locking his arm around her tiny waist, he lifted. Startled, she cried out, then cried out for another reason as his teeth closed around her nipple and tugged.

Abruptly his head lifted. "Did I hurt you?" Daniel asked, his voice hoarse.

Her eyelids blinked open. Her eyes were black with passion. "I—I—"

"Did I hurt you?" he repeated, his face an anguished mask.

Trembling fingers touched the rigid line of his mouth. "N-No. I was just surprised. I never knew. I never knew," she said, replacing her finger tips with her lips.

"Mad—"

Whatever he had been about to say vanished when her tongue touched his. He drew her to him again. One more kiss, and then he was out the door. He simply meant to teach her that she couldn't keep on provoking him. One more sweet taste.

He felt Madelyn's small hands on his bare chest and started to pull away. When had he unbuttoned his shirt?

Warm lips closed gently on his hard brown nipple. He groaned instead. When his shirt had been unbuttoned no longer mattered. He was wildly glad that it was.

Her head lifted, and he found himself torn between regret and salvation, then her tongue licked the nub delicately, before she whirled her tongue around the turgid point.

He shuddered.

By the time she had moved to the next nipple, Daniel was holding on by a mere thread. His entire body was shaking with need. He had been a fool to start this. He had wanted her too badly for too long.

"M-Madelyn, we have to stop this."

She kept right on driving him out of his mind with her delicate little tongue, seemingly lost in the touch and taste of him. Thinking to stop her, he pulled her up to him and kissed her. She melted against him like honey on a hot day. Her unbridled response snapped the last thread of his control and sealed their fate.

She was a woman burning in his arms, and he needed her fire to survive.

Stopping was impossible. The need had built inside him, picking up force like an avalanche thundering down the mountainside, mercilessly taking everything in its wake, its power awesome and frightening.

He didn't know where the bedroom was, and it was pure chance the first door he entered held a bed. They tumbled on top of the covers. Daniel swiftly rolled, bringing her beneath him. Feeling her full length against him was pure ecstasy.

He wanted to taste her, taste all of her . . . later. Now he ached too much. He rolled again, this time standing as he unzipped her dress. Thankfully she seemed as impatient to undress him.

Sweeping the covers aside, he lay back down, taking her with him. He prepared himself, moved her thighs apart, and thrust into her.

The thin barrier easily gave way. Disbelief tautened his body.

No, she couldn't be! Wide-eyed he stared down into her strained features. Her lips were tightly pressed together, her eyes shut.

She had been a virgin.

Cursing, he started to withdraw. She arched against him, locking her legs around his hips.

Breath hissed through clenched teeth. His forehead rested on hers. "Please don't move, Madelyn."

She heard him. She just wasn't able to stop trying to find some ease from the feeling of being stretched and filled. It had been so nice before— Maybe if she lifted her hips.

Control slipped beneath the seductive call of her body. Daniel met her halfway. She tried to pull back but he followed, his body plunging deeper, then withdrawing.

Pleasure snuck up on her. Instead of shrinking from the intimacy, she was greedily demanding more.

Their mouths and bodies fused. Her arms wrapped around his neck, her legs locked around his hips, she met him stroke for incredible stroke. Madelyn felt her body spiraling out of control, the feeling frightening. Instinctively, she began to withdraw in mind and body.

"No, come with me."

The husky entreaty of his voice caused her fear to recede. Her fingernails bit into Daniel's perspiration-dampened back. Her head arched, her body tightened as she reached toward the spiraling sensation, knowing Daniel was with her.

As soon as the last aftershock left her body, Daniel rolled to one side and held her tightly in his arms. Madelyn snuggled closer. She had never felt so happy, so complete. She had known almost from the first moment he had held her that she would love him.

Feeling shy and bold at once, she ran her hand down his back. The stiffness of his muscles surprised her when she was feeling so mellow. "Daniel, what's the matter?"

Suddenly he released her and sat up on the side of the bed, his broad back to her. "I'm sorry."

The tiny ray of fear receded. He was only concerned about her. "You didn't hurt me," Madelyn said, sitting up in bed and clutching the sheet to her breasts. She reached out to touch him.

He jerked at the contact, stood, and began dressing. "Yes, I did. In ways you don't even understand yet."

"Daniel, what's the matter?" Fear crept over her, stronger this time. "Did I do something wrong?"

"No. Never think that." Finally he faced her, his face tortured. "This shouldn't have happened."

She flinched, but kept his gaze. "I-Is that all you have to say?"

"What else is there to say?" he questioned, roughly buttoning his shirt.

"How about 'Madelyn, I'd like to see you again.' Or 'Madelyn, this was just a one-night stand.'"

His grim expression told her he could say neither of those things. "I tried to warn you in San Antonio I'm not the staying kind."

"So you did." Hurt beyond measure, Madelyn glanced away. "I'm sure you can find the front door. You seem to have excellent radar in finding the bedroom."

"I didn't mean for this to happen."

"Goodbye, Daniel." The words were tight.

"Mad—"

"Just go."

For endless moments he stared at her, then her huddled form turned away from him. The sight tore at his heart. He was already reaching for her when he realized his mistake. If he touched her, they'd probably end up doing the same thing she was crying about now.

A virgin. He hadn't expected that. She had been too responsive and somehow knowing in his arms. There hadn't been any of the awkwardness he'd have expected from an inexperienced woman. She had come to him with fire and passion, making his feeble attempts to deny himself her sweetness impossible.

Even now he still wanted her. Yet more than the wanting of her body, he wanted to see her smile, hear her laugh.

"Mad—" He broke off abruptly. The instant he began speaking, she flinched and curled tighter into a fetal position.

Guilt weighing heavily on his shoulders, he turned to leave and saw the teddy bear he had won for her in San Antonio. The animal's flat black eyes seemed to stare at Daniel accusingly.

Closing his eyes, Daniel glanced upward. What had he done? How could an innocent like Madelyn deal with something like this? No answer came. Opening his eyes, he left.

Madelyn heard him leave and wondered how she could still breathe with her heart ripped out. The front door opened and—after what seemed a lifetime—closed.

With a whimper of pain, she tucked her chin into her chest.

Chapter 6

Head bowed, Daniel's hand clamped and unclamped around Madelyn's front doorknob. He couldn't leave her like this. Not in misery after she had trusted him.

But what could he say? Do? He valued her gift, the generosity of her sweet body, but he had been the wrong man to give it to. A sound from the direction of the bedroom had him whirling sharply.

Crying. No, crying wasn't the heart-wrenching sounds he heard. She was sobbing. He'd hurt her. A hurt he didn't know how to mend or fix or even if it were possible to correct such a wrong.

It didn't take a genius to figure out that she probably thought she cared about him. In her inexperience she had confused lust with love. A woman didn't wait that long and then give herself to a man unless she thought there was some permanency to the relationship.

She had picked the wrong man. Marriage was out for him. Even when two people loved each other, it wasn't enough. Madelyn was looking at her brothers and her parents as examples. Unfortunately he had his parents as examples.

Love hadn't kept them together. They couldn't live together and couldn't live apart. They'd tried dozens of times to make it work, until a couple of years ago. The final break had been physically and mentally hard on both of them . . . and on him and his sister, Dominique, who hurt for them both.

No wonder neither his nor his sister's plans included marriage—although Dominique had had to learn her lesson the hard way.

The wrenching sounds from the bedroom gave no indication of lessening. Daniel's hand rubbed the back of his neck. Jewelry, flowers, or a designer original wouldn't fix this. She'd probably try to stuff it down his throat if he tried.

All he had was the truth and the hope that she'd understand. Slow steps took him to the bedroom. His knuckles rapped softly on the wall by the door.

"Madelyn?" The sobs stopped abruptly. "Can I come in?"

"Go away."

"Madelyn, please."

"You don't want me. What could be plainer?"

He stepped into the doorway. The sight of her sitting with her back pressed against the headboard, her knees drawn up, frantically wiping tears with the corner of her sheet, tore the words from his throat. "I wanted you. I still want you."

Her head jerked up. Hope flashed in her teary brown eyes. He clamped down hard on the need not to hurt her anymore and let her believe for just a little while. "But I don't love you."

She seemed to shrink and retreat before his eyes. He locked his legs and forced himself not to go any closer. "I made up my mind a long time ago that love and marriage weren't for me. I grew up watching the misery and heartache my parents put each other through—and I promised myself, I wasn't going to fall into that trap."

Finally Madelyn lifted her head. "It doesn't have to be that way."

"You're so naive and innocent, I should have seen it before. Love doesn't always survive."

"It can if the people love each other enough."

"Don't confuse lust with love. I wanted you, and love had nothing to do with it." She flinched again, but he was determined to get through this. "I was as cocky as that creep you took down tonight in thinking I could control the situation, that I was actually teaching you a lesson. Instead I took something from you that can never be replaced.

"The only reason I got farther was that you trusted me. I broke that trust. I know you can't stand the sight of me. You probably hate me, and you have every right. What I did was unforgivable. I ask you only one thing: Don't blame yourself. You expect everyone to be as open and as honest as you are. Some of us aren't."

Madelyn didn't know what to say. No matter how he phrased it, he didn't love her. Worse, he wouldn't even try. She was in love with a man who couldn't love her back. Her head fell forward.

"Are you all right?"

She heard the concern in his voice, saw it in his coal-black eyes when she lifted her head: concern, not love. She had given him all she was going to. Somehow she managed to speak with only a minor quiver in her voice, "No, but I will be."

His hands clamped. "I'll call tomorrow."

"I'd rather you didn't."

"I'll call."

The first call came a little after nine Sunday morning. Madelyn lay in bed listening to Daniel's voice and vacillated between anger at herself and at him. She'd known his reputation, and she had let herself get caught up in the moment anyway.

She had never known a kiss could render you mindless, make your body crave for so much more. Once his lips touched hers, thinking became impossible. All her senses took over. Daniel dominated every one.

The touch, the taste, the scent of him wrapped around her—and all she wanted was for the sensation to continue. His voice had dropped to a deep, velvet whisper that sent shivers through her. At the sight of him, his hair hanging down his back, his eyes dangerously alive, she had wanted time to stand still.

The answering machine clicked. She sent the machine a hard glare, then rolled to her side to stare out the sliding glass door leading to her small patio. The large teddy bear Daniel had won for her stared reproachfully back at her from the other side of the glass.

"You're not getting back in here any more than he is," she told the stuffed animal, then tucked her head into the crook of her folded arms. Unlike last time, there wasn't a whiff of Daniel's cologne to send her stumbling out of bed. She hadn't stopped until she had laundered the sheets and the pillowcases. She wanted nothing to remind her of her stupidity.

Of all the guys who had tried to talk her into bed in high school or college, she hadn't been tempted, not once. Daniel didn't even have to ask. In the bright light of day, that galled and angered Madelyn more than anything. She had let her feelings for him overshadow every other consideration.

He wouldn't get another chance. She had learned her lesson. But she had paid a high price.

The phone rang. Somehow she knew who the call was from. Her father's cheerful voice came through loud and clear.

"Hi, Kitten. When are you coming home? Seems like a year instead of a month. I guess you're at Sunday school. Today's the pastor's anniversary, and your mother went early to help out." He chuckled. "Probably doing a lot of bragging on how well our baby girl is doing. I better go before I'm late. You know how she hates that. Don't know what time well be home, so we'll call back. Bye, Kitten."

The answering machine clicked.

"Oh, Daddy. Your baby girl messed up, and I don't know what to do about it."

"Madelyn, since you won't answer the phone, I'm coming over. I'll be there in twenty minutes."

Madelyn sprang up in bed and stared at the answering machine as if it had turned into a snake. Why couldn't he leave her alone? He had gotten what he wanted.

The thought caused her to wince. She had been ridiculously easy for him. But once she learned something, she never forgot.

Scooting to the edge of the bed, she stuck her foot into her clogs, grabbed her purse off the dresser, and headed for the door. He thought he was so smart. She'd show him.

A smug smile on her face, she turned from locking her door. Her mouth gaped.

"You move faster than I thought," Daniel said.

He was less than ten feet in front of her and closing fast. She glanced toward her car, then back at Daniel. She'd never make it. "I don't want to see you anymore."

"I know and I don't blame you," he answered.

She frowned. "Then why are you here?"

"Because you've been hiding in your apartment and I didn't want that."

"How could . . ." Her voice trailed off as he pulled a cell phone from his pocket. "You've been out here since nine?"

"Actually since eight. I didn't know if you went to early church service."

She couldn't take it in. "I don't understand."

"You're a good, caring woman. What happened last night goes against everything you've been taught. You won't easily forgive yourself, although the fault was mine."

"I was so easy," she whispered in anguish.

Strong hands gripped her shoulders. "Don't say that. Don't you ever say that."

She recoiled. His hands dropped, and he stepped back. "It wasn't your fault. Get that through your head. You depended on me, and I let you down."

There was a question she had to ask. "Did . . . did you plan for . . . for it to happen?"

He gazed at her with steady eyes. "No. I lost control for the first time in my life. I'm not happy about it. Saying I'm sorry won't change things, but I don't want you beating yourself over the head."

She glanced away. "I can't help it."

"Would it help if you beat me over the head instead?" Her gaze jerked back around. "I have a training room in my house."

"No." She had faced disappointments before and survived. She'd survive this time. She had some pride left. He'd never know how much she hurt inside. She held out her hand. "Goodbye, Daniel."

"Take care of yourself." His hand closed around hers.

Nodding, she pulled her hand free and walked to her car. She hadn't missed the electric awareness between them. From the sudden narrowing of his eyes, he hadn't, either. At least she no longer felt used and discarded. She just wished she felt loved.

Daniel watched Madelyn drive away and wondered why he felt worse instead of better. The animosity between them was gone. She had left instead of retreating back into her apartment. He had almost accomplished what he had set out to do. She hadn't smiled or laughed, but she would.

The only problem was, he wouldn't be there to see or hear it.

Madelyn didn't know where she was driving to, and she didn't care. Knowing how hectic the Houston freeways could be, she took the off ramp and simply drove aimlessly until she saw Meyer Park and pulled in.

Too restless to sit, she got out and soon found herself in front of the duck pond, her mind still on Daniel. He was right. She was more angry with herself than she was with him. He had offered nothing, promised nothing. She had wrongly assumed that he felt the same way she did.

He had felt only lust.

Her fault. Despite the idea of being called antiquated by some of her friends, she had always expected to wait until she married to make love. That's why none of the other men in her life ever tempted her to go farther than a few heated kisses.

The moment she had kissed Daniel at the street fair in San Antonio, she had known he was the one she had been waiting for. There was a connection there that even he couldn't deny.

He hadn't tried. She might be inexperienced, but she knew he still wanted her. He just wasn't going to let himself be swayed by his emotions the way she was.

She had three choices: mope and hide from life, chalk

up the experience as a bad decision, or go on and pray one day he might stop running from a commitment. Since the possibility of her feelings toward him changing wasn't an option, she really didn't have a choice.

Like her mother, she somehow knew she'd love only once. Considering Daniel's coming over this morning to check on her, and his statement that she was the only woman that had ever made him lose control, things weren't as bleak as they could be.

Returning to her car, Madelyn drove home. Without replaying the messages on the answering machine, she called her parents later that afternoon. At the sound of her mother's voice, her throat stung. The sensation became worse when she talked with her father.

She'd always been Daddy's girl. She'd follow him anywhere. She'd learned to drive by sitting in his lap, caught her first fish with his favorite pole, served him her first mud cake.

Her eyes stinging, she looked straight into the glassy black eyes of the teddy bear. Swallowing, she made up her mind what she was going to do.

After promising she'd be home the following weekend, she put the bear back in the corner of her bedroom. She wasn't a quitter or a coward. Somehow she'd find a way to change Daniel's mind—and maybe, just maybe, win the heart of a falcon.

This has got to stop. Splashing cold water on her face, Madelyn took deep breaths and tried to keep her stomach from emptying anything more. Her lunch was already gone, but that hadn't seemed to matter to her stomach.

The women's rest room door opened, and Cassandra Lincoln came in. "You're feeling better?"

Madelyn sucked in another breath before she answered. "I'm not sure."

The petite blonde frowned. "Today is the second day in a row you've thrown up your lunch. Maybe you're getting an ulcer?"

With one hand on her stomach, Madelyn straightened. "Probably a virus. I've been sick the last couple of mornings also."

Cassandra's blue eyes narrowed, then she smiled. "If I didn't know better, I'd think you might be pregnant."

Madelyn spun toward the other woman, horror written on her face. "What?"

Cassandra held up her hands. "Just kidding. Everyone knows you're the straight-arrow type. I better get back. If you're still sick by tomorrow, you should see a doctor."

Clutching her stomach, Madelyn stared at the closed door. She didn't have to see a doctor for a little virus. She certainly wasn't pregnant. She couldn't be.

Snatching a paper towel from the dispenser, she dried her face and repaired her makeup. She felt better already.

Once at her desk, she went back to working on the specifications for a deep well.

There was a brief knock on her open office door, then Mr. Sampson came in. "Madelyn, I need you and Floyd to fly down to the Gulf. Number fifty-eight is ready to be plugged up and abandoned."

Just the thought of riding in the helicopter sent her stomach into a spasm. Unconsciously she clutched it.

He frowned, coming farther into the room. "You sick?"

She swallowed. "I've picked up a virus."

"That lets you out." He peered at her closely. "Maybe you should stay home tomorrow."

"I'll be fine," she said. "Besides, I'm almost finished with new designs for the deep well in zone eight."

"Really?" His eyes brightened. "Then I'd certainly want you to stay and complete that. Cassandra can take your place on the Mexico trip."

"I'll have the report to you by tomorrow afternoon," Madelyn said, her voice wavering only slightly.

By three the next day, Madelyn was trembling and flushed, yet somehow she had managed to finish the report. Despite drinking only a carbonated beverage, she continued to feel queasy.

Mr. Sampson took one look at her when she handed him the report and told her to go home and stay there until she was well. All he needed was the rest of his staff to get sick.

This time she didn't argue. She had never felt worse. Opening the door to her apartment, she stopped only long enough to grab a carbonated beverage from the refrigerator.

Two sips later she was running to the bathroom. After emptying her stomach, she looked into the mirror, refusing to believe what her body was telling her. Eyes shut, she tried to keep the suspicion from forming into thought.

It was useless.

The word formed. Hammered against her skull.

Pregnant.

Unsteady legs refused to hold her. She slid to the cool tile of the bathroom floor. This couldn't be happening to her. She had done it only one time. One time.

No. Her eyes snapped open. Something else was wrong. Maybe she had caught some virus? Her cycles had always been erratic. It was only a coincidence that the Petroleum Ball was a little over six weeks ago. There was no need to panic.

She was overreacting. Daniel had used protection. Just because she had been nauseous for the past few days didn't mean anything. Her breasts being tender was probably due to some hormonal imbalance due to her irregular cycle.

Yes, that was it.

Feeling better, she got up from the floor. The wan, frightened face staring back at her wasn't reassuring.

"I'm not. I'll prove it."

Washing her face and brushing her teeth, she grabbed her purse and rushed out to the car. Not daring to let anyone know her suspicions, she drove to a drugstore on the other side of town.

She sat in the busy parking lot a full five minutes to make sure she didn't see anyone she knew before she went inside. Unwilling to ask a clerk for directions, it took her two frantic minutes of looking over her shoulder before locating the home pregnancy kits.

Grabbing the first one, she went to the counter. When the clerk bagged the kit in a plastic bag and handed it to her, she quickly stuffed it into her purse and left. *You'd think stores would use paper sacks for bagging personal items*, she thought irritably.

Knowing she was being irrational didn't help her to calm down. Always a safe driver, she ran two caution lights and kept the speedometer on seventy on the freeway. Once the test came up negative, she'd be back to her normal self.

Thirty minutes later Madelyn stared at the blue indicator, a growing knot of fear tightening her stomach. No. It was wrong. The kit must have been faulty.

Grabbing her purse again, she went to her car. This time she was too anxious to go very far. She stopped at the first drugstore she saw. Minutes later she was back in the car with three different brands.

The results were the same. Lined up on the marble vanity were four pregnancy tests: each blue, each positive. She was going to have a baby.

"No, I can't—I can't be pregnant. Please, I can't be."

Shoving her hands through her hair, she sat down on the cool floor. One time. She had friends in high school and college who played musical beds and never got caught.

Why her? Why did she have to get pregnant?

She didn't want to be a single mother. Raising a child was a big responsibility. She wasn't ready to be a parent. How could she have been so irresponsible and careless?

Her parents. Her eyes shut tightly. Her parents were so proud of her. How could she tell them that she had messed up? She couldn't. The news would devastate them. She was their sweet little baby girl. Sweet little baby girls didn't have one-night stands and, if they did, they weren't careless enough to get pregnant.

What about her job? She was so proud of her accomplishments and looking forward to being in management by next year. Next year she'd be up to her eyeballs in diapers and formula. It wasn't fair—it just wasn't fair.

Her head dropped into her open palms. Tears freely fell. Lifting her head, she forced herself to get up. She made it to her bed and lay down, curling into a tight ball.

How was she going to get through this?

Madelyn awoke feeling fuzzy and thickheaded. Her mouth was dry. Her eyes hurt. Before she was completely upright, she remembered. Her gaze shot to the bathroom. Anger propelled her across the room.

With an angry swipe of her arm, she swept the test results into the wastebasket, yanked up the plastic lining, and securely tied the end.

She was squeezing the bag when she realized what she was doing. Shame, then guilt, struck her.

"I'm sorry. I'm sorry." Dropping to her knees, she released her hold on the bag.

Her anger was misplaced. The tiny life growing within her wasn't to blame for this. It had nothing to do with its conception.

She had made a decision, consciously or unconsciously, to make love with Daniel. Now she had to take responsibility for the results.

A baby.

Her gaze dropped to her waistline. A life was growing inside her. A life she and Daniel had created. Slowly she reached down and rubbed her abdomen.

"We'll get through this. It's not your fault." Leaning back against the wall she closed her eyes. If she had almost freaked out, what would Daniel's reaction be?

Chapter 7

"I'm pregnant."

Whatever words Daniel Falcon had expected to hear from Madelyn Taggart's forbidden lips, those definitely were not part of his unwanted fantasy.

With the same control with which he'd held himself since she first walked into his office, Daniel's face reflected none of his anger, his disappointment. Both hands remained negligently atop his neat desk, his face expressionless.

Not that it mattered because once Madelyn had tossed out her bomb, she had tried to take a chunk out of her lower lip, then centered her attention on the bank of windows on the other side of the room. Sunlight poured into his downtown office in Houston like spun gold. He seriously doubted if Madelyn noticed.

"Are you sure?" Daniel asked.

"Yes." Was that a smile or a grimace that quickly swept across the profile of her beautiful face? He couldn't tell. Her dismal expression made it difficult to remember her quick smile, the excited burst of laughter from her mouth, the sparkle in her big brown eyes.

All that was gone now. And it was his fault.

All because that same smile lit up his heart, that

same mouth tempted him beyond measure, those same eyes reached inside him and touched his soul. Despite knowing better, he had crossed a line he had no business crossing. "What do you plan to do?"

She looked at him then, her eyes wide. Her teeth clamped down on her lower lip again.

"Stop shredding your lips, for goodness' sake," he told her, the anger he had been trying to control slipping its tenuous hold.

She flinched, and he clenched his teeth to keep the curse words locked behind them. Unable to remain seated, he surged to his feet. Because he wanted as desperately to hold her as much as he wanted to shout at her for being so careless, he shoved his hands in his pockets. "What a mess."

Down went her head again, and he wanted to kick himself. Hell, he should kick himself. This was his fault more than it was hers. Her naivete was alluring to jaded men like him. He had shattered her illusions, and now she was paying the price.

But she had also shattered an illusion he had of her. His fists clenched as a wave of jealousy swept through him. "Have you told the father yet?"

She went as still as a shadow. Daniel could almost feel her pulling into herself. His control slipped. In seconds he was kneeling in front of her, his hands clamped around her upper forearm. "Did that bastard hurt you? Tell me? Who is he?"

Daniel didn't understand the sad smile that transformed Madelyn Taggart's face, but he did understand the words, "You are. You're the father."

Madelyn stared into the stunned face of Daniel Falcon and fought to control the tears that always hovered these days. He had just insulted both of them. "We never really knew each other, did we?"

His face cold, he pushed to his feet. "I can't be the father."

"Biologically or morally?" she managed to choke out.

"Both," he said tightly. "I'm not careless in that area. A man in my position can't afford to be."

Unconsciously Madelyn's hand went to her waist. Daniel saw the gesture and wanted to break something. She had gone straight from his bed to some other man's.

Her memory had never been far from him, and he hadn't meant a damn thing to her. Rage curled inside him, but he had the power to lose it on the woman huddled in front of him or subdue it. He had done enough to her.

"I know this must come as a shock. It was to me," she said quietly, remembering the crazy mix of emotions from fear to sheer terror on watching the tester turn blue. Dark, hopeful eyes lifted to his. "You're the father, Daniel. Nothing is foolproof except abstinence. Failures happen."

Daniel clamped down on the surge of excitement before it could materialize. He wasn't the father. "That's just it, Madelyn. It's never happened in the past."

Madelyn fought against succumbing to the misery and pain and anger assailing her from all sides. Of all the scenarios she had gone over in her mind, denial of paternity was not one of them.

In spite of everything, somehow, in the back of her mind, she had thought he would shout with delight on hearing the news. She had only been fooling herself. Since the morning afterward he hadn't tried to contact her in any way. He had walked out of her life and forgotten she existed.

Her initial instinct was to just get up and leave his

office, but she had never been one to walk away from anything, no matter how painful. More than her pride was involved. There was a child to consider.

"Have you told Kane or Matt yet?" Daniel asked abruptly.

Her fingers clutched the handbag in her lap. "No."

"That explains why I'm not in the hospital."

Her sharp gaze locked on his. "My brothers have nothing to do with this."

Daniel snorted. "We both know they'll come looking for me when you tell them."

"I have no intention of telling anyone at the moment," Madelyn said quietly. "As the father I thought you should be the first to know."

"I'm not the father," Daniel repeated adamantly.

Hurt and anger filled her eyes. "I saw the doctor Wednesday, and I'm between seven and eight weeks' pregnant, Daniel. If you'll check your calendar, you'll find that the Petroleum Ball was eight weeks ago tomorrow. You haven't forgotten what happened when you followed me home, have you?"

Pictures of them entwined on her bed flashed into Daniel's mind. His body hardened. He'd go to his grave remembering the softness of her body, the drugging taste of her skin, the soft cries she emitted as he sank into her moist heat.

From the slight parting of her lips, she remembered as well. She had been all the woman he wanted or needed. He hadn't touched another woman since that night. Too bad she hadn't felt the same way.

"What about the next night or the night after?" he asked.

Madelyn flinched. She stared at him in stricken horror. "Are . . . are you saying . . . But you know you were the first."

"It's been my experience that first doesn't always mean only or last," he said tersely.

His words stunned her. She opened her mouth, but nothing came out. Daniel had no such problem.

"How many people do you think are still with their first lover—and if by some miracle they are together, how many of those have remained faithful?" he asked sharply.

"I don't know and I don't care. But I wasn't raised like that. *I'm* not like that—I could never be like that," she told him, her voice rising in anger with each word she spoke.

"And that's the only reason this conversation didn't end the moment you told me why you came. By now you'd be talking to my lawyer."

Outraged, she gasped.

"But good women make bad decisions. I know how naive you are, how hurt you were. You obviously trusted the wrong man."

"Obviously," she said coldly, her meaning all too clear.

A muscle leaped in his jaw. "Do you honestly think you're the first women to walk through my door and make such a claim?" His expression harshened. "I've had two other paternity suits brought against me. The last one less than six months ago. Both claims were proven false."

His implication sent a shaft of red-hot anger through her. "Because their claims were unfounded doesn't mean that you aren't the father of this baby." Hurt beyond measure, Madelyn continued despite the agony she felt. "They probably wanted money. I haven't asked you for anything, nor will I ever."

"They didn't either at first," Daniel said with derision. "Each one went on and on about how they only wanted their child to know its father."

"And you believe I'm just like those women? Trying to get what I can?" The anguish was unmistakable in her thin voice.

"Whatever your reasons, I don't make mistakes like that," he said with biting finality.

"You just made the biggest one of your life. One day you'll realize just how big." Standing, she yanked her purse strap over her shoulder.

Disbelief etched itself on his bronzed face. He took a step toward her. "You're going to have a paternity test and try to bring a suit against me?"

"What kind of woman do you think I am?" she asked, infuriated, then continued before he could answer. "To do that I'd have to have testing done now. Amniocentesis can be dangerous, Daniel. I won't risk my baby's life for anything. And despite what you might think, being pregnant and single is not something I want to broadcast to the world."

His black eyes narrowed. "Then what are you going to do?"

She stared at him a long time before she answered. "You gave up your right to ask that question."

His entire body jerked as if he had been struck forcibly. "Don't play games with me, Madelyn."

"I never did and I never will." He was entitled to his doubts, but that didn't mean he could attack her character and suspect her motives. Her chin lifted. "Thank you for seeing me."

His brows bunched in surprise. "You're leaving?"

"I see no reason to stay. There's nothing left to be said. I'd like to remember our last meeting together at least ending cordially."

His eyes rounded at the full implication of what she was saying. Pleased to leave him looking confused and not so sure of himself, she turned and started from the room.

Dizziness swept over her. She swayed. In her haste to leave, she had forgotten what sudden moves did to her.

"Madelyn!" Daniel's hands circled her forearms.

Eyes closed, she waited for the spinning to stop.

"Madelyn—say something."

The frantic desperation in Daniel's voice more than anything enabled her to open her eyes. "Please take your hands off me and don't shout."

Dismissing the first request, he told her in a commanding tone, "Then stop scaring the hell out of me."

"I wish I could. It's not something I'm overly fond of, either." Her eyelids fluttered closed again.

"Damnit, Madelyn, don't do this to me again."

"The world doesn't spin so much if I keep my eyes closed," she explained.

Quickly picking her up, he carried her to an overstuffed chair, then carefully set her in it. Her head rested against the high cushioned back. "I'm calling your doctor. What's his name?"

"Dr. Scalar—and Daniel, do you think you could stop talking and asking questions for a few minutes?"

He didn't want to, but he kept his mouth closed. He wanted to help her, and he couldn't do that unless he had more information.

The feeling of helplessness was new to him and completely unacceptable. He was a man of action, used to seeing a problem and correcting it. But this was completely out of his realm of knowledge. Damn, he didn't know anything about pregnant women!

Except they weren't supposed to get excited. Guilt struck him in the chest like a powerful fist.

He gazed at the beads of perspiration on Madelyn's forehead, her trembling lips, and wanted to strangle the man responsible. His hand flexed and felt her smaller one in his. Tentatively his other hand brushed across her forehead.

Perhaps he should call the doctor. She might not want his help, but obviously she needed someone. Seeing her needing help and being unable to give it tore at his gut. He'd give her exactly one minute. Sixty seconds and if she didn't—

Her eyelids slowly fluttered upward. She moistened dry lips with the tip of her tongue. "Sorry."

"Can I get you something to drink?"

"No, it will only come back up again," she said and slowly sat up. "I can stand now."

He hesitated only a few seconds before assisting her to stand. His attention remained focused on her face to note the slightest change.

"Does this happen often?" he asked when she was completely upright.

She let out a trembling sigh and swept wisps of hair from her cheek. "Depends on what you call often."

"Madelyn," he said in a tight voice that proclaimed he was unwilling to settle for anything other than a straight answer.

"It's more of a nuisance than anything else," she told him, shoving the strap of her handbag over her shoulder.

Black eyes continued to study her. "You're sure you're well enough to leave?"

"I'm fine now."

He frowned, obviously unconvinced. "You don't look fine."

He hit a nerve. Unlike in San Antonio, this time it was *his* fault she wasn't looking her best. "You try being pregnant with your hormones going crazy and throwing up your toenails all the time, and see how great you look."

The sudden tightening of Daniel's features told her she had let her anger undo any ground she might have gained with him in the last minutes. Anger and accusations would solve nothing and perhaps damage what could be salvaged in time.

One of them had to resist the urge to strike out at the other. From the hard glitter in Daniel's eyes, it wasn't going to be him.

He had just shown he wasn't completely indifferent to her. Maybe he just needed time. From the beginning he had told her he didn't want long-term commitments. She couldn't think of anything more long term or more of a heavier responsibility than becoming a parent.

If she didn't believe that he was in heavy denial just as she had been initially, that he'd finally accept the baby as his, she wasn't sure she wouldn't sit down and wail like a child. But that didn't mean she'd hang around waiting until he did.

"Goodbye, Daniel." This time she made sure she didn't make any sudden moves as she left. The door closed softly behind her.

Her body trembling, Madelyn drew in a shaky breath and slowly made her way out of his outer office and down the hallway toward the elevator. She could get through this. She had to.

Daniel stared at the closed door. Emotions swirled through him like a dark cloud. Madelyn had left as quietly as she had come, leaving behind the elusive scent of her perfume and a rage churning inside him.

One tightened his body in remembered pleasure; the

other tightened his fists with the almost irresistible urge to smash something.

He silently battled to push both from his mind. He succeeded, but then something more disturbing appeared. Madelyn, faint and pale. That picture would not go away.

Stalking to his door, he jerked it open. "Gwen, cancel my appointment with Ames. Explain to him something came up," he instructed his secretary without breaking his long strides past her desk. Opening the door leading to the hallway, he was just in time to see Madelyn step into the elevator.

Madelyn stepped into the crowded elevator with a sigh of relief. While waiting, the feeling of light-headedness had returned. She had never been sick in her life except for colds, and she was becoming tired and aggravated with her body.

The elevator stopped two floors later, and a well-dressed man in his late fifties wedged himself on despite the sharp looks of the other passengers. Madelyn was just glad the elevator was moving again . . . until she became aware of the cloying scent of his cologne. The muscles of her stomach clenched in protest.

Eyes closed, she started to inhale deeper, caught herself before making the mistake, and exhaled instead. As soon as she breathed in again, the queasiness returned, only worse.

She swallowed, swallowed again. Nothing helped. She needed to get some fresh air. Leaning her head against the cool paneled wall, she opened her eyes and kept her gaze locked on the lit panel clicking off the floors.

Finally the panel blinked 1. Seconds later the doors slid open. Straightening, she started from the elevator.

A wave of dizziness hit her halfway across the busy lobby. She paused, blinking her eyes in an attempt to clear her head.

She had to get to her car. She took another step, then another. Faintly she heard someone ask if she was all right. She tried to answer, but found her tongue as uncooperative as her unsteady legs. The last thing she remembered was someone shouting her name.

Time stood still for Daniel when he saw Madelyn falling.

He raced toward her, catching her just as she would have hit the marble floor. Her eyelids were closed, her lips slightly parted.

Daniel thought his heart had stopped. His legs were shaking. Hell, his whole body was shaking. What if he hadn't been worried about her and decided to follow?

Pulling her close, he quickly carried her to a couch on the far side of the spacious lobby and laid her down. Going down beside her, he took her limp hand in his. "Madelyn, please open your eyes."

"Should I call an ambulance, Mr. Falcon?" asked a uniformed security guard who had hurried over.

"No. Just see that we have some privacy." The middle-aged man moved away, but Daniel didn't notice. All his attention was centered on the woman lying so still. "Madelyn—Madelyn, please say something."

Long black lashes fluttered, then opened. "Daniel? W-What happened?"

"You fainted. You can't keep scaring—" Shutting his eyes, he drew in a deep shuddering breath. He jerked them open when he felt the tentative brush of fingertips against his cheek.

"I didn't mean to scare you again. Pregnant women do silly things sometimes."

A soft gasp from behind a crouched Daniel caused Madelyn to glance upward. Directly behind him was a stunning African-American woman elegantly dressed in a pale pink suit.

The gold buttons had the distinctive interlocking CC of Chanel. She wore her short, dark brown hair in a breezy cut that complemented perfectly the contours of her oval face. She appeared to be in her early forties.

Catching Madelyn's gaze on her, the woman smiled and placed a slim, manicured hand on Daniel's shoulder. The square-cut emerald surrounded by diamonds on her ring finger sparkled like green fire. "I see you have been keeping secrets from me again."

Daniel tensed at the sound of the crisp Bostonian accent. He almost groaned. She was supposed to be in New York. But when had Felicia Ann Everett Falcon ever done what was expected of her?

Of all the times for his mother to return unexpectedly, this was the worst. He didn't have to see her face to know she was ecstatic with thoughts of finally getting to bounce a grandchild on her knee. So far he and Dominique both refused to give her any.

She might as well know it wasn't going to happen. He glanced up at her. "It's not what you think."

"I-I'm all right now." Madelyn struggled to rise. "Thank you, but I'll be late meeting my husband."

The smile left his mother's face. She sent Daniel an accusing look.

Daniel didn't know whether to thank Madelyn or shake her. He did know he wasn't letting her out of his sight until he made sure she had stopped all this fainting nonsense. "Can I take the car?" he asked his mother.

"Of course, dear. I'll get a cab back to the house."

He turned his attention back to Madelyn. "Do you think you can walk, or do you want me to carry you?"

"I'd rather not be on the ten P.M. news."

He glanced around the lobby. The security guard might have kept the crowd back, but he and Madelyn remained the center of attention "Point taken."

Easing her legs over the side of the couch, Madelyn slowly stood with Daniel's help. Thankfully she felt only a brief moment of dizziness.

"Don't you dare go out on me again," he ordered anxiously.

She looked at the frowning woman before answering. "You don't hav—"

"Yes, I do. Ready?"

Madelyn was too conscious of the people watching them, of the unknown woman only a few feet away, to protest any further. She only hoped no one connected with the media was around.

On the sidewalk Madelyn saw the big, silver Mercedes and the chauffeur rushing to open the back door. Her steps faltered. Now she understood what he had meant about "take the car." She had some pride left. "I'm feeling better. I can drive home."

"Humor me. I'll take care of your car after I've taken care of you. Now stop dragging your feet." Exerting more pressure on her arm, he started her toward the waiting sedan.

She didn't protest any further. She was too tired. As soon as she leaned against the luxurious buttery soft leather seat, her eyelids drifted downward. "I hate this."

"Don't blame the baby," Daniel said, a hint of censure in his deep voice.

Thick, black lashes swept upward. She stared at the man she had so easily fallen in love with, the man who didn't love her in return, the man who didn't understand her, the man she was coming to realize she didn't understand, either.

"We never really knew each other, did we?" she said again.

"No," he agreed.

"Well, Daniel Falcon, know this. This child will never hear blame or hatred or mistake or fault or any other words that make a child feel he or she did something wrong. Because I don't want to think of the life growing inside me in those terms. I may have acted irresponsibly, but I plan to take responsibility for my child."

"Raising a child isn't easy," he told her evenly.

"Life isn't easy," Madelyn said and closed her eyes again.

Daniel studied her closely. Was she shutting him out or sick again? He didn't know, but he felt easier since her forehead was dry, her breathing even.

She never acted the way he expected. She hadn't blamed him when she told him of her pregnancy; rather she had informed him. One hell of a difference.

There were so many questions he wanted to ask her— only he wasn't sure if he was ready for the answers. Her betrayal cut deep. Until this afternoon he would have believed it of any woman in his past, anyone except Madelyn.

Although he had known her for only a short while, he had known her brothers for over two years. Kane and Matt Taggart both possessed high standards of integrity and honesty. And while it didn't necessarily mean their sister possessed those same qualities, since they always spoke so highly of her, Daniel hadn't thought differently while he was with her.

But he had been wrong.

Whether out of passion or anger or need, she had

gone to another man. In the past Daniel had insisted on loose relationships because he wanted no ties. He wanted to be able to move on whenever he was ready. Although he had wanted Madelyn with a hungry urgency he had never experienced before, he still wasn't ready for anything long term. Ties and commitment didn't fit into his plans.

His parents had shown him how destructive love could be, but it was Jeanette who made sure he never forgot. Poor needy, pitiful Jeanette. She'd wanted so much to be loved and hadn't the foggiest notion of how to love in return.

Madelyn hadn't behaved like Jeanette or any of the other women who had come and gone in his life over the years. Most of them were fascinated with the public's perception of Daniel Falcon, and not the man. He understood their reasons and used them for reasons of his own.

Greedy, selfish women weren't likely to be hurt when a relationship was over. They were in it for the kicks, the prestige, and the benefits of being on the arm and in the bed of a powerful man. The game was to make it seem as if the parting was mutual. Then they'd move on to the next man and the next. "Night crawlers," Luke used to call them.

Daniel glanced at Madelyn. She had been too innocent for him—in mind and body. Yet somehow she had touched him more than the most experienced woman.

Her body had responded to his as if they had always been lovers. There was a knowing, despite the hungry desperation that made each touch, each caress fuel the need for more. Loving her had been the most powerful and the most humbling experience of his life.

No one had ever given him so much of themselves so freely or wanted to please him so much.

That's why he didn't understand. He knew there was a small failure rate using only a prophylactic, but he also knew they hadn't failed him in the past.

Not once.

So why had Madelyn chosen to name him the father and not the real person? He didn't know, but he'd find out who the man was—and if he had done anything to hurt her, Daniel would take care of him in his own unique way. The smile that crossed his face would have chilled a seasoned soldier.

The man should have protected her better. Hell, *he* should have taken better care of her. If he hadn't made love to her, none of this would have happened. No matter who the father was, her life had been irrevocably changed.

Just as no matter how it ate at his insides to think about her with another man, Daniel couldn't leave her alone. That meant he had to stop thinking about the other guy or he'd go crazy.

Yet the craziest thing of all was that he hadn't been able to forget the brief flash of joy he felt when she had told him she was pregnant.

Chapter 8

"Madelyn. Madelyn. We're here."

Opening her eyes, Madelyn lifted her head from the seat with difficulty. Although she wanted nothing more than to be able to lie down and stretch out, she couldn't get her body to cooperate.

"Let me help." Once again she was in Daniel's arms. Knowing protest was useless, she leaned her head against his wide chest and closed her eyes. Once inside she'd send him on his way.

"Do you think you can open the door?"

From somewhere she found the strength to open her eyes. Thankfully she found her keys without digging through her perpetually cluttered purse. Key in hand she leaned over. Dizziness struck. Closing her eyes, she slumped against Daniel.

"Easy, Madelyn. Higgins," Daniel called.

"Allow me, miss." Gently the keys were removed from her hands. The lock clicked.

"We're in," Daniel informed her. "Hold on. You'll be in bed in no time."

Madelyn swallowed and remained silent.

With profound tenderness, Daniel placed her on top

of the floral comforter. "We'll have you undressed in no time, so you can rest."

Madelyn's eyes blinked open, glad to see at least that the "we" didn't include Higgins. She wasn't quite so sure about the closed bedroom door.

"Just tell me where your nightgown is."

She attempted to sit up, but dizziness and Daniel defeated her.

"Be still. I'll get it for you." He crossed the room and pulled open the top drawer of her triple dresser. "Bingo." The nightgown spilling from his big hand, he came back to the bed.

"Daniel, this is not going to work."

Kneeling on the carpeted floor, he slipped off her dark brown suede heels. "What are you talking about?"

"I'm not about to undress in front of you," she explained, eyeing him wearily.

He stared at her. "You can't do it by yourself. You can hardly raise your head off the pillow."

She couldn't argue with him there. "Maybe after I rest for a little while, I'll feel better," she said, trying not to let herself be lulled into forgetting her decision of sending him home.

"Do you really believe that?"

"I want to believe it," she told him softly.

His hand lifted toward her brow, only to clamp into a fist midway there and settle on the bed. "How about if I help you out of the suit and turn my back while you do the rest?"

Somehow she knew that was as good as she was going to get. Besides, she was too tired to argue. Once she was in her gown, he'd leave. "All . . . all right."

His hands went to the tortoise buttons of her orange suit jacket. "After I finish, I can fix you something to eat."

Her stomach lurched. "Please, I don't want to talk about food."

"Madelyn, I don't think that's an option." Another button slipped free.

"I can't, Daniel."

He stopped and looked at her. "Yes, you can. There isn't much you can't do."

"Once I would have agreed with you," she said slowly.

"Meeting me changed that." Regret flashed across his face. "If I could change things. Go back."

Somehow his words hurt more than they helped. Tears pricked her eyes. She didn't want him to see her weakness.

"Don't cry," he said anxiously. "Everything will be okay."

"Will it, Daniel?"

Not waiting for an answer, she bent her head and slipped the last button free on her jacket, then began unbuttoning her blouse. His fingers were quicker. Despite her intentions of getting this over with quickly, she was glad he didn't try to remove her blouse once it was unbuttoned.

She hesitated only a second before reaching for the side hook on her coffee-brown skirt, then she slid down the zipper. Too vividly she recalled the same rasping sound as Daniel slid the zipper down the back of her gown the night of the Petroleum Ball. As if her mind had a will of its own, she lifted her gaze.

Tight-lipped, he spun away from her. Madelyn didn't have the luxury of trying to figure out if he was angry with her or himself, but angry he was. Shrugging out of her blouse, she pulled her lacy camisole over her head, then unsnapped the front fasteners of her bra, trying to ignore Daniel's presence less than a foot away.

Impossible. Especially when, despite everything,

she wanted nothing more than to pull him into bed with her and let him hold her. She wanted, needed to be held. She needed to be told everything was going to be all right. She had never felt so in need of another human's touch in all of her life.

"Everything all right?"

No, she wanted to say. "Yes" slipped out instead.

Grabbing the ecru-colored nightgown on the bed, she slipped it over her head. The heavy satin material pooled in her lap. Now all she had to do was find enough energy to raise up and get out of her skirt and panty hose.

"Decent?"

"Yes, but—" Her words trailed off as he turned. His gaze swept her, instantly seeming to size up her problem.

Standing, he scooped her up in his arms. "Lean against me, and I'll draw the comforter back."

She did, inhaling his scent, glad it didn't make her stomach queasy Sad because in her weakened state it made her want to keep hanging on.

"I'm going to lay you down again."

He removed her arms from around his neck as soon as her bottom touched the bed, a bottom without her skirt.

Surprised eyes lifted to his. He had the audacity to look pleased with himself. She didn't want to think of how many women he had undressed to perfect such a task.

He pulled the covers over her legs. "Soup, okay? I'm not much good in the kitchen."

"I don't want anything. It'll just come back up."

Hands on his hips, he stared down at her. "What did Dr. Scalar say?"

The fact that he had remembered her doctor's name

didn't surprise her. "That it was normal. He gave me some pills, but I can't keep them down, either."

A frown worked its way across his forehead. "How long has this been going on?"

She closed her eyes. She didn't want to see his face when she gave him the answer. "Off and on for several days."

The explosion she expected didn't come. She slowly opened her eyes and cringed. His eyes were saying everything quite eloquently. None of it good.

"Has the dizziness passed? I'd like to talk."

Now she understood why he hadn't said anything. The man never forgot a thing. She scooted down farther in the bed. "I'm really tired, Daniel."

He stared at her a long time. "I'll be here if you need me."

"You don't have to stay." Yet in spite of everything she told herself earlier, she wanted him to. She didn't feel alone when he was with her and being kind.

"Is there anyone who will stay with you if you called?" he asked.

Her lashes lowered. "No. I mean there is, but no one who wouldn't ask questions that I'm not ready to answer."

He nodded. "Then I guess I'm it until you're well enough to throw me out." Bending over, he unnecessarily adjusted the bed covers again. "Close those big brown eyes of yours and go to sleep."

After a moment's hesitation, she turned on her side and did just that.

Now that he was here, Daniel didn't have the foggiest notion of what to do. Hands on hips, he glanced around the small rose and white kitchen. He had mentioned soup because he'd always heard of people trying to give you soup when you were sick. He didn't know if that was what he should be giving Madelyn or not. Obviously she wasn't going to help.

The logical person to ask was another woman who had been pregnant. His mother came to mind. Bad, bad choice.

Leaning against the white countertop, he tried to go through his list of female acquaintances and came to the conclusion that was another bad idea. He could imagine the questions and the gossip to follow.

He was on his own. Looked like soup was on the menu.

Pushing upright, he started opening cabinet door after cabinet door. To his surprise he didn't find any soup or much of anything else. The refrigerator wasn't much better. He thought women stocked food like there was no tomorrow. Obviously he had been misinformed.

He'd have to go to the store. Buying one can of soup didn't seem to make much sense. Madelyn was just going to have to cooperate and give him a list of what she needed.

Opening her bedroom door, he quietly went to the bed. She slept with both hands under her face. She looked peaceful. He pulled the covers back over her shoulder. There was no way he was going to wake her up. He'd just have to find out on his own.

In the living room, he looked for the keys the efficient Higgins would have placed somewhere easy to find. A set of keys was on the cocktail table along with a brass planter filled with a sprawling silk ivy, several women's magazines, and a couple of hardcover books.

He reached for the keys. Inches away his hand paused. Beneath the keys was a book on pregnancy.

The thick book was an unwanted reminder of the guilt and anger he was trying to deal with, but it would also contain the information he needed to take care of Madelyn.

He picked up the book. He was flipping through the glossy pages when he saw the chart on fetal growth and development. Everything inside him stilled for a long moment. Without allowing his gaze to drift down the page, he turned the next page and the next until he reached the index and looked up nutrition.

Fifteen minutes later he left with a list of foods.

"Daniel, I don't want any."

"Come on, Madelyn, just a little," he coaxed. "It can't be good for you not to eat."

She eyed the spoonful of clear yellowish liquid inches from her lips, then Daniel. "I don't remember having any chicken broth."

"I stopped by the store on the way back with your car—now open." He moved the spoon closer.

She opened her mouth to say something, and the broth went in instead. She swallowed. It tasted warm and soothing to her dry throat.

"See, have some more."

She opened her mouth. Maybe the nausea had passed. Several bites later she knew she had deluded herself. She barely made it to the bathroom in time. When her stomach was empty, she wanted nothing more than to curl up into a little ball and roll away in embarrassment.

"I-I'm sorry," she murmured.

"For what? You have no control over being sick." Pulling her gently into his arms, Daniel sat on the side of the bathtub with her in his lap. He ran a moist washcloth over her face. "Better?"

She finally looked at him. He didn't appear disgusted at all. "Yes."

"I'm the one who should be sorry for forcing you to

eat." His hand brushed across her moist forehead. "I'll help you brush your teeth, then I'm calling your doctor."

"Daniel, I don't know."

"I don't, either—that's why I'm calling the doctor," he told her, then prepared her toothbrush and handed it to her.

Immediately after she finished she told him, "I feel better already. There is no need to disturb Dr. Scalar on a Friday night. You go on home, too. I'll probably sleep until morning."

He handed her a washcloth to wipe the toothpaste off the side of her mouth. "The book said to call."

"The book?"

Taking the washcloth from her, he placed it on the towel rack, then carried her back to bed. He didn't answer until she was beneath the covers again. "The book on pregnancy," he answered, then he was gone.

Seventeen minutes after Daniel had called Dr. Scalar's answering service, the ob-gyn had yet to return the call. It was six thirty. To Daniel, who was worried he had done more harm than good by forcing Madelyn to eat, it wasn't a good sign. Maybe he should have Madelyn get a new doctor—one who answered calls.

When the phone did ring, he jerked it up. "Yes."

"Dr. Scalar returning your call."

"About time. Madelyn can't keep a thing down, and she fainted twice. I gave her some broth like the book said, and she threw it up. You have to do something now to make her feel better."

"And to whom am I speaking?"

"Daniel Falcon." The name slipped out without a moment's hesitation. He wasn't above using his name to get the man moving.

"And what's your relationship to Madelyn?"

This time the answer came more slowly. "I . . . I'm responsible."

"I should have known that the minute you started rambling. Let me speak to Madelyn."

He never rambled. "She's resting."

"That may be, but until she gives me permission to discuss her case with you, I can't do so," the doctor said evenly.

Daniel wasn't pleased by the man's obstinance. "But I told you I'm responsible."

"I heard you the first time, Mr. Falcon," Dr. Scalar returned calmly. "And I know you've made quite an impression on our city, but your name is not on one piece of information Madelyn filled out—and until it is, I'm going to speak only to her."

"Hold on," he said in rising irritation. Entering the bedroom, he picked up the phone on the nightstand, then touched Madelyn's shoulder. Her eyes opened almost instantly. The weakness in them tore at his heart and dissolved his anger.

"Tell the doctor it's all right to talk with me, then you can try to rest."

Without rising, she took the phone. "Dr. Scalar. It's all right. No, the pill didn't stay down this morning or yesterday. Since Wednesday evening. I don't—" She handed the phone back to Daniel.

"Yes?"

"All right, Mr. Falcon, this is how I see things. Madelyn hasn't been taking care of herself because she's too tired, and the nausea and vomiting are only compounding the matter. Pregnancy is rough when it's planned. Unplanned it can be ruthless on the body. You follow me so far?"

Daniel liked the doctor even less. "Yes."

"Good. You did right to give her broth and to call

me. If she had been able to keep her pills down, I don't think this would have happened. Give her the pill again with just enough water to get it down. Four hours from now give her a couple of sips of carbonated soda; do the same four hours later."

He paused briefly then continued. "Give her the medicine in the morning as directed. Thirty minutes later give her a couple of saltines and a small amount of carbonated beverage. If she keeps that down, give her some of that chicken broth or something else light. Do this to make up five or six small meals. If it all stays down, good. If not, call me back. Understood?"

"What if she doesn't keep it down?"

"Don't get worried until I get worried. I saw her Wednesday. She's fine and the baby's fine. Anything else?"

Daniel glanced at Madelyn, who was watching him with those big brown eyes of hers. "No, we can take it from here. Good night."

"Good night. By the way, I've known Madelyn since she came to Houston. I'm glad you're there with her. Good night again."

Daniel replaced the receiver.

"What did he say?"

He explained everything the doctor had said, except the possibility that the nausea might continue.

"Didn't you explain you didn't stay here?"

"It wouldn't have mattered. Tell me where the pills are, and I'll get you some fresh water."

"Daniel, I didn't mean for this to happen." She sounded miserable.

"I know."

Thankfully, after a few anxious moments, the pill stayed down. Madelyn was so relieved and so pleased with herself, it didn't take much coaxing on Daniel's part to get her to slide back under the covers.

Switching the lamp on the bedside table to its lowest setting, he walked back into the living room. He hadn't intended this to happen, either, but somehow he was squarely in the middle of Madelyn's life and that of her child.

He didn't want to be there—he just couldn't think of any other place he'd rather be.

Except for one scary moment at Madelyn's second meal, she did fine. Saturday and all during the day. She had ceased worrying about Daniel being there and was just thankful he was. She couldn't have taken care of herself.

She had friends in Houston, but as she told Daniel, she wasn't ready to share her pregnancy with anyone else. She went to sleep Saturday night, feeling better than she had in weeks.

She awoke sometime during the night. A muscular arm was flung possessively across her waist, anchoring her to the sculptured male perfection of Daniel's body. His beautiful thick hair tumbled across his powerful bare shoulders. He still wore his pants. Obviously his intent had been to get some rest, not to seduce.

By the light from the lamp on the nightstand, she studied the incredible beauty of his face inches from her own. Since the eyes that had always fascinated her were closed, her gaze centered on his lips. Lips that could steal a woman's will and give her incredible pleasure.

Tentatively her finger traced the shape. His arms tightened, drawing her closer still. She smiled. It seemed natural and right that he would be there for her and their baby. Snuggling closer, she went back to sleep.

Sunday arrived and she continued to improve. Instead of a quick shower, she took a long bath, then ate lunch at the kitchen table. Daniel insisted she rest afterward, and she let him have his way.

Waking later that afternoon, she didn't see him. Curious, she got up and pulled on her robe. Since he had brought her home, he had never been far from her side. She missed him.

She found him in the kitchen. She smiled. "There you are."

He glanced up, then went back to unloading the various sacks spread out on the counter. "Dinner's almost ready."

Going to his side, she opened one of the containers. "Baked chicken. It smells delicious. I'll set the table for us this time."

He shifted uneasily, then looked at her. "Do you think you'll have any trouble from here?"

The smile slid from her face. Trembling fingers set the hard clear plastic container down. "No."

"I'll be going then." He reached into his shirt pocket and pulled out a business card. "My private number is on there. Call me if you need anything."

Her hand clutched the card. Unable to speak, she nodded.

She watched him almost run for the front door. Misery welled up inside her. "Oh, Daniel."

A tense Daniel sat in the backseat of the Mercedes as Higgins pulled out of Madelyn's apartment complex. Daniel hadn't wanted to leave. But he had had to. She possessed the unique ability of slipping past his defenses. Remaining emotionally detached while caring for her was impossible.

He had been doing all right until she became restless Saturday night. He thought he heard a noise coming from her bedroom, so he had gotten up from the sofa where he had been sleeping, pulled on his pants, and went to check on her. She was turning one way, then the other as if she couldn't get comfortable.

Things had started off innocently enough by him feeling her forehead, then her cheek to see if she had a fever. Almost immediately she had pressed her cheek against his hand, deepening the contact, and murmured his name.

The next thing he knew, he was in bed with her, holding her, inhaling her scent, whispering nonsensical words about him being there and she could rest. Unexpectedly, being with her calmed him as well.

Waking her every four hours for her meals hadn't been difficult because he had been unable to sleep. Holding Madelyn, he had slept way past his usual hour of rising at six in the morning. He realized then he had to leave.

Sharing the warmth and comfort of another's body could be as addictive as sex. Staying around her would only complicate matters. He had helped her when she needed it, now it was time to get on with his life and she hers.

As soon as the car rolled to a stop in front of his two-story country French mansion on the outskirts of Houston, Daniel got out. He took the four curved brick steps by two, then opened the leaded glass front door and entered the house.

Impatient steps rang loudly on the marble floor as he crossed the seventeen-by-seventeen foyer. He headed for the elegant wood spiral staircase, unmindful of the bright stream of sunlight pouring through floor-to-ceiling windows on the fifty-foot wall of the living room to his immediate right.

He needed a shower and a change of clothes, and to make a phone call. Canceling an appointment ten minutes before time with a man who owned one of the largest rig-manufacturing firms in the country wasn't done. Especially when Daniel needed rigs to bring up oil and gas, and rigs were in short supply and high demand since the energy boom. But not for one second did Daniel regret his decision.

He hit the stairs running, then groaned on seeing his mother coming toward him. Although she enjoyed an active social life and was dressed in something soft and flowing, he didn't hold out much hope she was going out. Because more than anything else, she'd enjoy having a grandchild.

"Good evening, Mother."

"Good evening, Daniel. I'm going to be disappointed in you if that young woman really is married."

It certainly hadn't taken her long to start in on him. "Mother, stay out of it."

She turned and followed him up the stairs. "Don't take that tone of voice with me, Daniel Falcon. I don't care how many boards you sit on."

"I thought you were going to stay in New York until the play you were backing opened," he said, hoping to change the subject.

"Seeing my favorite son is much more important," she said, accompanying him down the wide hallway. "Looks like I returned just in time."

"Mother, unless there's something you haven't told me, I'm your only son, and I'm tired." He opened the door to his room. "Do you mind?"

Apparently she did because she smiled sweetly and stepped past him. Still smiling she sank gracefully onto the maroon silk coverlet on his immense four-poster bed, then crossed her legs at the ankles.

Lilac chiffon fluttered and settled midcalf. "I hope she's feeling better. I never had morning sickness with Dominique, but you were a trial." Her eyes narrowed. "You still are."

A clean shirt in his hand, Daniel paused at the wardrobe, caught between learning more about morning sickness and keeping his mother out of his business. The keenness in her gaze decided him. He'd get the rest of his things later. "I'm going to take a shower."

Leaning back, Felicia braced her hands on the bed. "I suppose I can have Higgins retrace his route and talk to her myself."

He stepped a few feet from the bathroom door. "Mother, please."

"I want to know her. You might as well give in."

Gripping the shirt in his hand, he faced her. "It's not mine."

His mother clearly didn't appear convinced. "You want me to believe that you spent the last two days nursing a pregnant woman—and you're not involved?"

"I'm going to fire Higgins." Daniel had had the chauffeur come back on Saturday to check to see if she needed anything, then Daniel had called him to pick him up this afternoon.

His mother's smile returned. "You can't. I pay him out of my money. Besides, you care for him too much."

"Sometimes I do things I don't want to," Daniel said with suppressed anger.

Rising from the bed, she went to her son and placed a soothing hand on his tense shoulder. "You're an honorable man. Whatever mistakes your father and I might have made in our own lives, we raised you and Dominique right."

He stared out the window draped in maroon silk

damask to the towering pin oaks in the distance. "Some-times I wonder."

"Did this young woman start you to wondering?" she questioned softly.

He glanced down into her expectant face. "You're not going to let this go, are you?"

"No."

He admitted defeat. "Her name is Madelyn Taggart."

"I guess her family is here in Houston," Felicia probed.

"No, she's by herself." The moment the words left his mouth, he knew his mother was going to interfere. "Mother, stay out of this."

"Oh, look. It's almost six." She glanced at the Piaget eighteen-karat gold watch on her slim wrist. "I better let you get your shower or dinner will be late." She hurried from the room.

"Mother."

She kept going. Daniel said one explicit word under his breath.

Chapter 9

Monday afternoon Madelyn groaned on hearing her doorbell. She didn't want to talk with anyone, had left work early for that very reason. She had a lot of thinking to do.

Whatever ideas or options she came up with, Daniel wouldn't be a part of them. Foolishly, while he had cared for her over the weekend, she had begun to think he had accepted the baby as his and wanted to be a part of their lives. His quick departure Sunday afternoon proved her wrong.

The doorbell chimed again. Madelyn ignored the sound. He'd left so fast, he probably singed the soles of his expensive loafers.

The memory angered her as much as it confused and saddened her. Who was the real Daniel? The compassionate man who bathed her face and coaxed her into eating or the hard-eyed man who thought she had gone from his bed to that of another man's?

Whatever the answer, his loss.

She didn't want a man who thought her so lacking in morals. He honestly didn't believe her. In his life's experience women moved from man to man with a shameless disregard for propriety—and always, always with an ulterior motive. True, Daniel hadn't known her long, but she felt he *should* have known her character.

She had expected his reaction to be her reaction to their relationship, one of complete faith and trust—and yes, love. She had been so wrong. She should have listened to what he said and not to her own foolish heart.

The bell sounded for the third time. Sighing, Madelyn pushed up from the sofa. Obviously the caller wasn't going away.

Determined to quickly get rid of the person, Madelyn opened the door. Surprise narrowed, then widened her eyes. Her determined visitor was the woman from the lobby of Daniel's office building.

"Hello, Madelyn," the woman greeted with a warm smile. "May I come in?"

Madelyn wasn't in the mood for a confrontation with one of Daniel's lady friends—although so far this one wasn't spitting venom.

"I'm rather busy. What's this about?"

"That's what I was hoping you could tell me," the woman said.

This one might be older and more sophisticated than the other two, but that didn't mean she wouldn't turn into a spiteful shrew. "Could you be more specific?" Madelyn asked, glancing over her shoulder at the sound of a cheer from the TV set.

"Is your husband home?" the woman inquired.

Unprepared for the question, Madelyn answered before she thought. "I'm not married."

The woman beamed. "I knew it. Please, may I come in? I don't think we should talk out here."

"Then you had better tell me your name and what you want," Madelyn told her.

Astonishment flashed across the other woman's attractive brown face. "Daniel didn't tell you?"

The queasiness that had been absent for the past two days returned. "No."

"I'm sorry, I thought you knew." She extended her manicured hand. "I'm Felicia Falcon."

Stunned, Madelyn stared at the other woman in utter horror. Only her grip on the doorknob kept her upright. "You're Daniel's wife?"

"Mother. You better sit down." Stepping inside, Felicia closed the door and led Madelyn to a chair and hovered over her. "Better?"

"Yes," Madelyn answered, unable to keep from staring at the youthful-looking woman. "You're his mother?"

Felicia's smile was one of pleasure and indulgence. "I married when I was eighteen."

Madelyn absorbed the information. Daniel's mother didn't look to be older than her midforties. He was thirty-three. Face-lift or good genes? "Any cosmetic firm, including my brother's, would fight to get you as a spokeswoman."

Felicia laughed, a bright, soothing sound. "Whenever I need a pick-me-up, I shall have to come and see you."

"Why are you here now?" Madelyn asked.

Felicia's gaze touched Madelyn's trim waist before meeting her eyes. "I've come to ask you something. Something my son says I have no right to ask, but I've never been one to listen to what other people think I should do or say." She paused for only a second. "Are you carrying Daniel's baby?"

Madelyn flushed, then straightened. "I don't want to be rude, but Daniel is right. The answer to that question is none of your business."

To her credit Felicia didn't appear upset by Madelyn's statement. "May I sit down?"

"Of course." Good manners won over nervousness.

Felicia sank gracefully into the jewel-tone floral sofa by Madelyn's chair. Once seated, she placed her black quilted calfskin handbag in her lap, then crossed her long legs at the ankles.

Today she wore another Chanel suit, this one in black minicheck. Deeply etched, small drop sterling silver earrings dangled from her ears. Understated and elegant.

Madelyn sat up even straighter in the antique, Duncan Phyfe armchair given to her by her maternal grandmother and refinished and reupholstered by Kane in seafoam green. She wished she had on something besides a red and white cotton knit striped short set that clashed with her purple slipper socks. At least her hair was combed.

"I have two beautiful children whom I love very much. Dominique is in Paris doing a photo shoot. She says she's having the time of her life." Felicia pressed her lips together. "Sometimes I think she almost believes it herself."

"Mrs. Falcon, perhaps you shouldn't be telling me this," Madelyn said.

Felicia sent her another smile, just not as bright. "I'm not saying anything to you I haven't said to Dominique. Then there is Daniel: aggressive, smart, intelligent, fearless. He took over my father's business interests when he graduated from Harvard, magna cum laude, with an MBA. He has more money than he can spend in ten lifetimes, and he has no one to share it with."

"Mrs. Falcon—"

"It's my fault," she interrupted, her fingers now wrapped around the top of her bag. "Two years ago I would have flayed alive anyone who suggested such a thing to me. Loneliness has a way of making you face the truth."

In his mother's black eyes, Madelyn saw as much misery as in her own. She wondered if Daniel's father loved Felicia as much as she loved Daniel.

"I made mistakes being a mother. I'd like to think I won't do the same with grandchildren," Felicia said softly.

Madelyn moistened her lips. "I didn't say this was Daniel's child."

"You didn't say it wasn't, either," Felicia said, then continued. "Daniel said you have no family here. Is that right?"

"Yes." There was no harm in answering that question.

"I presume you haven't told anyone on your job?" Felicia leaned forward in her seat.

Madelyn's hands clutched in her lap. "No."

"Then you have no one you can talk to about your pregnancy. I'm volunteering." Felicia's eyes sparkled. "I'm not a patient woman by nature, but I promise to try and not badger you too much," Felicia said.

"Daniel won't like us seeing each other." She couldn't believe she was actually considering his mother's proposal.

"Contrary to popular belief by some, Daniel doesn't rule the world," Felicia pointed out with a graceful arch of her brow.

Madelyn laughed, something she hadn't done freely in a week. The take-charge feistiness of Felicia was what Madelyn needed. She wouldn't mope when she was around, and she'd have someone to talk with about the baby.

"I was about to have dinner. Would you care to join me?" Madelyn stood.

Felicia came to her feet, her face wreathed in a wide smile. "I'd love to."

* * *

"Where have you been?" Daniel asked as soon as Felicia stepped inside the foyer. "It's almost eight thirty."

Felicia kissed her hard-looking son on the cheek, said good night, and headed for the stairs.

Daniel was right on her heels. "You've been with her, haven't you?" He tossed the words in accusation.

"By her, do you mean Madelyn?" Felicia started up the stairs.

"You know da—"

His mother whirled, her sharp gaze cutting off the word. Heat climbed up Daniel's neck. Although she knew he didn't curse in front of her, knew he had probably been going to say "darn"—which he was—she also knew one pointed look from her could always make him feel like horse manure. She wasn't above showing him she still had power over him.

"I asked you not to see her."

She smiled, forgiving him. "I'm the parent here."

"You don't understand," Daniel told her.

Folding her arms, she casually leaned against the railing. "Then perhaps you'd like to explain things to me."

Daniel raked his hand through his hair. "Don't you see, being with her only complicates matters?"

"I'm afraid I don't see how it complicates matters any more than when you spent the weekend with her," his mother replied.

A muscle leaped in his jaw. "There was no one else."

His mother's sigh was long and eloquent. "Daniel, if you think that is the only reason you stayed with her, then you're in deeper trouble than I thought."

His hand clamped down on the polished wood of the banister. "Just promise you won't see her again."

Felicia turned and continued up the wide staircase.

"I'm afraid I can't do that. We're having dinner tomorrow night."

"Mother, I don't want you seeing her."

At the top of the stairs, she stared down at her son. "There's nothing you can do or say that will keep me away from Madelyn and my grandchild."

"It's not your grandchild," he gritted out.

Sadness touched her face. "As long as there is the slightest possibility it is, I plan to be a part of their lives. You're like your father in so many ways. Please don't make the same mistake." Then she was gone.

He started after her to ask what she was talking about, then decided he'd do better with Madelyn. His mother could be bulldog stubborn. He'd just have to call Madelyn.

Breathless, Madelyn answered on the sixth ring. "Hello?"

"Why didn't you answer the phone sooner?" Daniel barked, her labored breath sending waves of jealously through him.

"I was finishing my exercise. What do you want, Daniel?"

His relief was short-lived. He almost looked at the phone. Madelyn had never sounded impatient with him in the past. "I don't want you seeing my mother."

"Tough."

"Tough?" he repeated incredulously.

"We had a great time talking about fashion, movies, and sometimes just nonsense. I thoroughly enjoyed her company and the baby has a right to know its father's mother."

His grip on the phone tightened. It was all he could do not to tell her again he was not the father.

"Daniel, I have another call coming through. Good night."

The line went dead before he could tell her not to hang up the phone. Angrily he pushed the redial button, only she didn't switch over to talk with him. He barely kept from banging down the phone. He knew what his mother was trying to do. Let them talk and meet all they wanted, but it wasn't going to matter to him.

"Daniel doesn't believe the baby is his," Madelyn said as she sat next to Felicia on the couch, a bowl of unbuttered popcorn between them. Exactly one week had passed since she came into Madelyn's life.

"So history repeats itself." Sighing, Felicia removed her size-six feet from the cocktail table where Madelyn had insisted she place them to get the best effect on watching the black-and-white movie classic on TV.

Madelyn turned wounded eyes to her. "Felicia, I promise I'm not lying. I'm not like those other women who wanted only money from Daniel. This is Daniel's baby."

Felicia's delicate hand covered hers. "Of course not. You misunderstood. I meant Daniel. You see, he was born four months and three weeks after I married his father."

Madelyn's mouth gaped.

"I see I shocked you. It came as a shock to my parents, too. They fully intended me to marry some successful man of my race who was of the same social circle, not fall desperately in love with a full-blooded Muscogee Creek who was as poor as the proverbial church mouse." Felicia sighed. "One look at John Henry, and I knew he was mine.

"As the only child of wealthy parents, 'no' wasn't a word I accepted. I always got what I wanted. My father used to say I demanded my way from the day I was born, and I wouldn't stop until I had it, or those around me would pay."

"You must have changed," Madelyn offered—she hadn't seen Felicia do one selfish thing. She went out of her way to be kind and helpful to Madelyn. She was accepting, nonjudgmental, and respected Madelyn's privacy.

"Thank you, but not until after I lost Daniel's father," she confessed.

"So what happened to make the two of you get together?" Madelyn asked, curious and hopeful at once.

Felicia smiled with the memory. "I sent him a letter, saying my parents were shipping me off to England to marry one of my father's business associates' sons and told him, if he wanted me and his child, he better come and get us."

Madelyn laughed, liking the woman's style. "So he came running."

"In a flash. Two days later I woke up one night with a hand over my mouth. John Henry kidnaped me. We left in his beat-up pickup and were married when we reached Oklahoma. Of course I wasn't that easily gotten back after the way he acted, so he took me to a little cabin and proceeded to try and win me back. I can't ever remember being happier. He ate every bite of burnt food I set before him."

"How romantic," Madelyn said, smiling.

"My parents didn't think so. The only reason they didn't call the police and file kidnaping charges was because they knew I was pregnant and in love with John Henry." She wrinkled her nose. "It probably helped that I called every day for a couple of weeks and sent them a copy of the marriage license."

Madelyn's dark brows drew together. "Obviously they came around."

"Only after Daniel was born. I begged John Henry to call my parents. They fell in love with Daniel and decided they'd rather try and get along with their poor but proud son-in-law than give up their daughter and grandson. I left the hospital thinking all my dreams had come true."

This time it was Madelyn who placed her hand over Felicia's. "You could call him."

"I'm afraid it will take more than a phone call. You see the new improved Felicia. I could be a real rich-bitch when I put my mind to it." Her voice trembled. "I pulled that stunt one time too many. He walked out of my life two years ago, and I haven't heard from him since."

"Does Daniel or Dominique?"

Felicia nodded. "All the time. They split the last Christmas holidays between the two of us. They love their father very much. I wonder why sometimes that they don't hate me for driving him away."

Madelyn remembered Daniel's poor concept of marriage based on his parents' stormy past. She understood him more being around Felicia. Madelyn just wished she loved him less.

"You're too vibrant to hate, and your grandchild is going to love and adore you." Madelyn stood, unwilling to admit there wasn't hope for both of them. "I know what's wrong with us. No butter on the popcorn."

Somehow Madelyn wasn't surprised to see Daniel lounging against a big black truck as she pulled into her parking space in front of her apartment two days later. He looked handsome and dangerous in a black Stetson, white shirt, and sinfully tight jeans.

Truthfully she had expected him or a phone call before now. She and Felicia saw a lot of each other.

Yet, by unspoken agreement, John Henry and Daniel's names were never mentioned in their conversations since Monday night. From his hard expression, Daniel hadn't come to declare his paternity or his affection.

Since she didn't want the entire complex to know her business, she opened her front door and stood back for him to enter. "Daniel."

"Madelyn."

"Have a seat. I have to get out of these heels."

"You should be wearing sensible shoes anyway."

Midway across the room she turned. "What did you say?"

He yanked down the Stetson. "Never mind. I came to talk about my mother."

She was across the room in no time. "Is she all right?"

"Of course she's all right," he admitted, not sounding the least happy about it. "I haven't seen her this happy in a long time. That's why I'm here. You can't keep on giving her false hope."

Madelyn slipped off one of her heels and resisted the urge to throw it at Daniel's head. "I think you better leave."

He didn't budge. "Why are you doing this?"

"Why do you think? I'm not trying to trap you into marriage or ask for a chunk out of your portfolio. I have no reason to lie."

He gave the brim of his Stetson another good yank. "Maybe the father's a jerk."

Slipping off the other shoe, she said, "There's no maybe to it."

His mouth flattened into a straight line. "My mother spends more time with you than she does with me."

"That's because you're out every night."

"Business," he told her and watched her roll her eyes. Gritting his teeth, he gave his hat another yank. He didn't have to hide anything. His life was his own—at least until Madelyn came into his life.

He couldn't stop thinking about her, worrying about her. The women he had taken out hadn't helped. They only made him miss Madelyn more. He could hardly wait to take them home.

Madelyn folded her arms across her chest. "If there is nothing else, it's after seven and I have to get to the gym."

"What! Are you crazy?" he yelled, outraged. "You can't do tae kwon do classes in your condition! What's wrong with you?"

"They're pregnancy exercise classes, Daniel," she said patiently.

"Oh." Damned if he didn't feel his face flush. Flushing, for goodness' sake! She made him act like a raving fool.

"I really must get going."

His gaze locked on her soft lips—lips he was desperately trying not to remember how good they felt on his, how much he wanted to feel them again.

She was too close. The light fragrance she wore beckoned him to lean closer. He had to get out of there before he did something stupid. The book said a woman's breasts changed during this time, becoming more sensitive, larger. The areolae darker.

He wondered. His hand lifted toward her red jacket.

"Daniel, are you all right?"

He snatched his hand down. Disgust rolled through him. He was turning into a pervert. "I'm late for an appointment."

He almost ran from her apartment. He didn't dare look back.

* * *

Daniel fully expected his mother to grill him over seeing Madelyn when he arrived home. He had no doubt she knew about his going to see her. He was ready for the interrogation, the prodding. Only his mother wasn't there.

He didn't need to guess where she was. His own mother had gone over to the side of the enemy. She didn't even pretend to be on his side.

He always knew his mother could be stubborn, and he was realizing just *how* stubborn. Her father had told Daniel more than once how stubborn she was. She had grown up thinking everything she wanted, she should have. Usually she wasn't disappointed.

The way the story went, she had seen his father at a Native American rodeo in New Mexico, and that was that. None of them could believe a pampered young woman who had always had servants had lived happily in a little two-room cabin for almost five months, cooking meals over a wooden stove and sweeping the floor with a straw broom.

John Henry had taken Daniel there once, and he hadn't believed it, either. The log cabin was on a dot of land that scorpions shunned. His father had had to drive fifteen miles one way over rutted roads to work as a ranch hand.

They had certainly loved each other, endured hardships to stay together—yet they hadn't been able to hold their marriage together.

Getting up, Daniel went to stand by the window in his study downstairs. If not for him, they might never have gotten married. Their worlds had collided instead of merging when they left that cabin.

He didn't want that for himself. Or Madelyn.

He had learned at a young age what happened when love wasn't enough. The lesson was reinforced each time his father couldn't take the pressure of his mother trying to turn him into something he wasn't and took off for Oklahoma. Daniel had grown up knowing if not for him, his parents' lives might have taken a different, happier path.

What his parents hadn't taught him about was how easily love could turn into harshly spoken words and accusations, Jeanette had. She had been an expert teacher. Beautiful, vibrant, and poised, Jeanette had been so easy to be with—and then overnight he hadn't been able to stand the sight of her.

She had killed any love he might have had for her, then she had killed herself.

He was never going to let another person depend on him for their emotional well-being and happiness, especially when he knew the high failure rate.

Never. Snapping off the light, he slowly climbed the stairs and went to his room.

Whatever game his mother had going on, he was not going to play.

Daniel was already eating breakfast when Felicia came down the next morning looking elegant as usual in an ice-blue pantsuit. "Good morning, Mother."

"Good morning, Daniel." Kissing his cheek, she took her seat. Almost immediately a servant was at her elbow. "Just juice and toast, please."

Daniel set down his coffee cup. "Eating light?"

"I'm having lunch with Madelyn. I always over-indulge. She might be eating for two, but that's no reason for me to gain the pounds." She glanced up and smiled as the servant placed her juice and coffee on the table. "Thank you, Helen."

Here it comes, Daniel thought.

"What are your plans today, dear?" Daintily she lifted her cup and drank.

His smile was pure innocence. "Flexible."

"Good," she commented.

"Is there something you wanted me to do?" he asked, tired of the charade.

"Oh, no. You simply work too hard, and I'm glad you have a light schedule." Getting up from the table, she kissed him on the cheek. "Have a nice day."

Daniel watched his mother leave the room, then grinned. He had walked right into that one. She was enjoying herself at his expense.

Yet there was nothing she wouldn't do to protect her children.

The smile slid from his face. Once that had included almost destroying the man she loved.

Chapter 10

Pick up the phone, Madelyn, Daniel silently demanded. His fingers bit into the plastic when the answering machine clicked on. The deep, melodious tone of Kane's voice was starting to irritate him.

Disgusted, Daniel slammed down the phone. There was no sense leaving another message. She hadn't answered the three from yesterday.

Where the hell could she be this early on a Saturday morning? She wasn't at home, that was for sure. He had gone by there before seven this morning and late last night. Both times her Acura was gone.

When he tracked her down, he had something to tell her. This time he wouldn't choke. He'd make sure she understood he wanted her to stop seeing his mother. It was bad enough trying to forget her without his mother being a constant reminder of her.

"What was that noise?"

Daniel whirled to see his mother wearing a navy-blue and white pantsuit, standing in the study doorway. The frown cleared on her face on seeing his hand on the telephone. "Is something wrong?"

His mother would know. She looked too happy with herself for the past two weeks not to be in contact with the woman she thought was carrying her first grand-child. He wasn't going to ask her though.

She'd like nothing better than to see him and Mad-elyn get together. It wasn't going to happen in this life-time. Then the picture of Madelyn being hurt and alone somewhere flashed into his mind.

"I can't find Madelyn." Was that his voice that held a mixture of pique and desperation?

Frowning she stepped farther into the room. "Last night she didn't mention she expected to see you."

"You saw her last night?" he questioned, crossing the room. "When? Where?"

"We went to the movies together." His mother shud-dered delicately. "I can't believe some of the things that pass for entertainment these days. All that blood and gore."

"You didn't let her see anything that might upset her, did you?" he asked, his tone accusing.

She tilted her head. "I see you weren't worried about me."

He refused to back down. "You're not in her condi-tion." No matter how childish it was, he still couldn't say the word out loud.

His mother had no such problem. "By condition do you mean her pregnancy? Say it, Daniel. It won't turn you into stone."

But it would make him think of the unknown father. As long as he separated Madelyn from the baby, he was fine.

His mother patted his cheek when he remained si-lent. "Poor Daniel, one day you're going to have to make a decision on this, and I hope it's the right one."

He didn't want to talk about it. "What kind of movie did you see?"

"One that upset us both. A love story that ended

tragically. We both cried buckets. Life does imitate art." She looked sad for a moment, then started toward the small dining room off the kitchen.

Daniel didn't know if she was talking about her love life or his, but he was leaving both alone. "If you saw her last night, then you know where she is."

"Of course I do. I must eat breakfast, I'm going sailing this morning," she told him as she entered the dining room.

"Where is she?" he asked, pulling out a peach-covered chair for her.

She took the seat and was immediately served. "Why, she's gone, dear."

The word caught him off guard, plummeting him downward. "Gone?" He plopped into a chair. She couldn't leave him—she couldn't.

"Daniel, are you all right? Maybe Will can take a look at you when he shows up."

"Will?"

"He's a friend of Dr. Scalar and a dermatologist. Dr. Scalar introduced us," she answered, pressing the back of her hand to Daniel's forehead. "You work too hard."

"When did you meet Dr. Scalar?"

"Wednesday, when I went with Madelyn to her appointment," Felicia explained, helping herself to a blueberry muffin.

"Is something wrong?" His heart pounded in his chest.

"No, she's fine." She took a bite of the muffin.

"Then why did she ask you to go?" Daniel asked, still not convinced.

Felicia dabbed her mouth with her napkin before answering. "She didn't ask me to go. I asked her. I wanted to meet the man who's going to deliver my grandchild."

Daniel was caught between reminding his mother he

wasn't the father and gaining more information. "If Scalar's going to do the delivery, then why did she leave?"

"She didn't leave. She just flew home for her niece and nephew's birthday party," Felicia told him, sipping her coffee.

The tension snapped back into him. If Kane and Matt found out, there'd be hell to pay. If they upset her, they'd be the ones to pay. "To Hallsville. How long ago did she leave?"

Felicia glanced at the slim gold watch on her wrist. "Her flight left two hours ago, at seven. I offered to take her to the airport since her car wasn't ready as promised. I thought a tune-up was simple. People don't take pride in their work anymore."

Daniel didn't like the way his mother had looked at him when she made her last statement. "How did she get to the airport?"

"She said a friend would take her," answered Felicia. "The sweet thing didn't want me getting up so early since she knew I had a sailing date at nine thirty. Apparently he's an early riser."

"He?"

Now he was sure she was glaring at him. The cup clinked in the saucer. "The man who's taking her to the airport. And don't get that look on your face. You're just like your father. Women do have platonic male friends."

No way was he stepping into that one. "When is she coming back?"

"Her plane gets in tomorrow night around five. She didn't want to be too tired for work. I do hope she has a good time." Felicia looked worried. "She didn't say anything, but I could tell she was a little anxious about seeing her family." The thoughtful expression changed to one of pleasure.

"The only time she perked up in the last few days was when we were trying to stuff those piñatas full of candy to send to the twins." Felicia smiled at the memory. "She put a note on the outside of the box not to open until she arrived. I think she's planning to get a crack at them herself."

"A woman in her condition shouldn't be doing anything like that," he almost shouted.

"Daniel, there is such a thing as too much knowledge." She patted his hand as if he were a small boy trying to get away with something and had been caught. "Perhaps you shouldn't read any more of those books on pregnancy."

Black eyes narrowed. "How do you know what I've been reading?"

"I snooped of course," she answered without the least bit of remorse. "The surest way to get a mother's curiosity up is to try to hide something from her. Try to remember that in the years to come." With one final pat, she placed her napkin on the table and stood.

"I think you'll like Will. He's going to make a donation to the Children's Wish Ball I'm chairing. He's not as tall as I'd like, but he's quite charming and a good sailor I hear." She sighed. "You can't have everything."

"You can, if you try," Daniel said.

She shook her head. Sadness once again shimmered in her eyes. "No. No, you can't. I tried. Don't make my same mistakes."

Everything was going to be all right. No one suspected anything. Not even a twinge of nausea had hit Madelyn. If she felt guilty about not telling her family, she'd have to live with it. The twins' third birthday party was not the time to broadcast her pregnancy.

Besides, there hadn't been a moment's peace since

she had arrived at Kane's ranch house. Matt and Shannon were already there. Her parents drove up just behind her. She had been so happy to see them all. Breakfast was a loud affair, with everyone talking and catching up. Then they had all started trying to get ready for the party at two.

Everyone was given specific duties. They barely finished everything before the first guest arrived. Since then there hadn't been a quiet moment. The party was a roaring success.

Madelyn looked at the forty-odd children racing around the yard, trying to decide what they wanted to do next, and smiled. Unconsciously she placed her hand on her flat abdomen.

"You wonder how they get that much energy, don't you?"

She glanced around into the smiling face of Stewart Yates. Medium height and with nice shoulders and a kind face, Stewart had recently come to work for Kane at the ranch. His five-year-old niece was presently enjoying her third pony ride.

"I certainly do," Madelyn said, returning her attention to her job of watching the three children inside the recently constructed petting area. Only the children weren't doing as much petting as they were hugging the animals. The two goats didn't seem to mind.

"It's good having you back home again," Stewart said.

She smiled at him. "This isn't exactly my home, but it is good being with the family."

Calloused hands settled beside hers on top of the wooden rail. "Any chance of you moving back here?"

"No, I like my job in Houston. Excuse me." Opening the gate, she let the children out and three more in.

"Do you have any plans for tonight?" Stewart asked as soon as she returned.

"Plans?"

He looked uncomfortable. "I thought maybe you'd like to go out to a movie."

"She wouldn't."

Madelyn whirled to see Daniel standing a few feet away. Dressed in jeans and a white shirt and his signature black Stetson, he looked wholly dangerous and too tempting for words. He was also angry. She glanced around to see if any of her family might have heard him.

"I don't seem to remember asking you," Stewart said.

Madelyn swung her head back around. Stewart must have a death wish. Daniel looked ready to explode. "Stewart, do you think you could get me a diet soft drink?"

He didn't budge. "Maybe he'd like to get it?"

A smile crossed Daniel's face. "Good idea." In two strides he was beside Madelyn, taking her arm and leading her away. "Watch the children, would you?"

"Daniel, please," she cried, glancing over her shoulder at Stewart, who was caught between watching the children and coming after them. "That wasn't nice."

"I never said I was nice."

She swallowed. His hand on her bare arm felt too good. If he didn't touch her, she stood a better chance of remaining detached around him. That's the only thing that saved her when he came to her apartment the other day. "I'm assigned to be at the petting area."

"How long have you been on your feet?" He stopped. His gaze swept her. "It's hot out here."

Under his scrutiny, Madelyn's skin prickled in the white, loose-fitting sundress. The man had the most sinful eyes to go along with the rest of him. "I'm fine, but I can't abandon the children."

"That guy was trying to pick you up."

"And . . ."

"And," he shouted. "Have you forgotten you're—"

"Daniel!" she interrupted, looking around wildly. This time several people were watching them, including her two brothers and sisters-in-law. "I hope you're satisfied," she cried, and rushed back toward the petting area.

Hell, he was anything but satisfied. He had never been less satisfied in his life. He hadn't been satisfied since she ran dripping wet into him.

He scowled at her. She was wearing the same innocent-looking dress that had caused him so much trouble in San Antonio.

His gaze lifted to the immense blue Texas sky. Not a rain cloud in sight. His scowl deepened on seeing the other man move closer to Madelyn. He'd put a stop to that.

"Hello, Daniel," Kane greeted, extending his hand. "This is quite a surprise."

"Hello, Kane." Warmly Daniel shook his friend's hand. "I hope I'm not intruding. I was in the neighborhood, so I decided to stop by," Daniel said, almost wincing at his flimsy excuse for being there.

"Glad you did. I'd like you to meet my parents, and Shannon is going to wave her arm off if you don't go say hello." Taking Daniel's arm, Kane led him toward his parents.

Daniel threw one glance over his shoulder, glad to see the cowboy wasn't crowding Madelyn any longer, then turned back to Kane. "Matt might not like that," he said, remembering Matt as the jealous type. It didn't seem fair that Daniel was suffering the misery of the damned all by himself.

"I don't think you have to worry about that."

Daniel simply smiled.

Thirty minutes later Daniel wasn't smiling. He conceded he'd have to suffer by himself. Matt didn't appear the least bit jealous. He was a changed man—not for the better, either.

He didn't seem to be able to keep his hands or his lips off his wife. Kane was just as bad. They were letting themselves in for a lot of heartache, but Daniel wasn't going to tell them that.

Daniel glanced over to where Madelyn stood. The man had moved in again, and this time she'd stayed. Just wait until he got her alone!

"I think we have a problem."

"You noticed too, huh?"

"You'd have to be blind not to."

"I can't believe he thought you'd swallow the story that he happened to be in the area and decided to visit."

"He did tell it looking me straight in the eye. You have to give him points for that."

"He's been in the business world too long."

"Falcon is more than his name. It stands for what he is . . . bird of prey, merciless and ruthless when it comes to going after what he wants."

"That's what I'm afraid of. He won't scare off as easily as the others."

"Don't I know it."

"It might be fun to break his nose after all."

Kane glanced at his brother, Matt, and laughed. "You know he was never romantically interested in Shannon."

"I know, but at the time he gave me some rough moments." Matt pressed his knuckles into his palm. "Maybe Madelyn won't think he's so handsome after I finish."

"Or maybe she'll be as softhearted as Shannon and rush to patch him up."

Matt grunted. "What do you think we should do?"

From their vantage point from the side of the house, they watched Daniel watch Madelyn and Madelyn watch Daniel. "You have to give it to Stewart. He's pretending pretty good he doesn't know what's going on," Kane said. "I think he knows he's out of the running, but is just rubbing it in on Daniel."

"Yeah," Matt said. "At least baby sis and Daniel both look kind of tense. I don't think things have gone too far. Daniel still has that restless, edgy look about him."

"He better keep it until he puts a ring on her finger," Kane growled.

Matt agreed with Kane in principle, and knew Kane had waited until well after the wedding to claim his own bride. Matt hadn't been so gallant or patient. He didn't know if his big brother knew he'd jumped the gun or not, and he sure wasn't telling.

His gaze trained on Daniel again. He wore that same look of denial and desperation Matt knew so well. He had stared at it every morning while shaving. He'd fought his feelings for Shannon for all he was worth. Yet they had been too strong to deny. When they had finally exploded, nothing had been able to hold them back.

"Damn," Matt muttered. "We better have a talk with him."

In unison the men moved toward Daniel. "I'd like to show you something," Kane said.

Without waiting for him to answer, Kane grabbed one arm and Matt the other. Daniel lifted a dark brow, the corner of his mouth tilted. "I wasn't flirting with Shannon or Victoria."

"Wouldn't do you any good if you had," Matt answered.

"Then what is this about?"

"We'll talk in the barn," Kane said.

"Smile at Madelyn, Daniel. She looks upset. Any reason for her to look upset?" Matt asked mildly.

"Why are you asking me?" Daniel said as the three men stepped into the dimness of the barn.

Releasing his arm, Kane faced him. "Because since you've gotten here, you've spent your time between sending killer glances at Stewart and annoyed ones at Madelyn."

Daniel crossed his arms. "Then it seems to me you should be having this conversation with Stewart, since he's been with her since I arrived."

"So far he's the only one doing the looking." Kane thought the look on Daniel's face was much too smug. "But if that should change, he'll be standing where you are in a heartbeat."

Daniel's mouth thinned. Kane and Matt shared a look. It wouldn't hurt to let him know he might not have the inside track.

"I wasn't aware that my actions were being monitored so closely," Daniel finally said.

"Come on, Daniel. You're not talking to two fools. I've seldom seen you look at a woman more than twice. Yet you can't take your eyes off our sister."

He eyed a saddle on the rail. "She's an attractive woman."

Matt threw up his hands. "So are Victoria and Shannon, but you haven't done more than speak to either of them. And don't say it's because they're married, because two attractive women who aren't have been giving you the eye all afternoon, and you've ignored them, too. What's up between you and Madelyn?"

Unfolding his arms, Daniel faced Matt. "Whether something is up or not, it's between the two of us."

"What if I beat the crap out of you until I get the answer I want?" Matt challenged.

"You can try."

"He can try, but I'll succeed," Kane said, moving his huge body in front of Daniel, towering over him by a good two inches. "I want to know why you didn't mention something was going on between you and Madelyn when we talked. I want answers—and I want them now."

"If there is anything between us, it's none of your business," Daniel said. "But if you upset her, you'll have me to answer to."

"Is that a fact?" Kane snarled.

"Count on it," Daniel answered, not backing down an inch.

Kane suddenly burst out laughing and slapped Daniel on the back. He laughed harder at the bewildered look on the other man's face. "We've been waiting for a man we can't intimidate for our little sister." The laughter stopped and he pinned Daniel with dark, dangerous eyes. "But hear me, Daniel. I don't care about the new moral code. Madelyn is my sister. You step out of bounds, hurt her in any way, and I'm coming after you."

"And when he's finished, I'm next," Matt said.

"I never thought differently," Daniel said.

"Good. Now let's go join the party. It's time to bust the piñatas."

Madelyn was so nervous she had to force herself to keep from wringing her hands. Seeing Daniel and her brothers come out of the barn didn't help. The only two smiling were Matt and Kane. Since Daniel wasn't bruised, she was sure he hadn't told them about her pregnancy. But that left a lot to discuss.

"Time to break the piñatas," Kane yelled, motioning all the children to follow him.

Relief swept through Madelyn as she opened the gate and followed the children. She had to know what they had been talking about.

"I don't have a chance, do I?"

Madelyn turned back to Stewart. Maybe if she had met an uncomplicated man like Stewart, she wouldn't be going through all of the emotional gymnastics Daniel was putting her through.

"That's all right. You don't have to say it," the ranch hand said. "I can see it in your eyes."

"Is it that obvious?" Madelyn asked anxiously.

"Probably just to me, since I wish you would have looked at me that way. But at least I know he's not having an easy time, either, and he's rich."

"Money has nothing to do with anything."

"I know. That's why he's one lucky son of a gun."

She smiled tremulously. "I don't think he would agree with you."

"Some men go down hard—others easy."

"I'll try to remember that."

"I guess I better see if they need any help," he said.

"I hope you find the woman you're looking for soon. I'd say she's the lucky one."

His gaze flickered behind her, then he stepped closer. "I bet your lips taste sweeter than vine-ripe strawberries."

Madelyn's mouth gaped.

"I believe Kane wants you," growled Daniel.

Comprehension snapped Madelyn's mouth shut.

Daniel. Stewart had seen him and given him a little prod—only prodding Daniel wasn't recommended for a person's health.

"If there is dancing later on, save me a dance." Tipping the brim of his tanned straw hat, Stewart strutted away.

Daniel turned those lethal black eyes on her. "I hope you've enjoyed yourself this afternoon."

"I might have, if you hadn't shown up. Daniel, what are you doing here? Why did they take you to the barn?" she asked in a frantic rush.

"I came in case you decided to tell your family and needed some moral support," he said tightly. "Obviously you didn't need my help with Stewart hovering all over you."

"Daniel, you can be such a pain in the butt," she snapped and walked off. Unrelenting fingers caught her a few steps away.

"Slow down before you hurt yourself," he admonished. "Mother told me you're thinking about hitting that piñata. Forget it."

She stopped. "What?"

"You'll have to be blindfolded, and I won't have you swinging with a stick and possibly hurting yourself."

"You won't, huh?" Madelyn said, her hands on her hips.

Daniel gave her glare for glare. "No, I won't."

He was magnificent when he was angry, and this time his anger and concern were for her and the baby. *You're getting there, Daniel. Just keep coming.* "Since I want some of that candy, I guess you'd better take my place."

Daniel had taken her place after all the children had had several chances. Much to his surprise, he had enjoyed the encouragement of the children and the teasing from Matt about his pitiful swing. Finally he had landed a solid hit and broken the piñata. Kane had gotten the other one.

Instead of joining in the mad scramble for candy

along with the children, Madelyn had stood back smiling until she saw the boys were stuffing candy into their pockets, while the girls had only their hands.

Hitching up the hem of her dress into a makeshift pouch, she waded into the melee, showing the girls how to get more goodies. She was grinning from ear to ear and having the time of her life.

Her parents shook their heads indulgently at her. Her sisters-in-law cheered her on. Her brothers watched Daniel, and Daniel divided his time between sending lethal glances at her and Stewart.

Madelyn happened to glance up and look straight into Daniel's hard black eyes. The fun went out of her. He was more than angry about the candy—he simply didn't trust her.

That hurt. It hurt more to see him abruptly turn to say goodbye to her family, then walk away.

Hungrily her gaze followed.

No matter how much she told herself it shouldn't matter—to forget him—it did matter, and regardless of how hard she tried, forgetting him was impossible.

Chapter 11

It was all Madelyn could do to keep a smile on her face as she turned back to the children. She wasn't foolish enough to think that no one had noticed her reaction to Daniel's leaving.

She just hoped they didn't all pounce on her at once. She couldn't take that. Tears pricked her eyes. She was not going to cry. She was not.

Not once, no matter how hurtful the offense, had she ever cried in public. Not when Kali Jefferson invited every girl in the sixth grade to her birthday party except Madelyn; not when her date at the senior prom left her to take another, more willing girl home; not when she was repeatedly treated like a nonentity at Sinclair.

Not once. She was stronger than this. A tear formed, hovering on her lower eyelid.

"Madelyn, I need your help setting up things on the back porch," called Victoria.

Madelyn glanced up, blinking rapidly to clear the tears away. Not once, because she'd always known her family was one hundred percent behind her. Not once, because she had been taught to let no obstacle stand in her way. She sniffed. But Lord, she had never hurt this deeply before.

She sniffed again, her hands digging into the empty pockets of her sundress. Where was a tissue when she needed one?

"Madelyn, come on. I'll meet you on the back porch," Victoria told her, then started for the house. Kane followed.

Her heart sank. Interrogation time.

After walking only a short distance with his wife, Kane kissed her on the cheek and went to stand by his brother. "Baby sis, you better hurry or I might decide to take care of things in my own way."

Madelyn took off. It was a subtle warning. She was being offered a reprieve. The interrogation—and she was sure that was what it was going to be—would come later.

By the time Victoria reached the screened back door, Madelyn had it open for her. "Thank you."

"Don't thank me yet, he still wants to talk with you," Victoria said.

"Matt, too." Shannon Taggart walked up to them. "So do we smuggle you out the front door, or do you want Victoria and me to make the supreme sacrifice and find some other way to take our husbands' minds off their big-brother routine?"

Victoria's hazel eyes narrowed mischievously. "Speak for yourself about sacrifice."

Madelyn laughed as the three of them entered the house. Her brothers' wives were beautiful, loving, and unpretentiously wealthy women in their own right. Victoria owned a chain of six upscale lingerie boutiques called Lavender and Lace. Shannon had inherited her wealth, yet continued to work as a nurse practitioner on a voluntary basis in Jackson Falls where she and Matt lived.

What endeared them to Madelyn was their unfailing love and devotion to their husbands. Husbands who loved them just as much. Her smile died. That was something she might never have.

Shannon's hand gently touched Madelyn's. "Your business is your own, but for what it's worth, some men aren't easy to love or understand."

"Women, either," Victoria added. "Kane didn't give up on me even when another man would have walked away or shook me until my teeth rattled."

Madelyn looked at the two women. "What you're saying is that you have to fight for what you want?"

"If you can answer one question without hesitation," Victoria said.

"What?" Madelyn asked uneasily.

"Can you imagine living your life and being happy without him?"

No matter how much she wished otherwise, there was only one damning answer. "No."

"Then go after him with all you've got," Shannon told her.

"But . . . but what if I already tried, and it didn't work?" Madelyn bit her lip.

"Try again," Victoria said softly. "Kane never gave up on me. He taught me how not to be afraid to trust in loving someone. I never want to think of what might have happened if, at a crucial point in our marriage, we both hadn't put love above pride."

"Matt fought falling in love until the night he proposed," Shannon said with a hint of pride. "I admit I went after him shamelessly."

Laughter erupted. The whole family had been shocked to hear of Matt's engagement. His first marriage had been a disaster, and after swearing not to marry again, he had started going through women like water through a sieve.

"What's taking so long?" Grace Taggart inquired.

"The children are getting restless," Clair Benson added.

"Coming, Mrs. Taggart, Grandmother," Victoria said and rushed toward the kitchen, Shannon right behind her.

Before Madelyn could make her escape, her mother had her by the arm. She swallowed.

She had never been able to hide anything from her mother. She prayed today was the exception. "I'd better help."

"One more minute won't hurt," her mother said. "All I want to know is, was that talk your brothers had with Daniel necessary?"

Swallowing again, Madelyn cut a glance at Victoria's grandmother, Mrs. Benson, who appeared in no hurry to leave. As usual she was in lace and pearls even on a hot summer day. She was a sweet, no-nonsense lady.

"You had only to look at him to know the answer to that question," Clair Benson said. "He needs a haircut."

"He's part Native American," Madelyn said automatically.

Clair regarded her thoughtfully. "My great-grandfather was a Buffalo soldier who fought the Indians."

Madelyn didn't know what to make of that comment. "Yes, ma'am."

"In his diary he said he had never met a fiercer, more determined people. He said he thought they might be like the African tribes." Clair looked at Grace. "I don't know what was said in the barn, but it probably won't do any good." She opened the back door and went back outside.

"Addie," Grace said, her worry obvious in the reprisal of her daughter's old name. "I will be forever thankful for Daniel helping with arrangements for your brother's wedding, but I read the papers. His reputation with women is worse than Matt's used to be."

"And look at Matt now."

"But it took him a long time to find Shannon," her mother said, holding her daughter's gaze.

"Daniel and I are just friends," Madelyn said. The relief on her mother's face was instantaneous. "We better go help in the kitchen."

Grace Taggart palmed her daughter's cheeks. "I love you. If ever you need to talk, call. I'm not so old that I don't remember how it was to be in love and impatient."

"I love you, Mama," Madelyn said, wishing she had enough courage to tell her about her grandchild.

Daniel was in a foul mood. He was also as confused as hell. He had watched Madelyn laughing and giggling with the children, her skirt up over her slim legs, and had been caught off guard by a powerful surge of sexual hunger.

It hadn't mattered that her parents were there or her overprotective brothers or the dozen or so other adults, all he had wanted to do was drag her to him and to the nearest bed. Only he wasn't sure if he would have made it that far.

Lust had snuck up on him when he wasn't looking. It had to be lust. Initially he had been aware of her free, laughing spirit and sense of fair play. It hadn't been a matter of gender. If the girls would have been giving it to the boys, he didn't doubt that she would have waded in for the underdog.

She obviously loved children. She would make a wonderful mother. The sudden thought that he wouldn't be there to be the father hit him like a fist while he was still trying to deal with the lust.

The unexpected longing for her and the baby had sent him back to his rental car and to Meacham International Airport in Fort Worth faster than the lust. He was getting in way over his head.

Looking out the window of his private jet as it made its way to Houston, his mood hadn't changed. He had never run from anything in his life. And he had had plenty of opportunities.

Most of the students in the predominately Anglo-Saxon, prestigious private school in Boston hadn't known what to think of a boy of visible mixed African-American and Native American heritage. Although there were racial mixtures and African-American students, he was the only one of his mixture, an oddity, accepted by some and made to feel an outcast by others.

John Henry Falcon was unapologetically a Native American. He was more comfortable in jeans and a shirt than the suit and tie his wife and in-laws often demanded that he wear. His boots were run-down at the heel and were bought at the local Wal-Mart. No Italian loafers for him.

He believed in the Master of Breath, The People, his family, hard work. From Daniel's earliest memories, he recalled his father telling him stories of The People, of his tribe, the Muscogee Indians, called Creek by the white settlers because their settlement was near creeks. He never let Daniel forget his ancestors had been fearless warriors, brilliant tacticians, and daring leaders.

Daniel had grown up proud of his uniqueness instead of bewildered by the difference. He was sensible enough to realize his outlook might have been different if his maternal grandparents hadn't been wealthy or just as proud of their ancestors who had always been free.

They had migrated from the West Indies to England to America. Intelligence, fortitude, and business savvy had increased the wealth of each generation of Everetts.

His ancestors on both sides had a history of being displaced. His forefathers on his mother's side learned early what rank and wealth and influence could do when Elizabeth I tried to expel blacks from England in 1596. The expulsion movement largely failed, but it served as an indelible reminder that the majority of Britons thought people with dark skin were inferior.

In 1838 on the Trail of Tears, the Muscogee Indians suffered indignities and cruelties and numerous deaths. Then they were made to live on land that was foreign to them.

His ancestors on both sides were thought by some to be inferior, lazy, shiftless. Those small-minded individuals never thought of the intelligence, the perseverance, the determination it took to survive despite constant and overt discrimination and deprivation in a harsh and hostile world.

Both survived, passing down through generations their history through the spoken, chanted, or sung word. One branch of his ancestors had been more financially successful than the other, but both understood the problems inherent to people of color.

His maternal grandparents might have been snobbish in their own way, but they, like his parents, never let him forget money could get you only so far when the hue of your skin didn't come from hours in the sun or a tanning salon. The lesson was brought home one day when he went to the store with his mother, and they couldn't get anyone to wait on them.

Daniel hadn't understood until his mother gave him a smile and asked to speak to the manager. As soon as the man arrived and learned who she was, he had been all apologetic and so were the saleswomen. They left the store without buying anything.

It was only after they arrived home that he noticed his mother hadn't been dressed up the way she usually was. At dinner that night she casually mentioned the incident to his grandfather and suggested they close out the account. They never returned. His lessons had begun. He'd never forgotten.

He was a proud, almost belligerent, kid—big for his age and unwilling to take mess from anyone. If he hadn't had a conscientious teacher in kindergarten, one who ruled the classroom and the playground with rigid standards of fair play—no matter how much money the student's family had—he might have been expelled, or worse labeled "slow" and delegated to a backseat. Instead righteousness, truth, and honor prevailed as the only criteria for justice, in Mr. Kennedy's opinion.

By not being judged, Daniel had learned not to judge. He had no preconceived notions on meeting someone. The person's actions determined how they would be treated from that point on.

Some of his closest friends were still his kindergarten classmates. Since he admired intelligence, his friends were always at the top of the class. Interestingly, as the years progressed, they were the school leaders in academics and extracurricular activities.

Those same friends had grown up to be some of the most influential men in the country: men of integrity and long memory. Each year they got together for a think-tank off the Caribbean, where one of his former classmates owned an island.

None of them would believe that Daniel Falcon had run from a woman he could pick up with one hand. The problem was, after he picked her up, he didn't want to let her go.

Daniel had never in the past had any difficulty in figuring out when someone was trying to put something over on him. His logical mind was telling him he hadn't slipped up. Yet logic was also telling him there was always a tiny risk factor in forming any conclusion dealing with people and emotions.

He had based his decision on his previous experiences with women. But when he looked at Madelyn, as he had that afternoon, he saw an open, caring woman. Not the kind of woman who would name someone else as the father of her child.

That meant he had to reevaluate everything. It wasn't going to be easy—in fact, it was going to be the most difficult, the most gut-wrenching thing he had ever done. Because if he had made a mistake, the possible consequences were just as disturbing.

Something isn't right, and I am going to find out what it is, Bill Taggart thought.

Ever since Daniel Falcon had shown up unexpectedly at the twins' birthday party, people had been acting funny. First it was Madelyn, then his sons, now his wife. Grace bothered him most of all.

After forty-two years of marriage, a man learned to pick up on things if he wanted to stay happy. Grace hadn't asked for her camera back since she came to get everyone for cake and ice cream, nor had she gotten on to him for not snapping photos. She had more pictures of her grandchildren than all of her children put together— doted on the little rascals so much she had to stop going through the children's department to resist buying them something.

Now all her attention was for her daughter. She didn't seem to be able to pass without touching her head, her arm. The trouble was, their daughter was looking sadder and sadder.

His children might be grown, but a man never stopped being a parent until he drew his last breath. Something was wrong with his Kitten, and he was going to find out what it was.

"Kane, Matt—grab some trash bags, and we'll start cleaning up outside."

Bill's determination grew when he saw Madelyn tense and send a worried glance toward her brothers. What made him feel a little better was the slight nod of approval from his wife.

It had bothered him to think Kitten had a problem, and his wife hadn't come to him. He should have known better. They always talked things over. Grace wasn't the secretive type. His sons, on the other hand, could put a rock to shame on giving out information.

Outside he began helping his sons pull the pink and blue crepe paper from the lower branches of the oak tree. "Is Kitten in trouble or heading that way?"

"Daddy, I'm not sure it's either," Kane said. His extra three inches made it easier to remove the paper and not damage the branches. He paused a second, then faced his father. "I think she may be interested in Daniel Falcon, only I'm not sure how far it's gone or if it's going anyplace."

"So that's what the trip to the barn was about?" Bill asked.

"Yes, sir," Matt confirmed, a frown on his handsome face. "Only he isn't as easily intimidated as the others."

"He's not intimidated at all," Kane reminded him.

"Didn't I read he's in Houston now?" Bill asked.

"Yes, sir," Kane said, his sigh long and telling.

Bill stared into the distance for a long time before saying, "All you can do is try your best to raise your kids to know right from wrong, because one day you have to let 'em go on their own." His gaze turned to his eldest. "You were the easiest"—then to Matt—"You were always respectful, but you wanted to push everything to the limits."

Bill lowered his voice and continued. "You worry more about girls, but Kitten has never given your mother and me a moment of worry. I know some of that is because of you two, and I always loved you more because I didn't have to ask you to watch after her.

"Her mother is worried now. So are you two. But all of us jumping on her is not going to help, either." He held up his hand when Matt started to say something. "Sometimes talking makes things worse instead of better. The day Kane stopped talking and hauled you to Wade's ranch was the day you started to heal."

Bill's hand clasped his second child on his wide shoulder. "I hurt for you, but there was nothing I could do but be there for you. I think that's what we have to do now. Just be there for your sister."

"Daniel is my friend, but he can be a coldhearted SOB if he wants to," Kane warned.

Bill looked at his middle child. "So could your brother before Shannon. I want you two to leave Kitten alone."

"And if he hurts her?" Matt asked.

"Then you can have him, after I'm finished," the elder Taggart said.

Gradually Madelyn became aware she wasn't the center of attention anymore. The focus had shifted to Kane Jr. and Chandler. The two show-offs were demonstrating their riding skills.

Victoria, who by her own admission was afraid of

horses until she married Kane, was beaming as her children rode their Shetland ponies around the corral. Their father stood nearby, but no one doubted that if he had the slightest doubt of the children's abilities, he wouldn't have given them the ponies for their surprise birthday presents.

"Now we can go riding with you all the time, Daddy," Chandler said.

"Did you get Mama a horse so she can ride by herself?" Kane Jr. asked. "Shadow Walker must be tired of carrying both of you all the time."

Dropping her head, Victoria groaned. Matt whooped. Kane shot him a threatening look. "Shannon, you better get an ice pack ready"

"Now, children," Grace admonished sternly, her lips twitching. "What will Clair and Henry think of us?"

"That Victoria did the right thing when she asked Kane to marry her," Clair answered without a moment's hesitation. Her husband, Henry, not as outspoken as his diminutive wife, smiled in agreement.

This is how it is supposed to be, Madelyn thought. An outpouring of love and affection and warmth. This is what she wanted for her child. Her family might not approve of her single motherhood, but she didn't doubt they'd love her baby.

"That smile looks good on you," her father said, looping his arms over the top rail of the corral.

"Sorry, I've had a lot on my mind." They might love the child, but she wasn't ready to tell them yet.

"Whatever it is, you'll work it out. And if you can't, just remember your family loves you, and we're only a phone call away."

Slowly she turned and gazed up into the eyes of the first man she had loved. In his eyes she saw love just as great. There would be no interrogation.

She'd have time to work through this by herself. Once again her father had come to her rescue, just as he had so many times when she was growing up with scraped knees, broken bikes, back-stabbing friends, callous boys.

She swallowed the growing lump in her throat. "I'm glad you're my father."

"No gladder than I am." His hand left the rail and circled her shoulders. She leaned into him.

From the corral, Kane caught Matt's attention. Silent communication passed between them. For now they'd respect their father's wishes. But if Daniel hurt their baby sister, there wouldn't be much left of him for their father to worry about.

In his black truck, Daniel slowly drove into Madelyn's apartment complex. Catty-corner to her apartment, he backed in tail first, cut the engine, then tossed his aviator sunglasses on the dash. He wasn't happy about being here, but he hadn't been able to talk himself out of coming.

When he left—all right, ran from Kane's ranch—his primary concern had been with putting as much distance as possible between him and temptation. It was only later, as he had time to think on the flight, that he had thought how his abrupt leave-taking might affect her or make her brothers more suspicious.

She had enough to deal with without their butting in. He didn't delude himself into thinking he had fooled them or gotten them to back off. They were too stubborn and loved their sister too much. He wouldn't, if he we're in their place.

Daniel tossed his Stetson onto the seat beside him. Hell, he had been in their place. Even after all these years, the memory still enraged him. LaSalle had been

a smooth-talking snake. Daniel had taken great pleasure in pulling his fangs.

A white Lexus with gold mag wheels and gold trim
passed in front of his truck and parked in the space in
front of Madelyn's door. Daniel straightened.

The door on the passenger side of the car opened.
A jean-clad leg in white sneakers emerged. Moments
later the rest of Madelyn appeared, her face wreathed
in a smile.

Daniel's attention shifted to the driver. He finally
admitted the other reason he was there, to see her
"friend." He wasn't pleased.

The other man was of average height and build, and
dressed in raw silk black pants and shirt. A diamond
glinted in his ear. When he opened the trunk, Daniel
noted the heavy gold link bracelet.

Some women liked flashy men. He thought Madelyn
had more sense . . . until she laughed and swatted playfully at the arm of the walking jewelry store. Still
laughing, they went inside.

The truck's motor came to life. He finally admitted
the third reason he had come: to know if seeing her
helped him with the turmoil he had been going through
since his logic had hit him squarely in the face. It had,
only not the way he thought.

He should have trusted his first instinct. There was
nothing connecting him to Madelyn except white-hot
lust. Madelyn didn't need him, and he wasn't going to
make the mistake again of thinking she did.

"Thanks again, Sid, for picking me up."

"No problem. I'll be here at seven thirty to take you
to work," Sid said, setting her overnight case and gar-
ment bag on the couch.

"I appreciate it," she told him. "They promised to have my car ready by three tomorrow."

He grunted. "If they don't, let me know."

She grinned. Sid had been her neighbor and friend for two years. He'd passed inspection the first time he met Kane and Matt for the simple reason they could see there was nothing romantic happening. And his collard greens, candied yams, and hot-water corn bread were to die for.

The only boy and youngest child of five children, Sid had grown up with a strong protective instinct where women were concerned. His flight-attendant girlfriend, Gloria, was desperately trying to steer him to the altar. But Sid, an insurance adjuster, was having too much fun living the single life.

"You can depend on it," she finally said.

"See that you do. Hate to run, but the game will be on at six," he said, striding toward the door. "Sure you don't want to come over and watch the Sonics outshoot the Mavericks with me?"

"I'm not sure Gloria trusts me," she told him.

"Her problem. I'm not giving up my friends. Anyway, a relationship won't work without trust."

Madelyn's happy mood deteriorated. "Don't I know it."

He paused with the door open, his gaze openly speculative. "Something tells me you're not talking in generalities."

She studied the toes of her sneakers. "You'll be late for the ball toss."

He crossed back to her. Lean fingers lifted her chin. "Watch yourself, you hear?"

"I hear," she said, then closed the door after him and leaned against it. She heard. The warning had just come too late.

Chapter 12

Madelyn frowned on passing empty office after empty office Monday morning. She glanced at her watch: seven fifty-two. Usually everyone was at their desk by now. Putting her briefcase away, she peeped into Floyd Cramer's office. Empty. Dedicated, precise, and punctual to a fault, Floyd arrived at work earlier than anyone and was one of the last to leave.

Her frown deepened. There wasn't a morning meeting, Madelyn was sure of it—at least she hoped there wasn't. Her concentration hadn't been the best the last few weeks.

Hearing faint voices coming from Mr. Sampson's office, she slowly headed in that direction. Finding everyone crowded around a portable TV in her boss's office, she wrinkled her nose. If it was Daniel again, she wasn't staying.

"Good morn—"

Her greeting was shushed. She walked farther into the room. Daniel was hot news, but she couldn't imagine this type of attention.

"What's up?" she softly questioned Mr. Sampson.

His gaze remained fixed on the TV screen. "Mr. Osgood is about to make an announcement."

Madelyn placed her hands on Cassandra's shoulders and leaned closer. Osgood was CEO of Sinclair, and from all the TV stations and microphones jockeying for position, it had to be big news for the regular broadcast to be interrupted.

A distinguished, gray-haired man stepped to the podium and smiled. There was a collective sigh of relief from more than one person.

"Whatever it is, we'll still get a paycheck. Osgood rose up from the ranks. He wouldn't have that 'cat-ate-the-cream-look' if he was about to throw us to the wolves," Floyd announced.

Osgood straightened the mike and began speaking. "Sinclair Petroleum Company, because of its size and savvy, has always been a leader in the energy industry. So it is with great pleasure that I'm unveiling plans to build a two-billion-dollar chemical complex in Singapore, aimed at positioning the company as the low-cost plastics supplier in the booming Asian market."

"Gee whiz," muttered Scotty Jones, who quickly received a collective shush.

Osgood continued. "The four integrated plants in Singapore will eventually employ as many as one thousand people. The huge complex will produce petrochemicals and basic plastics used in a wide range of consumer products. Product prices are at their highest levels in years, and Asian demand is expected to continue to soar."

This time no one said a word.

"The state-of-the-art facility will be supplied primarily from an existing Sinclair refinery in Singapore, Sinclair Petroleum Company in Houston, and other soon to be announced regions." Removing his wire-rimmed glasses, Osgood placed them in his coat pocket. "Questions?"

He was bombarded with them. This time her co-workers weren't listening. They were too excited about the possibility of going to Singapore. Their excitement reached new heights when Mr. Sampson was called upstairs to a meeting.

When he returned two hours later, the first person he asked to see privately was Madelyn. Rising, she barely acknowledged the thumb's-up sign from Cassandra. She was too worried about what she would say if he did offer her a position.

Entering Mr. Sampson's office, she bit her lip and perched on the edge of the chair in front of his desk, "Yes, Mr. Sampson."

He smiled broadly. "I guess you know what this is about. I don't mind telling you, this is a coup for me as well." Leaning forward, he folded his arms on his cluttered desk. "My department has always had a reputation for having the best and the brightest. That's why I wanted you aboard—that's why I asked to see you first."

Madelyn swallowed. The knot remained in her throat and she barely choked out, "Yes, sir."

"Madelyn, you can take that scared look off your face. I didn't call you in here first to tell you you weren't going, but to offer you a position at the Singapore plant." His smile broadened. "Things are still being worked out, but I can tell you now, I'm putting you up for assistant supervisor."

This was worse than she imagined. She'd thought it would take another year before getting into management. Only now she wouldn't be able to accept the position after she had worked so hard.

Leaning back in his chair, he laughed out loud, his blue eyes twinkling. "I see I've shocked you. Well, say something so I can get the next person in here."

Her hand clutching her stomach, she said, "I-I can't go."

He snapped forward in his chair. His was smile gone, in its place was an expression of stunned disbelief. "What did you say?"

"I-I can't go." Saying it the second time wasn't any easier. "I'm pregnant and have no plans of marrying the father." Seeing the shock and disappointment on his face was worse than she'd imagined. "I can't possibly go, but I thank you for considering me."

He didn't say anything but continued to stare at her as if he didn't recognize her anymore. Taking a deep breath, she forged ahead. "I'd appreciate it if you didn't tell anyone else."

"They're going to know sooner or later," he finally pointed out gruffly, his hand clenched on a ballpoint pen.

"Does that mean you're keeping me in your department?"

Tight-lipped, Sampson leaned back in his chair. Leather creaked. "You're bright, intelligent, hardworking. I'm going to need all the help I can get since they asked for three of my top people. Yours was the first name I gave them."

"I'm sorry."

"So am I." He rocked forward. "Please send Kramer in."

Leaving, she did as requested, then went straight to the rest room to be alone. She didn't think she could go through telling anyone else she was pregnant. Certainly not her family. She felt too exposed. Her private sin made public—and it would only get worse.

The next day proved her right. Mr. Sampson, who had always been so warm, seldom acknowledged her unless necessary. Only Cassandra commented.

"He'll get over your turning him down. I'm glad you did, since I was the last one chosen from our department."

Madelyn wasn't so sure. The guilt she thought she had put behind her had risen up again. Even her theater date that night with the irrepressible Felicia couldn't shake her growing melancholy.

All during the two-act play, she thought of Daniel. His picture in the society page of the *Houston Chronicle* with a beautiful young woman tore at her soul. It was plain to see he had moved on with his life, a life that didn't include her and their baby.

She might not be able to imagine a life without Daniel, but he had no difficulty living without her. Somehow she had to do the same.

The next night she made herself go to the monthly church singles Wednesday night potluck dinner. There was always a lot of fun conversation and good food.

It soon became apparent the topic of choice that night was going to be the difficulty of a good woman finding a good man. Of course the men objected to being made the heavies. Where were the good women, they wanted to know.

Unlike usual, Madelyn didn't get into the middle of the heated discussion. Good was relative. Daniel was a good man, she was a good woman, they had created a life, yet they had no future together. Finding didn't count if you couldn't keep him or her.

Tired, she went home early and immediately went to bed. Before falling asleep, her last conscious thought was a wish for her life to be back the way it was.

Pain, sharp and intense in her stomach, jerked Madelyn from a restless sleep. Gasping, she balled into a knot, her arms circling her waist. Nausea sent her staggering to the bathroom. One hand on the toilet, the other clutching her stomach, she went limp when the twin agonies receded.

Breathing erratically, she tried to stand. Just as she pushed to her knees, a twisting pain in her abdomen sent her down again. In the midst of her torment, a mindless fear emerged.

She was losing the baby.

Felicia answered the phone on the second ring. The lateness of the call didn't bother her. She had called Dominique around noon Paris time and she had been out. When her daughter called back, Felicia had been at the club, helping to organize a benefit for literacy. The seven-hour time difference usually worked out well for them since she went to sleep late, and Dominique was an early riser.

"Hello." Popping a tissue from the holder on the bedside stand, Felicia sat up in bed and wiped away the last traces of the chocolate eclair she had indulged herself in. She frowned.

If this was a bad trans-Atlantic connection, there'd be static, not silence. Reaching for the TV remote, she clicked it off. "Dominique? Is that you?"

Hearing labored breathing, she started to hang up until she heard the word "hurt." Swinging her legs over the side of the bed, she stood. Alarm swept through her.

"Dominique! Dominique, say something," she shouted. Covering the mouthpiece, she yelled for her son, praying he had come home and she just hadn't heard him.

"Dominique, honey. It's mother. Talk to me."

"I-It's M-Madelyn," came the thin, wavery voice.

The panic Felicia felt receded only marginally. "Madelyn, what's the matter? I can barely hear you."

"Stomach keeps cramping. I-I don't know if it's the baby or not."

"Are you bleeding?"

"No," came the thankful answer.

"Don't worry—I'm on the way." Disconnecting the call, she dialed her chauffeur and instructed the sleepy-sounding man to bring the car around immediately.

"Where are you going this late?"

Felicia whirled around to see her son in the doorway and almost cried in relief. "Madelyn just called. She's having stomach cramps. She sounded as if she's in a lot of pain."

Terror ripped through Daniel. "Is it the baby?"

With all her heart, Felicia hurt for her son. Fear had done what his stubbornness wouldn't . . . allowed him to accept Madelyn's pregnancy.

Felicia prayed it wasn't too late. "She's doesn't know. She's not bleeding."

"I'm going with you," he said, grabbing his mother's arm and heading down the stairs.

Madelyn and the baby had to be all right. They had to be.

Daniel refused to accept any other possibility. He tried to think of another plausible explanation for her pain, which he might have read about in all the pregnancy manuals he had pored over—yet for the first time in his memory, his calm, concise mind deserted him.

He could form only one thought: *They had to be all right.*

Daniel felt his mother's hand holding his, knew she was offering support and comfort, yet he was unable to respond. It was as if he had been dropped in a black hole.

He exited the Mercedes before it stopped. An eternity

seemed to pass before Madelyn's door slowly swung open.

At the first sight of Madelyn, teary and trembling, clutching the doorknob for support, he came hurtling out of the blackness. Panic seized him.

Fear, remorse, guilt plummeted into him from all sides. He couldn't reach her fast enough, hold her tight enough.

"Honey, it's going to be all right."

She buried her face in his chest, her slim body shaking with the force of her sobs. "My baby. My baby."

"Don't cry," he begged. "Our baby is going to be all right. Dr. Scalar's service says he's at the hospital with a delivery, and he'll meet us there."

Scooping her up in his arms, he rushed back to the car. Felicia held the back door open. Once Daniel and Madelyn were inside, she closed the door and quickly got in front.

Higgins put the luxury automobile into a sharp turn and barreled out of the complex. During his youth he had raced stock cars all over the world. He hadn't lost the touch. In no time they were on the freeway, and he made excellent time in the light traffic.

Yet not good enough.

"It's coming again," Madelyn cried, her fingernails biting into the top of Daniel's hand.

Feeling utterly useless, Daniel murmured words of comfort, holding her in his lap, wishing he could take the pain himself.

At the emergency room, still holding her in his arms, he hurried through the automatic doors as quickly as possible without jarring her. "She's pregnant and having severe stomach pain," he told the first medical-looking person he saw.

"Is this Ms. Taggart?" asked the woman garbed in surgical green.

"Yes," Daniel quickly confirmed.

"I'm Nurse McKinnie. Dr. Scalar called." She indicated a wheelchair. "I'll take her back. You can go sign her in."

"I want to go with her," he cried, holding her tighter.

"Are you her husband?"

"No."

"I'm sorry. Regulations."

Reluctantly Daniel lowered her into the chair. She needed help he couldn't give her. The thought was a humbling and scary one. His unsteady fingers pulled her blue terry cloth robe back up over her shoulders. "I'll be here."

Looking small and frightened, Madelyn bit her lip. His last glimpse of her was of tears streaming dawn her pale cheeks just before the nurse wheeled her away through a set of heavy, automatic doors.

Being helpless wasn't something Daniel accepted easily or was used to. "I should be with her."

"Let's go sign her in."

Guilt-filled eyes lifted to his mother's. "How? I don't even know her birthday, her exact address, her . . ." Fist clenched, he swallowed.

"Then we'll do the best we can," Felicia answered reasonably.

He looked at the double doors through which the nurse had disappeared with Madelyn. "I should have been with her."

Daniel paced the waiting room. Luckily Madelyn had preregistered for her delivery, and they had been able to pull her up on the computer. The fact made him feel worse instead of better. His name wasn't anywhere. If she hadn't called his mother, he wouldn't even know she was here. The unsettling thought caused him to break out in a cold sweat.

He should have been with her all through her pregnancy instead of denying his paternity. It had taken this disaster for him to stop fighting what he had always known deep in his heart, his soul.

Duplicity wasn't in Madelyn's makeup. She was open and honest, sometimes too much so. Her sense of fair play was too ingrained for her to place false paternity. He had let his hardheaded logic, then fear of his feelings, then his jealousy at her apartment Sunday afternoon get in the way of that knowledge.

The baby was his. Stopping, he stared up at the ceiling. *Please, God, don't let it be too late for me to make this up to both of them.*

"Felicia."

Daniel whirled abruptly. A black man in his late thirties, in a white lab coat over green surgical garb and a white cloth cap, held out his hands to Felicia. His mother rose immediately.

"She's fine. Food poisoning. Several more of her church members are in the main ER," he said, his voice a smooth baritone.

"Thank God," Felicia said.

"Can I see her?" Daniel asked.

The man turned to him, his hands still holding Felicia's, "Daniel Falcon, I take it?"

"Yes. Dr. Scalar, I presume."

Deep black eyes twinkled. "You presume correctly. I don't suppose you can wait until I grab a cup of coffee? I've been here for ten hours."

"I don't want to, but since you helped Madelyn, I'll wait."

Dr. Scalar's gaze narrowed thoughtfully. "I can't imagine waiting is something you do well."

"No, it isn't."

"In that case, follow me."

"Give her my love," Felicia called.

Daniel followed the broad-shouldered man, resisting the urge to ask him to hurry.

"We've given her something for the pain and the nausea. Since she's in the first trimester of her pregnancy at almost eleven weeks, I'm keeping her in observation overnight," he told Daniel, pushing open a solid green door.

Seeing Madelyn on the bed, Daniel rushed past Dr. Scalar to her side. Unable to resist, he placed his hand on top of hers resting on her sheet-covered abdomen.

He frowned slightly as she removed her hand and put it under the covers. "Mother sends her love."

"I feel like a fool for worrying her. But I'm so relieved I could dance," Madelyn said. "Thank you, Dr. Scalar."

"You just be careful what you eat from now on."

Something was wrong. Her smile was too bright, almost forced. "Do you need anything from your place?" Daniel asked.

"No, we'll be fine now." She patted her abdomen. This time her smile was real.

Daniel wanted to place his hand on hers again, but wasn't sure of his reception.

"I'd better go. I have a patient in labor upstairs." Dr. Scalar gave Daniel a considering look. "The father is a wreck. I hope you hold up better."

"Someone else is going to be my birthing partner," Madelyn quickly said. There wasn't a hint of regret in her steady voice.

Dr. Scalar's face lost its warmth. "Whomever you

choose will be fine, I'm sure. I'll stop by before I leave the hospital."

The door swung shut. Daniel didn't know what to say. He suddenly had the feeling he had lost something infinitely precious, and he wasn't sure if he was going to be able to get it back.

"Daniel, I have to ask for your forgiveness," she finally said, her fingers playing with the seam of the sheet.

Surprise knitted his brow. "For what?"

"For being so righteous when I was telling you about the baby." She shook her head, seemingly unconcerned that her hair was spiked over her head like a porcupine. She had never looked more beautiful or precious to him.

"I was going to take care of the baby and not let it grow up feeling guilt or blame because it was unplanned. But the first time the pregnancy interfered with something I wanted to do, I resented it."

Her face clouded. "The last thing I remember before going to sleep tonight was wishing my life was back the way it was."

"That's understandable, Madelyn," he told her, wanting to take her in his arms so badly he ached. "Your life was changing, and you weren't prepared for those changes. My reaction to your pregnancy didn't help. I should have known the baby was mine. I'm sorry. I hope you can forgive me."

"That's the point I'm trying to make." She lowered her head for a moment, then shook her head. "I blamed you for the same thing I was unconsciously doing. Tonight I finally realized I was spouting words. The pregnancy hadn't really sunk in until it interfered with a job assignment to Singapore." She bit her lip.

"I felt sorry for myself. Then I woke up in pain. I was so afraid I was having a miscarriage. In an instant

I realized the best job in the world wouldn't make up for that loss. I had no right to expect you to jump up and down when I really hadn't accepted it myself," she said, condemnation heavy in her quiet voice.

"Mad—"

"No," she said, cutting him off. "This has to be said. I was so concerned about what my family would say, how the people at my job would react, how the parishioners at my church would treat me, that I forgot about the most important thing of all. The welfare of my child. Anything else is secondary." She glanced down at her stomach hidden by bedcovers and circled her arms protectively around it.

When she lifted her face, she glowed with happiness. "I won't forget again. I had never told my baby I loved it, only that I would take care of it. Thank God, I now have the chance. My baby is going to know it's loved."

Nowhere in her diatribe did she mention a need or a place for Daniel in her life with the baby. "I never doubted you'd make a great mother. The kids loved you at the twins' birthday party."

"I'm going to do my best," she said with absolute confidence.

Unable to resist, he brushed unsteady fingertips lightly across her cheek. "You better get some sleep."

Dutifully she scooted down in bed. "Would you mind asking the nurse if I could have a phone? Dr. Scalar doesn't want me to go to work tomorrow."

"I'll take care of it," he said, then added silently, and take care of you and the baby if you'll let me.

"Thanks, but I'd rather call," she told him, already shutting him out.

Not knowing what else to say, Daniel slowly left the room. He had tried to convince himself he didn't need Madelyn in his life, only to find out that he did. It was an unexpected twist of fate that she had taken a page from his book and decided the same thing.

The instant his mother saw him, she rushed to him, her face anxious. "Did something happen to Madelyn and the baby?"

"They're fine," he told her.

"Then why aren't you happy? Despite what's happened in the past, I know you care about both of them."

" 'Too little, too late,' as the saying goes."

Taking his arm, his mother led him out of the waiting room into the quiet hallway. "Will you please tell me what went on in there?"

He repeated their conversation. Each word was like a twisting knife in his heart.

"Daniel, I want to ask you something," Felicia continued when he simply stared at her. "Are Madelyn and the baby worth fighting for, worth locking that stubborn pride of yours in a closet and throwing away the key?"

"Yes." There was no longer any doubt. He wanted both of them in his life.

"Then don't make the same mistake I did," she told him fiercely. "Admit your mistakes. Do everything in your power to let her know you love her."

"You still love him, don't you?"

Tears crested in Felicia's eyes. "I must be a better actress than I thought."

"Then you just didn't marry him because of me?"

Shock widened her eyes. "Is that what you thought?" Her eyes closed briefly, then opened. "Naturally I was scared at first, but it didn't take me long to realize I had the means to make John Henry mine. I can see by your face you think I trapped him. At the time, in my selfishness, I didn't see it that way."

Gratefully she accepted the handkerchief Daniel offered her, then dabbed the corners of her eyes before continuing. "I loved your father from almost the first moment he grinned at me from the rodeo arena. Wonder of wonders, he loved me, too. But your grandparents' wealth sometimes made him uncomfortable."

Daniel's eyes narrowed. "Is that why you tried to make him over?"

"Partly. Although I knew he loved us, a part of him would never be satisfied and happy in tailor-made suits and Italian loafers. The idea of losing him scared me."

She bit her lip. "John Henry is the only man I couldn't wrap around my little finger. The knowledge infuriated as much as frightened me." Trembling fingers swept her hair back behind her ear. "I'm not proud of the way I tried to make him into what I thought he should be. I wanted him less proud, more needy. He took it until I did the unforgivable in his eyes."

Daniel had heard a lot of stories about the final breakup between his parents while his mother had been at a two-thousand-dollar-a-week spa in Florida, but both refused to discuss what had happened. Daniel wasn't exactly sure he wanted to hear.

"Don't look back on this months or years from now with regret," his mother said fervently. Her hand closed gently over his jacketed arm. "Don't follow in my footsteps."

Daniel's concern for his mother grew. He had honestly believed the final breakup hadn't affected her one way or the other for long, believed their forced marriage had slowly killed what love they once might have had for one another. It was a startling revelation to find out how wrong he had been.

He loved his parents, but saw no reason for them to be unhappy together when there was some chance for happiness apart. Now he knew that wasn't the case. "Mother, maybe I can talk to Dad."

Shaking her head, her hand dropped to her side. "Your father wouldn't appreciate your interference. I ruined my marriage. I don't want to ruin your relationship with John Henry."

"He's stubborn, but fair."

"No, and that's final." She hitched the strap of her handbag over her shoulder. She was his mother again—in charge, and not to be denied.

He'd forgotten she was as stubborn as his father. "Come on, I'll walk you to the car."

"And then what are you going to do?"

"What else? Go back in there and fight for another chance. I only hope it's not too late."

Chapter 13

"Here's the phone you wanted," Daniel said. Madelyn opened her eyes, a frown forming on her face as she raised up on her elbows in the hospital bed. "What are you still doing here?"

"They're shorthanded and I decided to stay." The lie slipped out easily. Plugging the phone into the wall outlet, he handed the receiver to her. "It's not like I haven't pulled this duty before."

She accepted the phone, her attention still on Daniel. "I could barely lift my head then. Except for a little queasiness, I feel fine."

"Good." He pulled out a straight-backed chair and sat down near the bed.

"Daniel, I'm fine."

"I know." He leaned back in the chair and crossed one booted foot over the other. "Just let me get used to the idea. You scared me again."

"I scared myself," she confessed softly.

Standing, he brushed back her hair, his eyes searching hers. "I know."

Brown eyes misted. "I don't know why I'm crying."

"All the tension finally caught up with you." The pad of his thumb caught a tear and wiped it away.

"I suppose." Dialing, she talked briefly with her boss, then hung up.

"You told him?" Daniel asked, gathering as much from the one-sided conversation.

Nodding, Madelyn leaned back in bed. "He wanted me to accept one of the positions in Singapore at the new petrochemical plant Sinclair is going to build. I was the first person he asked once he came back from his meeting."

Daniel placed the phone on the bedside table, then adjusted the bedcovers. "From your expression, I take it he didn't greet the news very well."

"He's really a very nice man. He has a reputation in the company for having the best and the brightest." She picked at the open weave on the blanket. "I let him down. He likes for us to go out and shine."

Casually Daniel picked up her soft hand. "So you'll shine in Houston instead of Singapore."

She sent him a bright smile. "You can count on it. I'm after his job."

"Something tells me you'll get it," he told her with absolute confidence. "Now rest. I'll be here if you need anything."

Uncertain brown eyes watched him. "You really don't have to stay."

"Yes, I do. Now close your eyes and get some rest before they kick me out of here."

"Daniel," she said softly after she had lain down and closed her eyes. "I'm glad the baby's all right, and I'm glad you're here."

His chest ached. A lump formed in his throat. To-night could have ended much differently. "So am I."

"Daniel, go home. You look ready to drop."

"Felicia's right, Daniel," Madelyn agreed, resting

comfortably in her own bed the next morning. "You look more in need of being in bed than I do."

"There's nothing wrong with me," he told them. "You're sure I can't get you something else?"

Madelyn smiled. "No, I think the magazines, candy, and flowers you picked up in the gift shop this morning just about take care of it."

"Daniel, go home and go to bed," Felicia ordered, bodily leading him by the arm out of the bedroom. "I'll be here."

He rubbed the back of his stiff neck. "I guess I could use a shower and change of clothes."

"Don't you dare come back here before this afternoon."

He frowned down at her. "I thought you were on my side."

"I am. That's why I'm sending you home." Felicia regarded him critically. "How much sleep did you get last night?"

"I don't remember."

She pounced on his answer. "Exactly." Opening the front door, she urged him through. "Goodbye, Daniel." She was still laughing when she reentered the bedroom. "I thought he'd never leave."

"He was so sweet and attentive," Madelyn said, a trace of laughter in her voice. "You should have heard him giving the nurse instructions on pushing my wheelchair into the elevator so I wouldn't be jarred. When he went inside the gift shop, the nurse leaned down and told me she hoped she was off the night I delivered." She sobered. "I guess she thought he'd be there."

"He will be, if he knows you want him there," Felicia said softly.

Madelyn shook her dark head. "Daniel has to go the rest of the way on his own."

The doorbell interrupted any comment Felicia might have made. "If that's Daniel . . ." Ruefully shaking her head, she went to open the front door. Instead of her son, a couple in their midsixties stood there. "Yes?"

"Good morning," greeted the gray-haired woman. "We're Mr. and Mrs. Sampson. Is it possible that we see Madelyn for a moment?"

"Is she expecting you?"

"No, but she called last night and told my husband about her illness," the elderly woman explained.

"You must be her boss." Felicia smiled warmly. "Daniel said she called you last night."

"Daniel. Daniel Falcon?" the man questioned, his voice rising in apprehension.

"Who is it, Felicia?" Madelyn called from the bedroom.

"May we see her?" Mrs. Sampson asked. "We'd like to give her these flowers. We promise not to stay long."

"This way." Felicia led them to the bedroom. "You have visitors, Madelyn."

"Mr. and Mrs. Sampson, what are you doing here?" Madelyn questioned, forgetting about the magazine in her lap.

"Howard wanted to tell you something," Mrs. Sampson said.

Madelyn tried to take comfort in the spring bouquet Mrs. Sampson was holding. It wasn't likely she was being fired if they were bringing her flowers, but being asked to transfer to another department would be almost as bad. "Of course. Felicia, could you please excuse us?"

Felicia saw the anxious expression on Madelyn's face and gave the Sampsons a pointed look. "The doctor doesn't want her disturbed."

Jane smiled. Howard remained uncomfortable looking. "I'll add some water." Taking the bouquet, Felicia left.

"Howard?" Jane prompted.

What little confidence Madelyn had that the situation wasn't dire plummeted. Being at a loss for words or unable to speak his mind was not a characteristic of her boss. "Is this about my job?"

"Howard, you're scaring the poor dear," his wife told him.

Mr. Sampson found his voice. "What do you think she did to me? She's the best production engineer I've had in years, and she tossed it all away."

"I won't apologize for my baby," Madelyn told him fiercely. "If you'd like for me to transfer to another department, I'll understand."

"Who said anything about a transfer?" he asked roughly. "You're still the best production engineer I've got."

"I don't understand," she told them.

He finally spit it out. "Babies and our jobs don't mix. We spend too many long hours away from home. You could have been tops in your field. The Singapore tenure would have given you more experience. Now you'll never get to the top."

Madelyn began a slow boil. Throwing back the covers, she got out of bed. The heavy silk blue pajamas more than adequately covered her. "Are you saying when this baby is born, I won't be able to do my job just as well?"

"You'll try." He shook his balding, gray head in dismay. "But the baby will be sick with this or that, and you'll have to take off."

"You better believe it," she said with heat. "That just means I'll have to work twice as hard when I return— something I'm very well used to."

His blue eyes narrowed. "I won't cut you any slack because of the baby."

"I won't ask you to."

Eyeball to eyeball they glared at each other. "Just so we understand each other. Tomorrow is Friday, you might as well take it off, too, because I want you fresh on Monday morning. Number eighty-five in East Texas struck gas and oil. They need the pipes like yesterday to bring up both. I want you to work with me on it."

Although excitement raced though her at the prospect of working beside him, her expression didn't change. "I'll be there at seven forty-five."

Nodding curtly, Mr. Sampson turned to his wife. "Let's go."

Jane smiled and whispered, "He really likes you or he wouldn't be so upset. He'll get over it though. We'll have lunch when you feel better."

Madelyn eyed her boss standing impatiently in her doorway. "Thanks for bringing him."

Astonishment touched Jane's round face. "You have it wrong. Howard isn't the type of man you can make do anything. I'm the Trojan horse, so to speak. He didn't like the strain between the two of you. He's not really as chauvinistic as he sounds."

Mrs. Sampson's eyes twinkled mischievously. "I'm depending on you to do what I and our four daughters and the other women who have worked under him with children have been unable to do—get him to admit motherhood doesn't diminish a woman's brain cells."

"You can count on it." The women shared a smile.

The doorbell rang. "Seems you have another visitor. We'd better go," Jane said.

Grabbing her robe from the foot of the bed, Madelyn followed them into the front room. "Daniel!"

His cutting gaze zeroed in on Madelyn, warmed when he nodded to Mrs. Sampson, then zipped back to Mr. Sampson. "Good morning, Mr. Sampson. Finding out already you can't get along at the office without Madelyn? I'm afraid you'll have to—the doctor wants her to rest."

Mr. Sampson's blue eyes widened.

"Daniel," Madelyn admonished, "you're meddling into something that is none of your business."

"Shouldn't you be in bed?" he asked her.

Madelyn sent Daniel a glare hot enough to melt steel. "Stay out of this, Daniel, or be prepared for the consequences."

"Mad—" Daniel began, then her eyes narrowed. He snapped his mouth shut.

"I apologize, Mr. Sampson. Mr. Falcon is a family friend, and he sometimes oversteps himself," Madelyn explained.

Daniel's mouth tightened.

A spat of erratic coughing erupted from the kitchen. "Some water would do wonders to clear your throat, Felicia. You met his mother earlier." A smile on her face, Madelyn opened the front door. "I'll see you at seven forty-five sharp, and thanks for the flowers."

Mr. Sampson almost smiled. He cut a quick glance at the silent Daniel Falcon. "You might make it after all."

"Of course she will, Howard. How else is she going to take your job?" his wife asked.

Mr. Sampson appeared exasperated at his petite wife, but Madelyn noticed he held her arm until he had seated her in their blue Cadillac, then gallantly lifted the hem of her floral print dress away from the door frame. He smiled down at her just before shutting the door.

His concern and love for her was obvious. For a moment Madelyn allowed herself to wonder what that must feel like, to know you were loved, wanted, needed.

"I overreacted again, didn't I?" Daniel asked, a note of caution in his voice.

Closing the door, Madelyn faced him. "Next time ask if your help is needed before you go charging in."

"That's a promise," he said, watching her closely as if she were a time bomb and he wasn't sure how to diffuse her. By slow degrees he took her arm, then gently led her toward the bedroom.

Madelyn started to remind him he hadn't asked, then decided to let him get by this one last time. A contrite Daniel was something you didn't see every day. "Why are you back?"

"I thought I recognized him, but it didn't hit me until I was several blocks away."

Pulling off her robe, she climbed into bed. "So you were practicing your rescue skills again?"

"Unnecessarily, it seems. I guess I keep forgetting you can take care of yourself."

"It's always nice to know you have backup if needed."

"What did he mean by exception?"

She made a face. "He thinks women can't cut it in the business world once we become mothers because we lose focus or have to take off too much with sick children." She smiled with satisfaction. "I know it won't be easy, but I can do it. I told him I'd take off if my baby needed me and still get the job done."

"I could help."

She was glad she had leaned forward to pick up a magazine and toss it out of the way. Her heart was almost dancing before she remembered he had taken care of her before until she was able to take care of herself, then he was gone. She didn't want a part-time father for her baby.

Grasping the magazine, she laid it aside. Her face expressionless, she said, "That won't be necessary." Yawning, she scooted down farther into the bed. "I'm really tired. Good-bye, Daniel."

"I'll see you this afternoon."

He informed his mother of the same thing on passing her in the living room. Madelyn was shutting him out again. He could take care of their child as well as anyone.

He'd show her when the time came. In the meantime he was going to swing that door wide open and keep it that way. Even as the thought came to him, Daniel knew it wouldn't be easy.

Madelyn wasn't going to be pushed. Self-reliant and independent, she might occasionally get down, but not for long. She was a survivor. He had never met a woman like her. She was the kind of resilient woman that could take on the world once she made up her mind.

She had made up her mind, only he wasn't sure if she still wanted him standing by her side when she did. He hated to admit it, but he wasn't brave enough to ask her the question in case she gave him an answer he didn't want to hear or accept. Opening the back door of the Mercedes, he climbed inside.

"Where to, Daniel?" the chauffeur asked, looking in the rearview mirror. Higgins had known Daniel since he was born. The elderly driver saw no reason to stand on formalities when they were alone or with just the family. Neither did Daniel.

"I don't know," Daniel said. He waited for a second, then asked, "Why are women so complicated?"

"Don't know. Guess that's why I'm not married. Couldn't find one who would put up with me," he answered.

"You want to run that by me again? Mother and some of her friends would try the patience of a saint. They talk incessantly and sometimes can't decide where they want to go or what they want to do." Daniel leaned forward in the backseat. "I've never seen you get the least perturbed with them. Even dour Mrs. Crenshaw calls you a dream."

Higgins chuckled, laugh lines deepening around his dark eyes. "She doesn't have to go home with me. I like my things to stay where I put them. Most women like a neat place. They say they're gonna leave your things alone—the next thing you know, you can't find a thing." Half turning in the seat, he faced Daniel.

"Nothing starts my day off worse than having to look for something I left out so I wouldn't have to look for it in the first place. A fussy woman can sure ruin a man's day. If I leave my Sunday shoes under the kitchen table, and my running shoes in the hallway, no one bothers them."

Higgins's comments clouded the issue rather than helped. Daniel didn't know how Madelyn felt about shoes left under the kitchen table, or if she usually woke up grumpy or smiling in the morning. The thing that had bothered him was the thought that he might never find out.

Exactly twenty-nine minutes after Daniel left, Madelyn's doorbell rang. She and Felicia exchanged looks.

Madelyn, sitting up in bed, voiced both their thoughts aloud. "Do you think it's Daniel again?"

"I wouldn't doubt it. Thirty minutes seems the limit of his endurance of being away from you," Felicia said, rising from the side of the bed. "But if it is, I'm going to put him over my knee."

"I want to see that," Madelyn said to Felicia's retreating back.

Felicia opened Madelyn's apartment door, still smiling over her shoulder at Madelyn's additional instructions from the bedroom to send Daniel home if it was him. When Felicia faced forward, time stood still.

Two beloved words whispered across her lips: "John Henry."

His impersonal gaze touched her briefly, dismissing

her as insignificant, then went beyond her to scan the interior of the room behind her.

Joy turned to pain. Trembling fingers gripped the doorknob as she fought to keep from crying out her anguish.

He was still everything to her, and she was less than nothing to him.

Yet some part of her was unable to dismiss him as easily. Hatless, his thick black hair hung straight down his back, framing a face as masculine as it was ruggedly beautiful.

"I was told I would find Daniel here."

The pain in Felicia's heart deepened. He refused to even greet her or say her name, but the deep timbre of his voice made her ache, made her remember its hoarseness as he'd painted erotic pictures of pleasure in her mind and made each one come true.

His searching gaze finally came back to her. She wished it hadn't. She could have borne his anger, withstood his hatred, but the blankness in his expression sent her deeper into despair. It was as if he had wiped her from his mind.

"Someone at Daniel's house said he was here with a friend." Deep grooves furrowed in his copper-toned forehead. "Is he all right?"

"Dad!" Daniel greeted in excitement from behind his father.

John Henry turned to be enveloped in a hearty hug, which he gave back full measure to his son. Stepping away from each other, they shook hands. Both were smiling.

Daniel couldn't have been happier that instead of leaving, he had walked around the apartment complex trying to figure out how to get Madelyn to let him into her and the baby's lives again. He wasn't any closer to a solution, but at least his delay hadn't caused him to miss his farther.

They hadn't seen each other since the Christmas holidays. Seeing him at Madelyn's door with his mother had been a wonderful surprise.

"You look well," his father said, thumping him soundly on the shoulder.

Daniel grinned. "You expected different?"

The deep frown returned to John Henry's face. Lines formed by time and sun radiated from his midnight-black eyes. "Last night I had a dream you were troubled and in pain. I called, but there was no answer. I got into my truck and started driving."

Daniel's hand tightened in his father's. John Henry had always possessed an uncanny sense of when his family was in pain or troubled. As a child, Daniel had thought it was cool, then as an adult he had rebelled against his father's interference. It had almost taken a tragedy for him to accept his father's gift and be thankful.

"Madelyn was sick," he answered, the memory still painful. "Come on, I'd like you to meet her."

Daniel turned and saw the empty doorway. His mother was gone. His puzzlement grew as he led his father inside the apartment and didn't see either woman. "Mother. Madelyn."

"We're in the kitchen," called Madelyn.

"Maybe some other time," his father said, his tone flat, his displeasure evident in his narrowed gaze and stiff shoulders. Guests were greeted, *if* they were welcomed.

Daniel didn't know what was going on, but he knew Madelyn wouldn't judge a man because he wore boots badly in need of a shine and new heels, and jeans and blue plaid that were thin and faded from too many washings.

John Henry's muscular arm firmly in his hand, Daniel

rounded the five-foot partition separating the kitchen from the living room. Felicia's rigid back was to them. Over her shoulder, he saw one of the magazines he had bought Madelyn.

Daniel frowned. He thought she'd be overjoyed to see his father "Mother?"

Madelyn in her robe and gown literally jumped up from her seat at the small table and extended her hand. "You must be Daniel's father. My name's Madelyn Taggart."

"So you're Daniel's friend," John Henry said, his gaze probing.

Withdrawing her hand, Madelyn gave Daniel's father a tight smile "And Felicia's."

John Henry grunted.

Madelyn lifted her chin. "You and Daniel must have a lot to talk about. I won't keep you," Madelyn said and started for the front door.

"She's the reason why you were so worried?" his father asked, his voice dismissive and puzzled.

Daniel watched Madelyn halt abruptly and spin around. His gaze went to his father and knew he was in one of his intractable moods. "Dad, please."

John Henry grunted and shrugged broad shoulders.

Daniel glanced around the room at the three silent people and had no idea how to ease the obvious strain between them. "Let's go to the house and get you settled in."

"I want my own room," John Henry proclaimed.

"Anything you say." Daniel swung back to his silent mother. "I'll ride home with Dad. Should I tell Higgins to wait for you?"

"No, we have some things to discuss," Madelyn answered for Felicia.

Daniel studied the hunched shoulders of his mother,

the gritted smile of his father, the narrowed gaze of Madelyn and left. After telling Higgins that Felicia would call, Daniel climbed into the passenger seat of his father's dented, faded blue truck.

The motor purred to life like a well-fed cat, which Daniel thought wasn't far off the mark. The outside of the vehicle might look like it had been rescued from a junkyard, but under the hood was the finest money could buy.

"Your friend is not a good woman."

"You're wrong. She's the best. Better than I deserve," Daniel said propping his elbow on the open window panel. "Dad, if you were trying to stick it to Madelyn and Mother back there for some slight, you're wrong," Daniel defended. "Neither deserves it."

Shifting the truck into gear, John Henry pulled off. "It wasn't as much fun anyway since I couldn't get a response from either of them."

"Were you trying to?"

"If you didn't care for this woman, I wouldn't have heard your pain." John Henry hit the freeway with a burst of power, the gears slipping smoothly and cleanly. "I wanted to see if she would make your heart bleed as the other tried to do."

"And Mother?"

"To see if she had learned to see with her inner instead of her outer one." Calloused hands tightened on the steering wheel. "She's only gotten worse in the last two years. She was too ashamed to look at me and take me to task as she used to do."

"Dad, you're wrong."

"I'm right—and I've finally come to a decision." He downshifted. "I'm divorcing your mother."

Chapter 14

As fast as Felicia wiped, more tears appeared. "I've lost him. I've really lost him."

Her chair pulled up next to Felicia's, Madelyn tried to console the seemingly inconsolable. "You don't know that."

"Yes, I do. I told myself it was over, but deep down I never believed he'd do it."

"You didn't even look at each other or speak. There's still a chance," Madelyn offered, unsure if she was right to offer hope when she wasn't so sure of the outcome.

Felicia looked up sharply, her lashes spiked with moisture. "That's just it. Even when we were ready to push each other over a cliff, we were never able to deny the deep attraction we had for each other. We may not have seen each other in two years, but for me at least, the irresistible allure is still there—stronger because I've missed and dreamed about him so much." Tears crested and flowed down her cheek.

"He made it clear he wants separate bedrooms. In the past we never slept apart under the same roof no matter how long we had been apart. John Henry would always say the bed was big enough for both of us." She sniffed delicately. "Sometimes during the night one of us would reach for the other, and blame didn't matter."

Madelyn knew what she meant. Finding Daniel in bed with her when she was ill had seemed natural, right. Curling up against his hard warmth had been instinctive, as if he completed her. She had felt safe in the haven of his strong arms. That kind of feeling could easily become addictive.

"I secretly hoped that when we saw each other again, the seductive pull we always felt for each other would overshadow the past and enable us to work things out." Felicia bit her lip. "As you saw, it didn't happen. He didn't even want to look at me."

"Maybe your wealth and background intimidate him?"

Abruptly the tears stopped. Felicia's shoulders in an elegant Chanel suit, this one in butterscotch, snapped back. She pinned Madelyn with a look. "John Henry's background to him is just as impressive as mine is to me. He's one of the proudest men I know. His master's thesis on the education of Native American children was published in several journals across the country."

"What!"

"He finished near the top of his class in his undergraduate and graduate studies at Oklahoma State University," Felicia said proudly.

"But the way he was dressed?" Madelyn questioned.

"Clothes have never meant that much to John Henry. At least he didn't try to fake you out the way he did my parents once we arrived back in Boston with Daniel." Felicia shook her head at the memory. "My father was laying it on a little thick about what we had and how grateful John Henry should be until John Henry had enough. I thought my mother would faint when he offered to buy her for his uncle.

"John Henry calmly related that his uncle's wife was toothless and unable to soften the animal hides for clothes and moccasins by chewing them. My mother, on the other hand, had an excellent pair of teeth."

Madelyn burst out laughing.

"My mother, who never drank anything stronger than sherry in her life, had to have a double brandy." Felicia dabbed another tear. "My father almost beat her to the bar when John Henry continued by saying since my father was so prosperous and the front lawn was so big, surely he wouldn't mind his relatives moving their many tepees there."

Madelyn erupted into another fit of laughter. "He doesn't like to be stereotyped. I know how he feels," she said. Perhaps she had misjudged him. On seeing Felicia's tears as she rushed into her bedroom, Madelyn had thought the worst of John Henry. Now it appeared she may have been too hasty in her judgment.

"That—and he knows it makes me crazy. The only thing he can do to make me crazier is to slurp his soup."

Fighting the smile tugging at her lips, Madelyn said, "Eventually your parents must have caught on."

"That only made it worse," Felicia said. "John Henry has a way of causing you to feel inferior with a grunt."

"I noticed," Madelyn said, leaning back in her chair. "No wonder Daniel is the way he is."

"Dominique is the same way," Felicia said with maternal pride, brushing away the last traces of tears from her cheeks.

Madelyn absorbed the information. No one in the Falcon family could be pushed, led, or prodded. Strong willed, a tad shy of arrogant, and as bold as the devil—intelligent and wily enough to give you a head start and then beat you to the finish line. Considering her family possessed some of those same attributes, Madelyn knew she was going to have her hands full raising her child.

Her hand cupped her still flat abdomen. "I'd say I have my work cut out for me."

Felicia finally smiled. "You won't be bored, that's for sure."

"Then I'm going to need all the help I can get." Madelyn's face became shadowed for a moment. "I don't know if my baby's father will be around much, but I'd like to be able to count on his paternal grandmother."

"Daniel cares about you and the baby," Felicia defended.

"He wants me, but a lasting relationship has to be built on more than lust." Madelyn groaned and closed her eyes for a few seconds. "I can't believe I'm talking to you this way."

"I assure you, I've heard the word 'lust' before," Felicia said.

Crossing her arms across her chest, Madelyn studied the other woman's flawless features. "It's because you don't look old enough to be his mother."

"It's in the genes. My mother doesn't look a day over sixty and she's pushing seventy-five. Dominique still gets carded sometimes unless she has on makeup, then watch out," Felicia told her.

Madelyn hung on to the word "parents." "Your parents are still living."

Felicia nodded. "So are John Henry's. So you see the baby will have a lot of people to spoil it."

"But not the father," Madelyn said softly. "And before you start on me about Daniel, I suggest you set your own house in order."

Sadness crossed the older woman's face. "There is nothing I can do."

"Bull," Madelyn said. "You've been handing out advice to me; take some for yourself. If you really are afraid he's going to ask for a divorce you'll have to act fast and get him back."

Tears crested in Felicia's black eyes again. Madelyn wasn't having it. "Crying won't get him back."

"I don't know what to do," Felicia wailed.

Madelyn stood and took the other woman by the arm. "We'll think of something. In the meantime we're going to stop all this moping and crying and do something just for us."

Felicia resisted every step into the bedroom. "I'm sorry, Madelyn, but going to a day spa would only remind me of John Henry's and my breakup."

"Who said anything about a spa?" Freeing the woman, Madelyn pulled a pair of faded sweatpants from the closet. "We're going to bake bread."

Most of the men Daniel knew relaxed on the golf course or in the gym. Daniel liked riding. There was something about a powerful animal beneath him, the elements around him, and the sky over his head that always calmed him.

Until today. He was worried about his mother. Although John Henry hadn't mentioned anything more about the divorce since he tossed the news out an hour ago, he wasn't given to making idle statements.

Slowing Wind Dancer, his Arabian stallion, to a walk, Daniel glanced over at his father. John Henry was an excellent rider. In fact, he had taught Daniel to ride when he was no older than three.

Whenever his father had taken off, he had always said good-bye to Daniel and Dominique and called every day. They had felt confused more than anything. They couldn't understand why their parents lived apart so much. When they were growing up, divorce hadn't been as prevalent among their friends.

"Dad, are you sure you should ask for a divorce?"

"The dead branch on a tree serves no purpose," his father answered.

This time Daniel knew his father wasn't being obtuse, but conversing in the wisdom of his grandfather. "What if the branch only gives the appearance of being dead? Maybe it just needs a little care."

"It's a wise man who will choose defeat over dishonor and the loss of an ear," John Henry said.

Daniel pulled his horse up abruptly. A Muscogee adulterer in the old days lost an ear. "You want to marry another woman."

John Henry solemnly faced his son. "One has asked."

Daniel hung his head. "You'll break her heart."

"I would never hurt Ann. How can you think that I would hurt any woman?" his father asked indignantly.

Daniel's head shot up. "I'm not talking about your *other* woman. I'm talking about *my* mother."

Sharp black eyes centered on Daniel. "Breaking your mother's heart is impossible. I embarrass her just by entering a room."

"Whose fault is that?" Daniel gestured toward his father. "Dominique and I took you shopping when we visited you for part of the Christmas holidays, and today you show up looking like you don't have two cents to your name."

His face impassive, John Henry remained silent for a long time, then he lifted a dark brow. "Who says I do?"

"All right, Dad, have it your way."

"I fully intend to." He gathered the reins securely in his gloved hands. "Now are we going to ride or talk?" he asked, his horse always a full length ahead.

* * *

"I'm sure she's all right," John Henry repeated for the second time in as many minutes as he sat beside Daniel, who was speeding back to Madelyn's apartment later that afternoon.

"Then why does she keep telling me she can't talk every time I call?" Daniel asked.

His father propped his elbow on the door. "Probably because she's busy."

"Doing what?" Daniel asked. "She's supposed to be resting."

John Henry sent his son a sharp glare. "You think there's another man over there?"

"If there is, there's nothing going on," Daniel said without a doubt in his mind. Madelyn was honest and up-front. He might learn slowly, but when he did, he didn't forget.

"So the baby she's carrying is yours," came the calm statement.

Daniel's gaze cut to his father. "How—"

"Watch the road."

Swerving to miss a Honda, Daniel gave his attention back to driving. Luckily they were near his freeway exit. "How did you know?"

"Prenatal vitamins on the kitchen table," John Henry said succinctly.

Daniel shook his head. He should have remembered very little got by his father—including the little dents and door dings he used to get on his father's car. No matter how far away Daniel parked, some nut would always park beside him and always leave his calling card on the side of the car.

"Why didn't you say something sooner?" he questioned, turning into Madelyn's complex.

"I wasn't sure how much you were involved."

"The baby is mine," Daniel admitted, the realization

still having the power to make him feel scared and proud at the same time. Parking, Daniel cut the motor and frowned on seeing his father settling back against the leather seat.

"Dad, come inside."

"Neither one of them probably wants to see me," his father answered. "I came only because I knew you were worried."

"Then come all the way," Daniel said softly. "Madelyn means a lot to me, and I'd like for both of you to get to know each other better."

John Henry hesitated only a moment, then opened his door. "When is the wedding?"

Halfway out the door, Daniel paused. "We haven't talked about it."

"Don't wait as long as I did. Felicia's parents never forgave me for her not having a big society wedding," his father said, meeting Daniel at the front of the truck. Silently they walked the rest of the distance together.

Daniel had a great deal more to worry about than Madelyn not having a big wedding. When her family found out she was pregnant, all hell was going to break loose. Once he could stand from the beating her brothers were going to give him, he'd be in front of some minister so fast, his loose teeth would probably rattle.

Frowning, he rang the doorbell. Somehow they'd have to understand he cared for her and the baby, but marriage wasn't in his plans. He—

His thoughts stumbled to a halt as his mother answered the door. The always perfectly groomed Felicia had flour on her face, more flour and some pasty-looking substance on the oversized black T-shirt with the Houston Sonics emblazoned on the front, flour-coated sweatpants—and ugly, shocking green knitted booties on her feet.

His mother's eyes widened. Her gaze jerked to John Henry, and Daniel knew if he didn't do something, the door would slam in their faces. "Hi, Mother. Something smells good."

Putting his arm around her shoulders, he led her back inside, giving her a little squeeze to bolster her courage. "I-I'll go get changed."

"Not until you ice these cinnamon rolls," called Madelyn.

His arm still around his mother, Daniel walked to the kitchen. Madelyn, in a T-shirt with the Dallas Stars hockey team logo on the front, jeans, and another pair of ugly booties, had apparently also been cooking.

But she was considerably cleaner. Dishes were stacked in both sides of the sink, and the counter was lined with various types of tempting-smelling baked bread.

"I missed lunch. Mind if I have a croissant?" Daniel asked, already reaching for one.

"Help yourself," Madelyn said dryly, bagging a loaf of foil-wrapped bread.

"This is good." Mid-chew, he frowned, then swallowed. "I hope you didn't overdo it."

Madelyn rolled her eyes as if she had expected the comment. "Felicia did most of the work."

"I'm sure he can tell," his mother mumbled, her head bowed.

"Would you like a croissant, Mr. Falcon?" Madelyn asked, feeling sorry for Felicia. She had hoped he'd stay away until Felicia had her courage up.

"Call me John Henry. If you don't mind, I think I'd rather have one of the cinnamon rolls once Felicia finishes icing them." Pulling out a chair, John Henry took a seat.

Madelyn could tell Felicia wanted to run for it and

quickly handed her the bowl of cream cheese icing. "Here you go. I'll fix some coffee."

Daniel was already reaching for the pot. "I'll do it. You sit down."

She sat. "You're as bossy as Kane."

"Thank you," he said. Turning, he missed the face Madelyn made at his back.

His father didn't. She tensed until he smiled. "I see you are feeling better."

"Much," she said, hoping Felicia wasn't having too much trouble with the icing. Madelyn could certainly see how she had burnt John Henry's food—she was lost in the kitchen.

A glass of milk plopped in front of her. She shot a glance at Daniel, but he was already pulling mugs from the cabinet. She could only hope his father didn't catch on. John Henry and she were still unsure and circling each other.

"I'll get you a plate for your roll," Madelyn said.

A light touch of John Henry's calloused hand stopped her from rising. "Please, let her do it," he said softly. Louder, he asked Daniel to take a seat as well.

John Henry's gaze was locked on Felicia so fiercely that Madelyn didn't see why there wasn't a hole in the back of the other woman's T-shirt. The antagonism and animosity she expected him to display wasn't there. Instead there was a watchfulness that made Madelyn uneasy. She glanced at Daniel, but he was also watching his mother.

More than the icing of cinnamon rolls was at stake here. Madelyn tried to think of one thing that would get Felicia moving to face her husband. To her delight, Felicia took care of the situation herself.

"How many do you want, John Henry?" Felicia asked, her voice slightly shaky, her back still to him.

"Two. I missed lunch, too," he said.

After placing a platter of the iced pastries on the table, she handed him a dessert plate. He took the stoneware, and they stared at each other a long time before he said, "If these aren't burnt on the bottom, you didn't help cook them."

Felicia burst into tears and ran from the kitchen. Madelyn jumped up to go after her.

"Please, let me." John Henry turned to his son. "It seems you may have been right. Excuse me."

Madelyn watched him leave, sadness in her eyes. "I guess you were right, Daniel. Sometimes love isn't enough."

Felicia heard Madelyn's bedroom door open and close but didn't look up. She was too busy fighting another losing battle with tears. "I'm sorry, Madelyn. I just couldn't stand there and listen to him laugh at me."

"I've never laughed at you."

Everything within her stilled at the sound of John Henry's deep, rich voice. For him to see her so disheveled, and now in tears, completed her humiliation. She would have run into the bathroom and locked the door if getting up wouldn't have offered him another mortifying look at her.

Worn cowboy boots and faded jeans came into her line of downcast vision. "Why are you on the floor?"

The question seemed easier to answer than to think about her embarrassment. "I didn't want to mess up the bed or the chair."

"Felicia, always worrying about what is proper, about being clean and neat."

Instinctively she reacted to the slight censure in his deep voice. "All of us can't thumb our nose at convention the way you do."

"There's a difference between thumbing your nose and living by your standards and not someone else's."

She opened her mouth for a comeback, but out of the corner of her eye she saw him easing down on the floor beside her. Her thoughts scattered.

Pressing his broad back against the foot of the bed, John Henry stretched his long, muscular legs in front of him. Although they weren't touching, he was close enough for her to catch a faint hint of his Aramis cologne. The scent on him always made her want to lick her lips, then lick him . . . all over.

She chastised herself, but it did little good. John Henry had always fascinated her.

His muscular strength and size were never more in evidence. She'd always liked the way their bodies complemented each other: her slimness to his brawn. It was only later in their marriage that it intimidated her. Madelyn had it backwards—John Henry intimidated *her*. He was a man who didn't bend to her will.

Self-consciously, she wiped her cheek and felt the stickiness of the icing. Her desperation to flee increased. She moistened dry lips. "If you'll leave, I'd like to get dressed."

John Henry crossed his booted feet at the ankles and braced his large hand on the carpet a tiny inch away from her hip. "You and Madelyn still have the dishes to do, unless you plan to let her do them by herself."

"Of course not," Felicia snapped, hurt that he thought she was that inconsiderate.

"Then why change?" He nodded toward the Chanel suit hanging on the back of the closet door. "I don't think that was made to wash dishes in."

Felicia didn't know how to respond. She couldn't very well explain to him that she felt more in control in her own clothes. She never wanted him to see her at less than her best.

"Do you remember what a hard time I had getting you to wade in the creek at the back of the house?" Out of the corner of her eye she saw his sensual mouth curve upward. "You never liked being dirty or mussed. The only time you didn't care what you looked like was when we were making love."

Heat splintered through Felicia like a stoked furnace. Her hand clenched in her lap. Vivid images of them entwined in bed flashed into her mind. The sudden need, the hunger was almost unbearable. Unconsciously she pressed her legs closer together.

"I'm hungry. You want to go get a hamburger or something?"

She jerked her head around. "You're asking me to go to dinner with you?"

"I don't see anyone else, and I don't mean dinner where I have to dress up," he told her.

Felicia couldn't take it all in. He was looking at her, talking to her, asking her to dinner. "Yes, I'd love to." She was up in a flash, rushing across the room toward her suit.

"If we go, you wear what you have on."

She whirled just before her grasping fingers touched the linen. "What? You can't mean for me to go out looking like this?"

"I've seen how long it takes you to dress, and I'm hungry now." Gracefully he came to his feet, his black hair swinging around his wide shoulders. "Are you coming or not?"

Felicia heard more than the words spoken. She heard, "I won't ask again."

"I'll get my purse."

"You won't need it."

She looked at him, and his gaze was steady and hard. She couldn't tell if he wanted to see her humiliated further, or was simply being impatient. She knew only that she had to take this last chance, no matter the consequences.

Walking toward him in her flour-and-dough-stained T-shirt and faded sweatpants, her face almost as bad, took every bit of Felicia's courage. Moistening her lips, she tasted icing at the corner. The Joy perfume she had splashed on that morning was probably no match for the aroma of freshly baked bread. Swallowing, she kept going.

She didn't need a mirror to know what five hours in the kitchen had done to her makeup, her hair. In fact, she preferred not to see one.

"Can I borrow the truck, Daniel?" John Henry asked the instant they entered the kitchen. "Your mother and I are going to get something to eat."

The twist of irony of his father asking for the car keys while his date, Daniel's mother, stood by and stared at her booted feet, lifted Daniel's spirits considerably. He wished he could enjoy it.

Madelyn had sipped her milk and played with the crust of a croissant ever since she had tossed out her opinion on love not being enough. For once, Daniel didn't want her agreeing with him.

Daniel studied the uneasiness of his mother, the self-assurance of his father. He couldn't begin to guess how his father had managed to get his mother to go out in public the way she looked. No matter what his mother did, she did it with style.

And now she was going out looking as if she had been attacked by a bread machine and wearing the ugliest booties he had ever seen. His father didn't miss much, and it was a sure bet he knew what his mother had on her feet.

He flipped the keys. "No dents, no dings, no tickets. Be back at a reasonable hour."

His father merely lifted a heavy brow. "I'll listen to you as much as you listened to me."

Daniel looked uneasy. "Wasn't my fault other people can't drive."

"So you always said. Help Madelyn with the dishes." He turned to Felicia. "Let's go."

Felicia didn't say a word, just started for the door as if she had been given her last rites and she was walking the last mile.

Chapter 15

"Are you just going to sit there and eat another cinnamon roll?" Madelyn asked as soon as the door closed.

Daniel frowned, not liking the glint in her eyes. "What is it you want me to do?" he asked cautiously.

Chocolate-brown eyes widened in disbelief. Planting both hands on the table, she stood. "Go after them of course. Felicia was terrified."

Daniel blinked. "What?"

Rounding the table, she tried to drag him up by the arm. "I try to stay out of family business, but Felicia is my friend. Being a man, maybe you didn't notice, but she didn't look too happy to be going with your father."

Daniel allowed himself to be pulled to his feet because he didn't want her to hurt herself. "You really think Mother didn't want to go?" he asked, trying hard to keep the smile off his face.

"Of course she didn't," Madelyn told him. "Now go get her before they leave."

Settling both hands on her shoulders, he turned her to him. The smile he had been trying to hold worked itself loose. "Thank you for caring about my mother, but in the short time you've known her, has she ever done anything she didn't want to do?"

"No, but she wanted another chance."

"Exactly," Daniel said. "If we try to stop her from leaving with Dad, she's not going to be happy with either of us."

Madelyn glanced toward the door. "She looked so unhappy, Daniel."

Her continued concern for his mother touched him. "Probably because she's not looking her best. Have you ever seen her less than perfect?"

Madelyn's shoulders relaxed. "Come to think of it, no. I had to push her hands into the bread dough. But whenever I'd turn away, she'd wipe them on paper towels. She probably went through half a roll."

"Don't worry, Mother is fine."

Madelyn shifted restlessly under his hands. It felt good to have his hands on her again. "Do you think they can settle their differences?"

"I hope so," Daniel said, the pad of his thumb absently stroking her shoulder. "He said some other woman asked him to marry her."

"Oh, no," Madelyn cried. "Poor Felicia."

"Don't count Mother out. Some woman may have asked to marry him, but Dad didn't say he had said yes."

Madelyn's eyes brightened. "Then there's a chance?"

"There's always a chance," he said, looking down into her eyes.

Swallowing, she stepped back. "I guess so."

He wasn't buoyed by her mild agreement, but it was better than a resounding no. "You want to go out to get something to eat or cook in?"

Folding her arms, Madelyn lifted a delicate brow. "I wasn't aware of inviting you to dinner."

She looked so adorable and cute with a smattering of flour across her forehead, he wanted to take her into his arms and cuddle her. Too soon. "Dad has my truck."

"Felicia said you have a five-car garage, and all the bays are full. You had to move one out to make room for her Mercedes."

"True, but they're there, and I'm here and hungry." He smiled. Dimples winked. "If you'll recall, Mother gave Higgins the rest of the day off."

She eyed him for a long time. Was it possible that last night at the hospital heralded a new beginning for them? "If you stay, you're helping do the dishes and we eat out."

"You've got yourself a deal."

Felicia couldn't relax. She tried taking deep breaths, creating a soothing picture in her mind, closing her eyes. Nothing worked. She finally had John Henry to herself, and she looked like an apprentice baker on her first day.

"You're going to stretch Madelyn's T-shirt out of shape if you keep pulling on it," John Henry said mildly.

Felicia released the ball of black material and glanced out the window of the truck. This so-called date was turning into a disaster.

"What do you want to eat?" he asked, pulling up behind another vehicle in the drive-thru window of a fast-food restaurant.

"Nothing for me," she said, knowing the food would stick in her throat.

"Did you eat while you were baking?" he asked, shifting the gears and pulling up.

She shook her head. "I wasn't hungry then, either."

"Why? You're worried about Madelyn and the baby?"

"You know?" she questioned. "Daniel told you?"

"May I have your order, please?" asked the disembodied voice.

"A hamburger with mustard, no onions, a grilled chicken sandwich, two fries, and two chocolate shakes."

"Thank you. Please drive to the first window."

"John Henry," Felicia prodded. "How did you find out?"

Answering her question, he shifted to pull his wallet from his pocket and pay the cashier. Felicia's heart sank.

The only reason she had noticed the vitamins was because she had watched Madelyn take one that morning. There probably wasn't a speck of flour or batter or a myriad of other things on her that he hadn't seen.

"Hold these."

Taking the shakes, she sat quietly while John Henry pulled into a space at the far end of the parking lot.

"I hope she didn't forget the ketchup."

"You don't like ketchup on your fries," she said absently.

"You do. Here it is," he said, pulling the package from the sack. "Pop some straws into our shakes."

Felicia was peeling the paper from the straw before it hit her. "You don't like chocolate shakes, you like strawberry."

Coal-black eyes stared into hers. "A man can change his mind."

Felicia's breath fluttered out over her lips.

"Eat your chicken sandwich," John Henry said, unwrapping his hamburger. "Then maybe we can go someplace and talk."

Her eyes brightened with hope that displaced her growing fear and helplessness. She unwrapped her sandwich. "I'd like that, John Henry. I'd like that a lot."

John Henry decided Daniel's house was the best place to have their conversation. He wanted a place where both of them could seek some privacy if things went wrong. A lot could go wrong. Maybe he was setting himself up for another disappointment. Maybe Daniel was wrong.

Yet seeing Felicia this afternoon, all mussed and in disarray, had been so reminiscent of the day he had come home from work to their small house to see her grinning and so proud of a batch of misshapen biscuits she had baked for him. In that moment he knew she no longer regretted their hasty marriage, regretted being separated from her parents, regretted not having the luxuries he couldn't afford.

Knowing her family would use any means necessary to get her back, he had quit his job with the Bureau of Indian Affairs in Flagstaff and brought his bride to the tiny community in Oklahoma where he had grown up. The only job available was as a ranch hand. He had gladly taken it to keep Felicia with him.

The first weeks were nothing short of pure hell. Nothing he did pleased her except when they made love. He had left her asleep that morning after a particularly satisfying night of lovemaking and had expected to come home again to a silent, sullen wife.

Instead she had met him at the door with a kiss, a smile, and the worst-looking biscuits he had ever seen.

The biscuits were as hard as rocks and as tasteless because she had left out the baking powder and the salt. To him, it hadn't mattered.

He couldn't have been more pleased and proud. He had drowned them in syrup and eaten every one, out of love, out of not wanting her to eat one herself and get sick because she was four and a half months pregnant with Daniel.

Remembering that day, John Henry felt the familiar tug of happiness in his heart, the unwanted ache of loving a woman he had never been sure of.

They walked side by side without touching until

they reached the edge of the immense backyard. Felicia headed for the white wrought-iron bench under a hundred-foot oak.

"Let's sit over there."

Warily Felicia eyed the base of the towering oak tree with several of its foot-thick roots protruding aboveground. Without glancing his way, she walked over and sank down on the sparse grass, drawing her slim legs under her. "All right, John Henry, you've pushed and ordered and subtly threatened—so what now?"

He hadn't expected her to be agreeable for long. Even at the spa two years ago, when rage had consumed him, she had stood up to him.

"Were you having an affair with Randolph Sims?" he asked. It wasn't what he had intended, but he needed to know nonetheless.

"No," she answered softly. "But I wanted you to think I was on the brink."

"Why?"

Hands pressed together in her lap, she looked out across the well-tended lawn. "I-I thought you didn't care. I wanted to make you jealous."

John Henry remembered going to the spa to surprise her, and he was the one who had been surprised. "Try again. You didn't know I was coming."

"Yes, I did," she answered quietly. "Dominique had called me that morning."

"So you invited Sims to your suite," he said tightly.

Her head swung around. "I thought he was you when I answered the door."

"And I suppose you gave him no provocation to think his visit might be welcomed," he bit out.

She flinched from the anger in his harsh face, but she didn't look away. "I'm not proud of the way I behaved, but I gave him no indication to expect anything else."

Hands on hips, his long black hair swirling wildly around him in the wind, John Henry glared down at her. "No indication! Damnit, Felicia, you're not that naive. Randolph had wanted you as long as I can remember."

"I admit I was wrong. I'm sorry."

He gave a short bark of hollow laughter. "You flirt with a known womanizer, a man who likes to brag about his conquests, and you think saying 'I'm sorry' is supposed to rectify the situation?"

"I don't know what else to say." Her gaze searched his face. "At least it never got out."

"Because I waited until Sims came out of your room and promised him if he said one word about you he'd regret it," John Henry said, his face hard and unrelenting.

"Then you know he didn't stay," she said joyfully.

"Not that night, but what about the other nights before I arrived? You asked me to leave while he stayed. Do you know how that made me feel, to see slime like Sims smirking?" he questioned harshly.

She came to her feet, her face and eyes imploring. "Nothing happened that night or ever. You've got to believe me. You might forgive me a lot of things, but adultery isn't one of them."

"I could have killed you both," he said, his fists clenched.

"You could never physically hurt me, but I realized if you harmed Randolph, you'd be the one to pay. That's why I told you I didn't love you. You were too proud to want a woman who didn't want you." Tears sparkled in her eyes and rolled down her cheeks. "I've paid for my foolishness every day and night since then."

"I've paid, too," he said.

John Henry had lived with her rejection day and night for two years. It was a hurt, a pain that wouldn't go away, a pain that knew no source of comfort. How could there be when his beautiful wife sent him away while she prepared to take another man to her bed? "I hated you. I hated you as much as I once loved you."

"C-Can't we start over?" she asked.

"And what will you do the next time I don't heel when you snap your fingers?"

Anger blazed in her eyes to match his. "How dare you say something like that to me? You're the one who kept popping in and out of my and the children's lives. Heel, my foot.

"You don't know the meaning of the words 'submission' or 'compromise.' You're as arrogant and as proud as ever. Did you ever stop to think how I felt knowing that sooner or later you'd get restless and go back to Oklahoma to that farm you bought a couple of years after we were married? Or how I felt hearing my friends whisper behind my back about my glaring lack of ability to keep my husband satisfied and at home?" she raged.

"You and the children could have come, but you were too busy being Miss Society and living the pampered lifestyle your parents' money allowed you," he told her.

"I was not going to raise my children in a two-room cabin with the nearest school twelve miles away with only one teacher for each grade," she flared. "I wanted better for them."

John Henry's face contorted, rage mixed with despair. "So the truth is finally out. I was good enough to screw, but not good enough to take care of my kids."

Horror washed across Felicia's face. "No. I didn't mean it that way. I wanted them to have every advantage to succeed in life, and that meant the right schools, the right social standings."

"Things I couldn't give them," John Henry said. He stepped back and lifted his arms from his sides. "This is who I am, Felicia. A simple man, a Muscogee Indian. Not much to people like you, but I'm proud of who I am. I'll never be happy being anything else. I'll be damned if I'll try anymore." His hands lowered. "As quick as possible, I want a divorce. Get one or I will."

"John Henry," Felicia cried, tears streaming down her cheek, her hands reaching for him.

He stepped back. "I don't ever want to feel your touch again, to know that I let you trample my pride underfoot. Get that divorce—and when it's final, I'm marrying a woman who wants me the way I am."

With a soundless cry, Felicia crumpled. Sobs racked her body.

John Henry looked down on the woman he'd loved since the first moment his eyes touched her, the woman who had given him more joy than he ever expected, more sorrow than he thought at times he could bear. Through it all he had stayed because of that love, stayed because of the children, then after they were grown, he kept hoping he would be enough for her. He needed a woman who needed him. Felicia never would.

"You have two months." Turning, he walked back to the house.

Madelyn was impressed with Daniel's dinner arrangements that night, but she didn't intend for him to know. Opening her front door, she didn't act the least surprised to see a tuxedoed waiter with several silver domes on a serving cart and a second waiter behind him with a collapsible table. Her expression never changed.

In less than five minutes, the table was set with white linen, sparkling water was chilling in an ice bucket, and

Daniel was holding her chair for her. By her plate was a pink orchid.

She remained cool through her crab claws sauteed in lemon sauce—thawed a little when served her garden salad loaded with artichokes, mushrooms, scallions, and cucumbers. He made points, however, when he asked what she was digging in her salad for, and she said, "more cucumbers," and he gave her his.

She kept up the pretense until the first bite of the most mouth-watering lobster she had ever closed her lips over. She moaned. Ignoring Daniel's knowing smile, she kept eating. Dessert was something rich and decadent and chocolate. Stuffed, she managed only a couple of spoonfuls. Daniel had no such trouble. He finished off his and hers.

The best part of the dinner was she didn't have to clean up afterward or groan all the way to the car to drive home. Sitting on the couch, one hand holding the orchid, she watched Daniel let the waiters out. She didn't think she'd move until morning.

"Can I get you anything?" he asked.

Madelyn looked the long way up to his bronzed, smiling face. He'd been smiling all evening. The smile looked good on him. "Not unless you want me to pop."

He squatted down in front of her and took her free hand. "You're tired."

"A little," she confessed, then yawned.

He grinned. Dimples winked. He stood and pulled her to her feet. "Come on, and lock the door so you can get some rest."

"How are you going to get home?"

"I'll call Higgins. Dad certainly seems to have forgotten me," he said, his tone light.

Madelyn came to a decision. "Take my car. There's no reason to disturb Higgins."

"You're sure?"

"I'm sure." Going into the bedroom, she returned shortly with her keys. "No dents. No dings."

"I'll be extra careful." Leaning over, he kissed her on the cheek. "Good night."

Following him to the door, she didn't know why she suddenly felt sad. "Drive carefully."

"I will." He reached for the door, then turned back, drawing her into his arms. She went willingly. There was no need to urge her lips apart, to coax her.

Finally he lifted his head, his breathing labored. "I'd better go."

He was out the door before she remembered to say, "Please call and let me know if Felicia is all right."

"I will. Now go back inside and lock up."

"Good night," she whispered, then stepped back, closing and locking the door. If only it was as easy to close her heart against hoping for something that might never be. She prayed that Felicia's heart was safe.

Madelyn's had been lost the first time Daniel kissed her.

Felicia cried until there were no tears left. The whimpering sobs took longer to subside. She'd never known a despair so deep, so yawning with no hope. Always in life she had hope and the courage to take what she wanted.

Hope and courage were gone. She no longer cared.

"Felicia."

Something in her sparked before she realized the voice was Higgins's and not John Henry's. She curled tighter.

A frail hand patted her on the shoulder. "Now, now."

"Oh, Higgins. I was such a fool."

"Your parents indulged you too much. Told them to

let you throw a tantrum or two. They acted like I had asked them to lock you in a closet."

Sniffing, she sat up and leaned against him. "Maybe they should have."

"I've been thinking we'd take the car and drive down the coast to Galveston, maybe stay at this little bed and breakfast I read about for a few days," he suggested. "Just until you feel better."

"I don't think I'll ever feel better."

"Yes you will." Awkwardly he helped her to her feet. His frail arms around her shoulders, they started for the house.

Stoic, John Henry watched them approach the back of the house. He had stood and watched Felicia until he couldn't stand it anymore. He had called Higgins and asked him to go to her.

The chauffeur knew all the family secrets, and he could be trusted. He also loved Felicia like the daughter he'd never had. She needed someone who loved her. John Henry's love had never been enough.

Opening the glass door, John Henry took the path leading to the stables. He needed a long, hard ride. Maybe if he rode hard enough, fast enough, he'd stop hearing Felicia's sobs, stop tearing his heart out over a woman he couldn't stop loving.

Daniel sensed something was wrong the instant he entered the house. It wasn't just the quietness. It was something else he couldn't put a name to.

Taking the stairs two at a time, he went to his mother's room. The door was open. Seeing her packing, he knew. He crossed to her and took her in his arms.

"Mother."

He caught a brief glimpse of her defeated expression before she grabbed fistfuls of his shirt and pressed her face against his chest. "Your father asked for a divorce."

His arms tightened. He had hoped they could work things out. "I'm sorry. Maybe—"

"No. It's over. Please don't say anything else, or I'll start crying again."

Feeling utterly helpless, he continued holding her. "Is it all right to say I love you?"

He felt her nod against his shirt. "Higgins is taking me to a bed and breakfast in Galveston. I-I'd like to be gone before your father gets back."

Strong hands gently pushed her away. A frown knitted Daniel's brow. "Where is he? His truck is out front and so is mine."

"I don't know. Higgins said he saw John Henry tear out of the stables on one of your horses, but that was at sundown." Fear crossed her delicate face. "Daniel, you don't think he's hurt, do you?"

"Dad's the best rider I know. Don't worry," Daniel advised, but he was already turning away. His father knew better than to ride at night. Yet what if something had happened before nightfall? If the unthinkable had occurred, none of the horses had been stabled long enough to come home on their own.

Fighting a rising fear, Daniel ran into the stable and hit the light switch, already moving swiftly down the aisle, counting horses. Seeing one missing, his heart stopped—Jabel, the fiery Arabian stallion he had purchased last week.

"Daniel?"

He swung around to see his mother, her arms wrapped around her, her eyes begging him to say the word to put her mind at ease. He couldn't. "One of the horses is missing."

"No, no."

"Mother—Dad!"

Felicia whirled. With a shout of pure joy, she launched herself at John Henry, who was walking and leading Jabal by the reins to the stable; her frantic arms circled her husband's neck. Jabal shied from all the noise. Felicia didn't seem to notice John Henry had to release the horse in order to keep them upright, keep them from falling beneath the stallion's deadly hooves.

Daniel grabbed the animals dragging reins.

Felicia kept right on planting kisses on John Henry's dirt-smeared face and crying. It took her a minute to notice he wasn't kissing her back. Her body tensed.

Slowly her arms slid down from around his neck. She took one, then another step backward. Seeing his expressionless face, she ran out of the stable.

Fists clenched, John Henry remained unmoved.

"We thought you'd been thrown," Daniel said matter-of-factly. The look on his father's face said they should have known better. "You're dirty enough."

"I stayed out longer than I expected. Since it was dark, I walked the horse, tripped and fell."

Now Daniel was the one wearing a look of disbelief. "You see like a cat in the dark."

"I had other things on my mind," John Henry explained tightly.

Daniel had a good idea what those things were. "The main thing is that you're unhurt. We jumped to conclusions since Higgins had seen you ride out earlier. Mother stopped packing and followed me out here."

Surprise widened his father's eyes. "Packing?"

"What did you expect after asking for a divorce?" Daniel said, not bothering to keep the anger out of his voice. "Now you can marry what's-her-name."

"If only I could." Turning, John Henry left the stable.

Chapter 16

Felicia lay prone across the antique linen hand-embroidered bedspread. She hadn't thought she had any more tears. She had been wrong.

A hand lightly touched her head. She flinched. "Please, go away."

"If only I could."

Recognizing John Henry's voice caused the tears to flow faster. "Please."

The pressure of his calloused hand increased as he continued stroking her hair. "Do you know you're dirtying up Daniel's fancy bedspread?"

"That's what they have dry cleaners for," she sobbed, hating the almost aching need to press her head into his strong hand.

"Your suit will have to go to the cleaners, too. I guess you didn't think about that when you were hugging me."

"I thought you had been hurt. Who cares about a stupid suit."

"You were really scared, weren't you?"

Felicia stopped long enough to stare up at him in disbelief. "How can you ask such a question?"

"Because you always acted like I was an embarrassment to you."

She came up like a spring, her face horrified. "I never!" she began, only to stop, her eyes shutting as she recalled the conversation with Daniel at the hospital. Slowly her eyes opened. John Henry watched her intently.

The time for the whole truth had finally arrived. John Henry couldn't hate her any more than he already did. At least she might stop hating herself for what she had tried to do to him.

"I was never ashamed of you. But you were the only man I was never sure of." She swallowed. "At first I tried to make you over because I wanted you to forget about going back to Oklahoma. I was terrified you'd get tired of me and leave. Then I did it to protect you against snide, ignorant remarks."

A muscle leaped in his jaw. "Come on, Felicia. You know I never gave a rat's behind about what your family or friends thought about me."

"I know that's what you said. Sometimes you went out of your way to play the uneducated Indian, but I'd see you sometimes looking at a group of men in a conversation you were excluded from, and I'd ache for you."

He shook his head. "You had it all wrong. Most of the time I was thinking how bored I was or what a waste of time it was to be there." His expression grew hard. "Your friends might have been wealthy, but a lot of them were bankrupt in the real things that matter in life."

"Including me," she said softly.

"I tried to make myself think so, but I did a lot of thinking this afternoon and realized something." He glanced around the lavishly decorated room. "Daniel might have obtained this without the private schools and the privileged life, but he couldn't have grown up to be the man I'm proud to call my son without you. I'm just as proud of Dominique."

His gaze returned to Felicia. "Whenever I showed up, there were never any recriminations from either of them. They were always happy and eager to be with me, no matter how I was dressed or what I drove. They still are. They had to learn that from someone. We might not have gotten along at times, but you never tried to teach my children to hate me."

Felicia sniffed. "I hated the farm in Oklahoma. You seemed to need it more than me and the children."

John Henry's hand tenderly stroked her cheek. "I never acclimated to Boston. The weather, the crowds, the food. I felt utterly useless working a token job for your father, living in his house. A Muscogee is taught to take care of his wife, his children. I felt less than a man."

"Forgive me. I never knew."

"Looks like we both have a lot to forgive," he said, picking her up. Her eyes widened, but her arms closed around his neck. "I take it that door leads to the bathroom."

"Y-Yes."

"Good. Hope your bathtub is as big as mine."

"John Henry, what are you doing?"

"Hell if I know. I only know I have to make love to you or go stark raving mad." He stopped and looked down at her. "Any objections?"

She bit her lip. "I don't want to lose you again."

"Our track record hasn't been the best."

Felicia's hold tightened. "I'm willing to try if you are. I'll do whatever it takes."

Shoving the door open to the bathroom, John Henry set her on her feet and began unbuttoning the buttons on her suit. "Whatever covers a lot of territory."

Felicia's fingers went to his shirt. Her hands trembling,

her voice unsteady, she said, "I hope it does, because it's been two long years."

His hands stilled as the implication of what she had just said sank into him like tender claws. "I—"

"Sheee." Her lips gently grazed his. "You are the heart of my heart. I'll keep on saying the words until you hear it in your heart as well."

"Felicia, I can't lose again."

"You don't have to." Stepping back, she undressed for him, her eyes glowing with a desire that was matched in his.

He pulled her to him, his mouth and hands devouring her. "I've waited so long."

"So have I." Her hands began unbuttoning his shirt, anxious to feel the heat and muscled warmth of his body. "Don't make either of us wait any longer."

He didn't. Quickly he finished undressing and drew her down on their scattered clothes on the floor, joining them in one powerful thrust. Her body accepted him as it always had, with hungry eagerness.

Mingled sighs of pleasure escaped from their lips. Sensations, powerful and exquisite, ran through them. They stared into each other's eyes, not moving, prolonging the exquisite moment each had waited for, hoped for, prayed for.

Then his hips began to move, slowly at first, then with quick, powerful movements. Heat built like a raging inferno, sweeping them both down its path. Completion came too soon, shaking them both with its violence. But there was also a rightness.

Trembling fingers swept John Henry's heavy mane of black hair away from his perspiration-dampened face. "Welcome home."

"In my heart, I never left."

Tears formed in Felicia's eyes. Tenderly John Henry

kissed every one away, then moved to other, softer parts of her body. It was a long satisfying time before they got into the tub, longer still until they went to sleep locked in each other's arms.

In the other wing of the house, Daniel called Madelyn from his bedroom to tell her his parents were trying to work things out. He was glad she didn't ask for any details. His mother and father had been behind closed doors together in the past, but until tonight he had never actually considered what they might be doing. He didn't want to tonight, either.

Reluctantly he ended the conversation less than a minute later. Madelyn sounded sleepy. Lying down, his hands behind his head, he could almost see her curled up in her bed, her hands pillowing her cheek.

With a fierce yearning he wished he was there with her, to hold her, love her. Soon, he promised himself. Very soon.

"Not yet, Mrs. Falcon, wait until the batter bubbles and the ends turn up just slightly," instructed Mrs. Hargrove, Daniel's cook.

With all the concentration of a mother watching her child take its first steps, Felicia's eyes never left the four circles of pancake batter.

"Bacon needs turning. You want me to do it?" asked Mrs. Hargrove.

"No, please, I want to do this by myself." Giving one last look at the pancakes, Felicia turned the bacon, her attention zeroing back in on the grill. Taking a deep breath, she flipped first one, then the others over. They weren't the perfect round shapes she would have liked, but they held together.

"I did it—I did it."

"You certainly did, Mrs. Falcon. We'll have you cooking in no time."

"Thank you, I couldn't have done it without your help." Smelling the bacon, Felicia took it out of the skillet and placed the strips on paper towels to drain, then removed the pancakes, adding them to her stack. Picking up a bowl, she whisked the contents, eyed the butter heating in the skillet.

"It's ready," instructed the cook.

The egg batter began to sizzle the instant it hit. Using the spatula handed to her by the other woman, Felicia soft-scrambled the eggs.

"Mother?"

"Good morning, Daniel," Felicia called, her attention on her cooking.

"It's barely eight," he said. Since she went to sleep late, she usually slept until around ten unless she had an appointment.

"I know." Felicia put the food in the divided chafing dish, covered it with the sterling silver dome lid, then placed the dish on the tray beside a plate and a carafe of coffee. "I wanted to surprise your father with breakfast."

Daniel stared at his mother. She was glowing. She was also in a flowing aqua robe. In his memory she had never come downstairs until she was dressed. "You two are going to work things out?"

"I'm going to do whatever it takes to make him happy," she said, then blushed. "I better take this upstairs before your father wakes up."

"He's still asleep?" Daniel questioned. His father never slept past five.

Felicia blushed again, her hands tightening on the sides of the wooden tray. Her gaze dropped to the middle of his chest.

"Must be the long drive," Daniel said helpfully, trying not to think of the implication of the robe or the blush. "You better get going."

Nodding, Felicia turned away, walking slowly. Still slightly bemused, Daniel followed her into the dining room as she headed for the sweeping staircase. His mouth opened to ask her if she wanted him to help, but the words were never spoken.

His mother stopped, her gaze lifting. At the top of the stairs stood his father in jeans and an open shirt. For an interminable amount of time, they simply stared at each other, then his father quickly moved down the stairs. Without a word being spoken between them that Daniel could hear, his father swept up his mother in his arms, tray and all, and started back up the stairs.

Seeing them disappear, Daniel's thoughts returned to Madelyn. He wanted to be with her in the morning, to hold her, to eat breakfast in bed with her.

"Here's your coffee, Mr. Falcon. Breakfast will be ready in a few minutes," said the housekeeper, handing him a cup. She looked toward the empty staircase. "I've never seen a woman more happy to be cooking breakfast for her husband."

"Did Mother make this coffee?" he asked mildly, taking a sip. "It's not half bad."

"I bet your father thinks it's the best coffee he's ever tasted," Mrs. Hargrove noted before going back into the kitchen.

Daniel followed, his brow furrowed. He didn't particularly care for sweets, but he had downed a half dozen cinnamon rolls yesterday because Madelyn had helped make them.

He placed the cup on the counter. "Nothing for me, Mrs. Hargrove. I have an early appointment."

"You're sure?" she questioned. "The whole-grain muffins should be ready to take out of the oven shortly."

"No, thank you," he said, opening the back door leading around the side of the house to the garage. "My appetite is craving something sweeter this morning."

"Good morning."

No man had a right to look so gorgeous in the morning, Madelyn thought. His chiseled features were perfect. His glorious hair was secured at the base of his neck.

Daniel's smile faltered when she didn't say anything. "I didn't catch you at a bad time, did I?"

"No," she answered, wondering if she'd ever come close to stopping loving him.

He shifted uneasily. "I brought your car back, in case you needed it to do some errands, since it's Friday and you have the day off."

"Thank you," she answered, still not moving aside to let him in. Loving Daniel was one thing, opening herself up to more heartache was quite another. She held out her open palm.

"I thought we might have breakfast," he said.

"I don't feel like getting dressed."

"I could go get something."

"Too much trouble. Besides, breakfast food gets cold easily." She wiggled her fingers impatiently.

Another frown worked its way across Daniel's brow. "I bet Dad didn't have this much trouble getting Mother to cook his breakfast."

Madelyn's eyes widened. She pulled Daniel across the threshold and closed the door. "Felicia cooked breakfast?"

"Pancakes, bacon, sausage patties, the works." Daniel smiled. Dimples winked, and it was all Madelyn could do not to sigh and ask him to do it again. "Her coffee wasn't half bad, either."

Madelyn folded her arms and eyed him suspiciously. "And you thought you might come over for some of the same?"

A flush rose up in his face. Madelyn could just imagine what he was thinking. Trying to settle her own erratic heart rate, she said, "This may come as a surprise to you, but all women can't cook."

They looked at each other and burst out laughing. "With Felicia as a mother, I guess not. Come on, I'll see what we can find," she said.

After taking off his jacket, Daniel followed her into the kitchen. "If the selection isn't any better than when you were sick, we better risk it being cold."

Throwing him a frown, Madelyn opened the cabinet and took out a box of instant Cream of Wheat and grabbed a pot. "It'll have to be hot cereal, croissants, cinnamon rolls, and juice—if there's any juice left."

Daniel opened the refrigerator. Sounded like a plan to him. "No juice. You need milk with that?"

"Yes." Pouring a small amount of milk in the pot, she turned on the gas burner. "Grab the croissants and cinnamon rolls in the plastic container. I'll slice the bread for the toast."

In a matter of minutes, they were seated and eating. "How is it you can cook bread that tastes this good and not much of anything else?" Daniel asked, on his third piece of toast. The only thing left of his two cinnamon rolls were a few crumbs.

She grinned. "I love fresh-baked bread. I took time enough long ago to learn the old-fashioned way, before quick-rising yeast. The whole process soothes me."

"What were you and Matt doing while Kane was learning to cook?" asked Daniel.

An impish smile crossed her brown face. "Anything that kept us out of housework. I was Daddy's girl.

Loved tagging behind him and taking apart things to see how they worked. Matt loved doing anything on horseback, and the girls loved him. His mission was to make as many happy as possible"

Daniel chuckled. "Your poor parents."

Madelyn laughed and took the last bit of her toast. "They loved us and our differences. They're so proud—" Her face became shadowed.

Daniel saw the pain in her face, her hand clenched atop the table, and wanted nothing more than to never see her sad again. "I have a couple of hours before my first appointment this morning. You want me to take you grocery shopping?"

She smiled, but it wasn't as bright. "Bite your tongue. Shannon and Victoria are still trying to get my brothers into the grocery store and longer than ten minutes in a dress shop. They're too impatient. I imagine you're the same way."

"You need food," he answered simply.

"I'll do it later on this morning." She rose, gathering the dishes. "Anyway, it's about time for another care package from my mother."

Daniel took his plate to the sink. "Care package?"

This time the smile was real. "A tradition that started when Kane went to college of sending a box every month filled with goodies. It continued with Matt, and now it's my time."

"But you're out of college."

"Yes, but I work long hours, and my cooking skills aren't what they should be. Mama knows it." Turning on the faucet, Madelyn squirted dish-washing liquid into the rushing water. "She did the same for Matt until he got married to that woman." Derision coated the last two words.

Daniel knew "that woman" was Matt's first wife.

Her treachery had almost ruined Matt's career in the rodeo and had ruined his life until he met Shannon.

Opening a drawer, Daniel took out a dish towel and began drying the dishes. "The wrong woman can make a man's life hell."

Madelyn looked at him closely. "You sound as if you're speaking from experience."

He shouldn't have been surprised that she could read him so easily. "Jeanette Pearson. I met her when I was a sophomore at Harvard. Her family had recently moved to Boston. It wasn't until later that I learned they left San Francisco because of Jeanette's problem.

"She was beautiful, vivacious, manipulative, and possessive—only I didn't know it until I tried to break off the relationship after I got tired of her jealous rages. The next day she slashed the tires of my car." He balled the dishcloth in his fist.

"A week later she got into my apartment and trashed the place. She kept calling, begging for me to take her back or I'd be sorry. I thought she meant me personally." His eyes became shadowed. "She overdosed. She left a note blaming me."

"Daniel, no!" Madelyn cried, her hand gently on his arm, her heart aching for him.

"Her parents blamed me despite knowing Jeanette was mentally ill. She'd tried the same thing with a man in California. The maid found her." His hands unclamped and clamped. "Instead of getting her the help she needed, they tried to hush it up. She died for their stupidity and mine."

"How can you say something like that?" Madelyn questioned. "You had no idea she had mental problems."

"One part of me knows that—another part looks at the senseless waste of a life." He tossed the cloth on the counter. "Love can be as treacherous as it can be beautiful. Sometimes you don't know it until it's too late."

Madelyn fought hard to keep the despair from her face. He didn't believe in love—had been hurt by it, had seen his parents' misery because of it. Love to him was something to be avoided.

Daniel kept on talking, unaware that he was shredding her heart while he went on about how fortunate she was to have grown up with a happy, loving family. Didn't he understand that for her it would never take the place of being loved and cherished by him?

"I shouldn't have told you," he said. "Don't look so sad. It was a long time ago."

And you'll remember it always, she thought.

"Madelyn?" he questioned, his hand touching her cheek.

"I'm all right," she managed. "You'd better get going or you'll be late for work, and I need to get to the grocery store."

"You're sure you don't want me to go with you?" He frowned. "You don't want to overdo things."

"I promise to take things easy." Turning away, she went to the front door and opened it. "How are you getting back to your office?" she asked, striving for normalcy.

"Higgins is waiting for me." He seemed reluctant to leave. "I didn't mean to upset you."

"I know. Have a good day."

"I'll call you later. Rest after you come back," he told her.

"Good-bye, Daniel." He cared about her and the baby, wanted what was best for them, he just didn't love them.

Leaning over, he brushed his lips against her forehead, then walked to the waiting Mercedes. Stepping back, she closed the door, feeling empty and alone.

Chapter 17

Daniel didn't expect to see the "walking jewelry store" open Madelyn's door that afternoon. A Houston Sonics T-shirt stretched across an impressive chest. Daniel remembered his mother wearing one similar.

"Is Madelyn here?"

The man didn't move an inch. "Who wants to know?"

"I might ask you the same question," Daniel said, irritated by the man's attitude.

"Yeah, but I'm not moving until I get an answer," the other man said.

Daniel studied the broad-shouldered man. He wasn't a threat to him with Madelyn, and if he was that protective of her, Daniel could stand his rudeness. "Daniel Falcon. I believe she's expecting me."

A smile broke across his dark face. He extended his hand. "Hey, man. I have you to thank for helping Madelyn while I was out of town."

"She told you about being sick?" Daniel asked cautiously.

"Sure," the man said, breaking the handshake and standing aside for Daniel to enter. "My name is Sid Wright. I live two doors down. Madelyn told me you're a friend of the family."

"She did, huh?"

"Food poisoning is nothing to play with," Sid said, continuing to the kitchen. "I just got back into town this morning. Saw her car out front on a Friday and came over to check on her. After she told me, I figured she needed a good meal."

Daniel eyed the various simmering pots on the stove. "You cooked."

"Yes," Sid said laughing. "Mrs. Taggert's care package didn't come today. I thought I better chip in. You like fresh black-eyed peas, collard greens, and candied yams?"

The tantalizing aromas drew Daniel closer. "Her family must really appreciate you."

Sid's booming laughter filled the small kitchen. "Between you and me, I think it's the only reason her brothers didn't send me packing the first time we met. They knew I wouldn't let her starve."

Another person who cared. It wasn't difficult to feel protective of a woman as warm and gracious as Madelyn. "Thank you for caring for her."

At Daniel's fervent words, horror replaced the smile on Sid's face. "Geez, no."

"Is something wrong?" Daniel asked, already aware of the answer.

"You hurt her, and I'll be on you like white on rice."

"That was never my intention," Daniel said earnestly, wondering if others could read his feelings for Madelyn so easily.

"Keep it that way," Sid turned off all the burners and removed a covered roasting pan from the oven. "Madelyn is in her office, working on some project with pipelines. I told her I'd call her for dinner. She works with headphones on sometimes."

"You're leaving?" Daniel asked.

"Three's a crowd. Madelyn knows how to reach me." He opened the door. "I meant what I said about not hurting her."

"So did I."

"I don't suppose you can cook?" Sid inquired.

Daniel had to smile, liking the man. "About the same as Matt."

"Heaven help us all." Shaking his head, Sid closed the door.

A smile on his lips, Daniel loosened his tie, removed his jacket, and went to find Madelyn. Since there was only one other room he hadn't been in, locating her office wasn't difficult.

Headphones on, she was transcribing scribbled notes into the computer. Absently unbuttoning his shirt collar and rolling up his sleeves, he watched her work. She appeared totally engrossed in what she was doing. Every once in a while, she'd stop, prop both elbows on the desk, and stare at the screen, then back she'd go.

He hated being disturbed when he was working on something, but she needed to eat. Pushing away from the door, he walked over and gently tapped her on the shoulder.

Her slim hand did a flicking motion, which he was sure meant to leave her alone. Smiling, he tapped her on the shoulder again.

"Go away, Sid."

Gently he removed the headphones. "It's not Sid."

She jumped, swinging around. "Daniel!"

"Dinner is ready."

Moistening her lips, she rubbed her hands on her sweatpants. "Where's Sid?"

"Gone. He thought three was a crowd."

Her expressive eyes widened. "You told him."

"He guessed." Daniel laid the headset aside. "I'll go set the table."

Saving her file, Madelyn shut off the computer and followed. He looked better each time she saw him. "Felicia called before she and your father left for Galveston."

"They went in Dad's truck." Daniel opened the refrigerator, glad to see it stocked better than it had been that morning. "Higgins said Mother had on her first pair of blue jeans and was grinning like a kid on Christmas morning."

"I'm glad for them," Madelyn said.

"Me too. I called Dominique, and as soon as she wraps things up in Paris, she's heading home."

"That's wonderful," Madelyn said, pausing with the plate she had picked up in her hand.

Setting a glass of milk on the table, Daniel came to her. "Then why do you look as if you've lost your best friend?"

She studied the buttons on his blue pinstriped shirt. "Long day I guess."

His forefinger lifted her chin. "Then we both deserve something special."

His head slowly descended, his lips closing over hers. Somehow the plate was out of her hands, and they were free to go around his neck—her body was free to nestle against his.

Slowly his head lifted. "Very special. Now sit down before I forget my good intentions. Do you want some of everything?"

"Whatever you want," she said.

"A dangerous thing to say to a man who wants a woman as bad as I want you."

She tucked her head. *Want*—not love.

"When is your next appointment to see Dr. Scalar?"

"Why?" Her head came up.

"If you don't mind, I thought I'd go with you. I imagine I should know your exercise schedule as well."

She frowned. "Why should you want to know that?"

"I plan to go with you of course."

"You can't," she told him, her voice rising. "People would figure out in no time."

The plate of food plunked none too gently in front of her. "You don't want me with you?"

She heard the hurt in his voice, but she was hurting, too. "That isn't it. You're too well known."

He sighed. "All right. I'll start searching for a birthing coach who can give us private lessons."

"I-I've thought about that, and I've decided to ask Sid."

"No." The word was flat, inflexible.

"Dan—"

"No." Coming down on his haunches, his hand pressed possessively against her abdomen. "I know I messed up. I was a fool to doubt you. This is my child, and I care about the both of you. I know you have a right, but please, please don't shut me out."

"Daniel."

He kissed her on the eye, the lips, the arch of her neck. "Please don't shut me out." His mouth fastened on hers.

Thought slipped and faltered under the onslaught of his kiss, the disturbing heat of his touch. His body urged her closer. Her sensitive breasts pushed against his chest, causing them to ache sweetly. Needing to get closer, her arms slid around his neck, bringing him nearer, anchoring him.

The shrill ring of the phone was like a blast of cold air. Hastily withdrawing her arms, Madelyn looked into brilliant black eyes deep and intense with passion. The shrill, impatient ring came again.

Pushing to his feet, Daniel stepped back. Grateful to him and the caller, she went to answer the phone in the living room. "Hello."

"Addie, are you all right? Why didn't you call?"

"Mother."

"Why didn't you call and let us know you had food poisoning and had to go to the hospital?" Mrs. Taggart asked, concern and hurt mingled in her voice.

Madelyn moistened her lips. Sid must have called her mother. It was a good thing she hadn't mentioned being admitted. "I didn't want to worry you."

"Mothers are conditioned to worry," said her father. "On the other hand, I've got enough gray hairs."

Madelyn plopped down on the sofa, silently thanking her father for trying to defuse the situation. "I won't do it again."

"We're on our way. We just thought we'd call first," he said.

"No, please," Madelyn almost screeched, then sought to calm herself. So much for thanking him. "I've never felt better. My boss gave me today off, and we're starting on a new project Monday, and I need all the time I have to be ready."

"We won't be in the way," her mother said, the hurt returning to her voice.

"Mama, I didn't mean it that way. You know you're always welcome."

"We just want to make sure you're all right," her mother told her. "You never minded us visiting before."

Elbow on her knee, Madelyn propped her forehead in her open palm. "Mama, I don't mind your visiting. I'm just a little busy at the moment."

Daniel motioned for the phone. She shook her head. "Hello, Mr. and Mrs. Taggart," he called loudly.

"Who was that?" her parents chorused.

Glaring at Daniel, Madelyn gritted out, "Daniel Falcon."

Silence stretched for long moments before her mother asked, "Why is it all right for him to be there and we can't come?"

"He just dropped by. I was about to send him on his way when you called," she said.

The grin on Daniel's face was part leer, part recrimination—and all seductive. He held out his hand for the phone. She took great pleasure in slapping the receiver into his palm.

To her disappointment, he didn't even wince. "Mr. and Mrs. Taggart, this is Daniel Falcon. I believe I have the perfect solution. If I remember correctly, Tyler has an airfield. I can have her there and back in a matter of hours, saving you the drive, and she can work on a laptop during the flight."

"I see," Mrs. Taggart said. "Thank you, Mr. Falcon. May I speak with my daughter, please."

He handed her the phone, making a cutting motion across his throat. She caught back a giggle. "Yes, Mama?"

"He said he'd bring you, but I don't want you in one of those crop dusters," Mrs. Taggart said firmly. "Do you know anything about his plane or his skills as a pilot?"

"No, but I'm sure he's a good pilot." Madelyn wrinkled her nose as Daniel mouthed "the best."

"I don't want you flying at night in a small plane. Can he bring you tomorrow morning?" her mother continued.

She didn't need to ask. "Yes."

"Call with the time, and we'll meet you at the airport."

"Yes, ma'am. Good-bye, Mama, Daddy."

"I don't think your mother likes me," Daniel said when she hung up the phone.

"She doesn't trust you," Madelyn told him.

"She might have been right at one time, but I'll make things right, I promise."

Madelyn shook her head. "No promises."

His face grew harsh. "I wouldn't lie to you."

"I never thought you would." Sighing, she glanced at the phone.

"What's the matter?" He hunkered down in front of her.

"The reprimands and inquisitions aren't over."

"Kane and Matt."

"Exactly," she stated, and reached for the ringing phone. She closed her eyes on discovering both brothers on the line. It wasn't too long before they asked to speak to Daniel. He didn't look too happy when he hung up.

"Well?" she questioned when he didn't say anything.

"If you ever get sick again and I don't call them, there won't be enough left of me to . . . you get the general, gory idea."

"I'm sorry."

"The one who's going to be sorry is Sid. He's going to learn to keep his big mouth shut where you are concerned." Daniel headed for the door.

Madelyn was right behind him. "You don't know where he lives."

"He said two doors down. How difficult can it be?"

Following an irate Daniel out the door, she hoped one of them would listen to reason, but didn't hold out much hope. Sid, despite his easygoing manner, could be just as volatile as Daniel.

Luckily Sid wasn't at home. Unluckily she received three more phone calls from her family during the next hour. Daniel left by seven, saying he'd pick her up at ten the next morning.

When she received the next phone call from Matt shortly after Daniel had left, she informed her brother to spread the word that if they kept calling, she wouldn't be able to come at all because they were keeping her from working. If they were worried about Daniel, he had gone home. The phone calls stopped.

A little after ten that night, Madelyn climbed into bed. Thankfully she had advanced further on working out the specifications for the pipes than she had imagined. By Monday she'd be able to give some important data to Mr. Sampson.

The ringing phone set her teeth on edge. She jerked up the receiver. "This does it. I'm not coming home."

"Give 'em hell," chuckled Daniel.

Grinning, she scooted down in bed, her knees tenting the bedcovers. "They mean well."

"They love you," he told her.

"I love them, too."

"The both of you okay?"

A blossoming warmth unfurled beneath her heart. Smiling at the teddy bear across the room, she laid her hand across her stomach and mouthed, *he's getting closer.* Out loud she said, "Great."

"Then don't fret about tomorrow. Things will work out."

Worry she had tried to ignore crept into her voice. "They've always been so proud of me."

"With every right."

"That might change when I tell them."

"Nonsense. From what I saw at the birthday party and heard tonight, their love is the kind that gets stronger, not weaker, when there's a problem," he told her. "Parents aren't as harsh on us as we are on ourselves. They tend to want to heal rather than hurt. Mine included. Despite their differences, when Dominique and

I were growing up and making mistakes, I think they loved us the most."

"I guess I'll find out. Good night, Daniel."

"I'll be there with you. Good night."

Hanging up the phone, she shut off the light and lay down again, dreading the coming morning and knowing there was nothing she could do about it.

Madelyn's parents were waiting for them Saturday morning at Pounds airport in Tyler. The small Cessna Daniel piloted didn't appear to impress either of them. Grace Taggart pulled her daughter into her arms seconds after she reached her. Bill Taggart stared at mother and daughter, waiting patiently for his turn.

Daniel watched the three closely. There was no doubt that the trio loved and respected each other. It didn't sit well with him that he might have jeopardized their relationship. He didn't doubt that eventually they'd come to forgive, but the forgetting part worried him. Madelyn loved her family, and their love in return was paramount to her happiness.

"Good morning, Mr. Taggart."

"Hello, Mr. Falcon," Mr. Taggart said.

"Please call me Daniel," he said, extending his hand. The grip was firm, the eye contact direct. Here was a man Daniel could respect.

At the twins' birthday party, he had been too concerned with Madelyn to pay much attention to anyone else. He should have realized sooner, three extraordinary adults would have extraordinary parents.

"Mrs. Taggart, nice to meet you again," Daniel acknowledged, turning to the older woman.

"Thank you for bringing our baby home," she said, looking pleasingly plump and pretty in a soft blue cotton skirt and blouse.

Madelyn blushed. Her father chuckled. "Now, Mama, you know she doesn't like to be reminded she's the baby."

"Well, she shouldn't act like one," her mother admonished, her arms still around her daughter's still slim waist.

"I won't again, Mama," Madelyn promised, glancing around for her brothers.

"They're not here," her father said as if reading her mind.

Madelyn sighed her relief. "Thanks, Dad."

Her father stared at Daniel. "They said there wasn't a need."

Daniel accepted the hard gaze of Mr. Taggart. "They were very explicit and thorough in our conversation."

"Good, then I won't have to be," Mr. Taggart said, ignoring Madelyn's shocked expression. "Come on, the car is over here. By the way, what is it you do exactly, Daniel?"

Madelyn groaned. It seemed she was going to be spared the inquisition. Daniel wasn't.

Daniel—who hadn't been grilled by concerned parents since high school—answered the myriad of questions with ease. It wasn't until halfway through their lunch that he understood why. He honestly liked the Taggarts and wanted them to like him.

The reason was sitting across from him, happy and teasing, as he had seen her few times. She rolled her eyes as her father told him about having to hide his tools when she was growing up to keep her from taking the electrical appliances apart.

She was beautiful and alluring. She was also wearing another one of those gauzy, off-the-shoulder dresses she'd worn when he'd first seen her. His mind had no difficulty seeing her again, wet and tempting, her breasts high, her nipples proud and erect, her body lush. Glad he was sitting down, he gulped his tea.

Later, sitting in the comfortable living room, half watching a golf tournament, Daniel saw the many photographs of the Taggart children progressing from infancy into adulthood on the piano, the mantel, the side tables. Scattered among the photographs were pictures of their twin grandchildren and wedding photos of their two sons.

Graduation pictures of Kane, Matt, and Madelyn and their subsequent diplomas were proudly displayed on one wall. Daniel had given his diplomas to his parents as well. During the important events in his and his sister's lives, they had always been together. The family unit was important to children, and he planned to be there for his child.

A blip ran across the bottom of the TV screen, predicting severe storms moving into the area.

Instantly Daniel was alert and on his feet. "May I use your phone?"

"I'll show you," Madelyn said.

In less than five minutes, Daniel had the information he needed. "There's a storm cell moving in from the south—it shouldn't get here for another hour. By that time we could be in Houston."

"Then you think we should leave?"

"At any other time I wouldn't think anything about taking off, but storms can be unpredictable and with you and—" Her startled gaze alerted him they weren't alone.

He turned to see her parents standing in the doorway and explained the situation. "It's up to Madelyn if she wants to leave now or wait it out and go back in the morning."

"Of course you'll wait," Mrs. Taggart said.

"We're leaving," Madelyn said. "Daniel says we'll be back in Houston by then."

"No," her mother protested.

"You're sure?" Daniel's attention centered on Madelyn.

"I'm sure," Madelyn answered without hesitation.

"Is it safe?" Mr. Taggart asked, his eyes direct and probing.

Daniel faced her father. "I wouldn't take off if it wasn't."

The older man nodded. "Come on then, let's get you two to the airport. Every minute probably counts."

"I'll take care of her."

"You better," chorused her parents.

Madelyn watched her parents on the runway until they disappeared from sight. Her mother had looked terrified.

"We can still turn back," Daniel told her.

"I'm not afraid for us." She straightened in her seat. "I'm just sorry she has to worry."

"You have that much confidence in me?" he asked, clearly surprised.

She cut her gaze toward him. "A braggart and a fool you're not."

Daniel laughed. "That leaves room for a lot of other faults."

"I know, but I'm keeping quiet until you land this baby."

The flight and landing were as smooth returning as it had been going. Madelyn called her parents from Daniel's car. They didn't talk long because the predicted storms had reached Tyler, and there was lightning. She didn't want to tell her mother, but an unexpected storm was moving fast into their part of Houston as well. They barely made it inside her apartment before the hard rains hit.

"That's what I call cutting it close," she said, looking out the window at the torrent of wind and rain lashing the cars in the parking lot. "Out-running two storms in a day has to be some kind of record."

"I kind of hoped we wouldn't make the last one," Daniel said.

Jerking her gaze from the parking lot, she saw Daniel coming toward her, a dangerous glint in his coal-black eyes. She swallowed. "W-What are you talking about?"

His hands settled gently on her waist. "I like this dress. It reveals and conceals and tantalizes. You were wearing one similar when we first met."

"It was plastered to me," she said, then flushed with embarrassment in remembrance.

"I remember. You were beautiful. I wanted to take you away and do wicked things to your delicious body. I still do."

Madelyn trembled.

"Do you know, most of the day I've been fantasizing about your being wet and helpless in my arms."

Madelyn gulped.

He reached out one long finger and traced her nipple. The point immediately hardened. His head bent, his teeth gently closed around the turgid point to lave and tug.

Madelyn sagged in his arms, her breathing erratic.

He lifted his head slightly and stared at the results. "On second thought, I may like getting you wet better myself."

Chapter 18

The seductive inference of Daniel's words caused Madelyn's body to shake. She stared into his hot eyes and felt her resistance crumbling, then his mouth closed over her nipple again. She was lost.

All she could do was feel the exquisite sensations sweeping through her, but somehow it wasn't enough. She wanted his hot, knowing mouth on her bare breast. Even as the shock of her thought went through her, he was pulling the wet cloth away and granting her unspoken desire. His mouth closed on her taut nipple.

Her knees buckled. Her back arched. A ragged moan slipped past her lips.

His head lifted. If his eyes were hot before, they were a blazing inferno now. Swiftly he carried her into the bedroom, pausing only long enough to pull back the covers before laying her crossways on the bed, her legs hanging over the side.

Dry-mouthed, she stared up as he removed the band securing his hair and unbuttoned his shirt. Naked from the waist up, his thick hair hanging down his back, he looked like a magnificent warrior, strong enough to bend anyone's will to his. His gaze moved over her in blatant hunger.

Instead of fear Madelyn felt a rush of greedy antici-
pation.

Pleasure, not domination, was his intent. The irrefutable proof of his ability pushed insolently against
his pants. The thought should have sent her rolling from
the bed—instead heat and moisture pooled in her lower
body. Her heart drummed.

Slowly Daniel came down over her, bracing his
hands on either side of her face, holding his body away
from hers. "I've never wanted another woman as much
as I want you. I've never wanted to give as much as I
want to give to you."

As soft as a whisper, his lips touched Madelyn's. Instinctively she opened her mouth to his. He didn't take
her up on her offer, but was seemingly content to nibble
and taste her lips. Restless, she moved under him, wanting and afraid to ask until his lips moved away from her
mouth.

"No." Her arms left her sides and wrapped around
his neck, holding him to her.

"Tell me what you want, Madelyn."

She moistened her lips. "You know."

"I know I want to make a feast of every sweet inch of
you. I know I want your mouth greedy and hot on mine.
I know I want to bury myself deep inside your silken
heat, then do it all over again in a variety of ways, but I
don't know what you want."

Madelyn shivered from need, from his erotic words.
This time when they made love, she wouldn't be able to
tell herself she was swept off her feet. She wanted him,
and she was tired of denying herself.

Tomorrow could take care of itself. She just wasn't
ready to say the words. "How . . . how about all of the
above?"

"That'll do for a start."

She opened her mouth to ask what he meant, but then his mouth closed on hers again, his tongue plunging inside. Figuring she'd find out later, she joined in the blatantly arousing kiss.

Lifting himself away, he grabbed her dress and pulled it over her head, leaving her in only a strapless, ice-blue lacy bra and panties that were just as quickly disposed of. Before she could get nervous, he was kissing her again, drugging her with the ecstasy of his touch.

He began to slide downward, past her breasts, her stomach. The first touch of him *there* set her bucking. His hands beneath her buttocks kept her in place. Shock and pleasure rippled through her—she tried to scoot away, then his tongue flicked. She cried out—not in shame, but in rapture.

Helpless, her hips moved toward him, her hands clutched the sheet. All she could do was moan his name, and soon she could not even do that. When it was over, she lay sprawled on the bed.

"Open your eyes." Daniel's voice sounded strained, gritty. "Open your eyes."

From somewhere she found the strength to comply. His eyes looked like glowing coals. She shivered, then shivered for another reason as he began to slide into her. Unblinking eyes captured hers as he joined them completely.

His moan of intense pleasure heightened hers. Her legs locked around his waist, bringing him deeper, closer. His hips began to move, slowly at first, then with a relentless rhythm she matched effortlessly. This time they reached satisfaction together.

In the aftermath, her body sated and languid, reality came crashing back. Daniel's touch sent her heart racing, her thoughts tumbling, but he had yet to speak of more than erotic, hot sex, and a child between them. He loved her body, but did he love her?

Madelyn was already afraid she knew the painful answer.

She snuggled closer, fighting the agonizing knowledge. He was afraid to love. Loving meant being vulnerable. He'd risk anything except his heart, which he defended with an unshakable iron will.

She could wail against fate for letting her fall in love with a man who considered love a liability, or she could take this time together to build memories. Angling her head up, her lips sought his.

Daniel and Madelyn lay curled up together in her bed. They had made love most of the afternoon and into the night. Earlier they had taken a shower, then fixed a quick meal before tumbling back into bed.

Madelyn was so responsive and giving, he hadn't been able to keep his hands off her. She had been the same with him. The more he made love to her, the more his body wanted.

He loved the way her breasts responded to his mouth, his touch. Interestingly he also just liked looking at them—at her. The restless feeling he had with other women after sex didn't come—he was content to lie there with her in his arms.

"Marry me," he said, not realizing what he was going to say until it slipped out. He tensed, but hearing the words aloud didn't bring the fear and uneasiness he always imagined.

His lips brushed the top of her head. Moving her things to his place would be simple. The teddy bear could go into the baby's room. They'd have a good life—

"No."

Daniel's warm thoughts crashed to a halt with the softly spoken word. Jerking upward, he stared down at her in disbelief. "What did you say?"

"No." She had the nerve to say the word again, this time lifting her small chin for emphasis.

He couldn't believe what he was hearing. "You don't want to marry me?" he asked tightly, knowing anger was no way to get her to change her mind, but unable to help himself.

"I didn't say that," Madelyn replied.

"It sounded like it to me," he yelled, watching her through narrowed eyes as she pulled the sheet over her breasts. He felt an urge to snatch the bedding away. On top of rejecting him, she was hiding her body from him.

"Daniel, there's no reason to yell."

He stared at her. How could she be so calm when she had just blindsided him? She added insult to injury by patting his cheek.

"Come on and get dressed," she told him, climbing out of bed and showing him a tempting picture of the elegant curve of her back and lush buttocks before slipping on her nightshirt he had hurriedly removed an hour ago.

He gritted his teeth. One day he was going to have her naked and keep her that way.

"Daniel, move." She handed him his shirt. "I have to get rested for church early in the morning."

"You're throwing me out?"

She smiled as if she were talking to the simple-minded. "Don't be dramatic. I need my sleep."

He didn't move. "You can't sleep with me?"

"You might snore."

"I don't," he snapped, affronted.

"How would you know?" Not waiting for an answer,

she acted as if he were the simpleminded person again and put his arms into the shirt.

Finished, she handed him his black briefs with one hand and with the other patted back a yawn as if his naked body did nothing for her, while the sight of the narrow line of brown silken flesh between her unbuttoned nightshirt had him hard and throbbing. "I don't snore."

She picked up his pants and shoes and gave them to him. Once again he was the recipient of that smile. "Thank you for being so understanding."

Standing, he pulled on his briefs, pants, then shoved his feet into his shoes. If she didn't want him, he wasn't begging to stay.

"Good night, Daniel."

Brushing past her, he stalked to his car. She had thrown him out. No woman had ever thrown him out. Women had been trying to get him to the altar since he was eighteen, and the first woman he asked threw him out.

His jabbed the key in the ignition hard enough for it to snap, then he snatched it out and stalked back to her apartment. His fist pounded on the door. He was too angry for a doorbell.

Immediately the door opened. Her hands clutching her pink silk nightshirt, she stared up at him with wide eyes. "Why don't you want to marry me?" he asked.

"Because you don't love me." The door closed.

His fist hit the door again. He was through the door before it opened completely. "How can you say that? I'd do anything for you."

"I don't doubt you'd fight the devil to keep me safe, but there's one thing you won't do"—a weary determination came over her face—"give me your heart, totally, completely, with nothing held back. I won't trap you into marriage."

"You're not trapping me—I'm asking," he told her, aware he hadn't reassured her about loving her.

"You didn't want to ask me, Daniel. You were feeling warm and magnanimous after some good sex. You stiffened like a board after asking me." The memory still hurt. She had wanted to kick him out of bed—she had wanted to bawl her eyes out. Instead she had tried to act as if she weren't dying inside.

"The sex was fantastic, and I admit to being thrown a little at first, but I meant it when I asked you to marry me," he railed.

She had learned early when people were the loudest, they were often the most wrong or the most scared. "If I had said yes, you'd be back-peddling as fast as you could by now. As it is, you're upset because I'm refusing you."

"You're wrong."

"Daniel, I don't want to argue." She was tired to the bone and finally resigned to what she had to do. "I think it's best that we don't see each other."

"You can't be serious."

"I am. I'll let you know when the baby is born. You and your parents can visit as often as you want."

Anger flashed in his dark eyes. "You expect me to just walk out and leave you and my baby?"

"You didn't want me or the baby when I first told you," she reminded him.

"I was a cynical fool. I'll always regret not believing you, but the fact remains you're carrying my child. I have a right to be a part of his life before he's born. If I had the skill, I'd deliver our baby with my own hands when the time comes. Since I don't, I'm going to do the next best thing—be there when it happens."

She shivered. "No."

"Yes," he countered, looking dark and menacing, a warrior refusing to be denied.

Madelyn refused to cower. Her chin lifted again. "You don't own me, Daniel."

He stepped closer, bringing with him the heat and hardness of his body. "I don't own you, but you belong to me, just as I belong to you. That irrefutable fact has been between us since we first met, since our first kiss, since I first made love to you."

"I belong to myself," Madelyn said, her arms circling her stomach, glancing away.

"What's the matter?" he asked frantically, his gaze swiftly running over. "Are you sick?"

"I'm just tired."

"What a fool I am," he said, picking her up despite her startled protests and depositing her gently on the couch. "I forgot what a long day you've had. I didn't mean to make it worse."

Slowly, carefully, she clenched her hands in her lap and looked away from his anxious face. "Daniel, I really think we shouldn't see each other for a while."

"Tell me what it is you want me to do or say," he implored, frustration in every word.

"You'll have to figure it out for yourself."

"And if I can't?" he asked.

Biting her lip, she finally looked at him. "Good night, Daniel."

He didn't move. He couldn't. How did he prove to a woman he loved her when he wasn't sure he knew what love was between a man and a woman? He wanted her, needed her—he didn't know about loving her.

Love was infinitely scarier. Loving a person was dangerous. Jeanette, his parents, Dominique, too many friends to count had proved that.

"You've never said you loved me, either," he said, aware he was grabbing at straws.

She gazed at him a long time before saying, "Yes, I have. With every touch, every smile, every gesture, every tear." Her sigh was long and telling. "I loved you when you hurt me more than I thought I could bear, I'll love you until the day I die—but I can't love you enough for the both of us."

His head fell, his hair falling over his shoulders. Despair, like a brutal fist, closed around him. "Why can't you take what I can offer?" he asked in a hushed whisper.

"I deserve more." The answer was as simple as it was complicated.

Madelyn was like no other woman he had met. She was loving and generous and fiercely loyal. She was also independent and a fighter. She could have taken a secure job with her brother; instead she had struck out on her own, using her intelligence and her skills to make her own way in the cutthroat business world.

Her strong work ethic enabled her to accomplish a great deal in a relatively short time. She eagerly sought to achieve more. Motherhood wasn't going to stop her from reaching the top of her field.

Neither would a man called Daniel Falcon.

Pushing to his feet, he stared down at her downcast head. "I don't know how, but I'm going to win you back." Without another word, he opened the door and left.

Desolate, Madelyn curled up against the teddy bear, her cheek pressed against the prickly fur, her arms around the wide middle. She loved Daniel, wanted to marry him. But she wanted more than a "have-to" marriage.

Daniel was still holding back, protecting himself.

Until he could trust her not to betray him, take the risk of being hurt, they'd never have a happy life together. As she'd told him, she couldn't love enough for both of them. She'd grown up seeing how wonderful a marriage could be. Settling for anything less was unthinkable.

Madelyn wanted all or nothing. Untangling herself from the stuffed animal, she went to stand by the open doorway of her bedroom. The silent front door mocked her.

Looked like it was going to be nothing.

Daniel didn't sleep at all Saturday night and he was sure Madelyn hadn't fared any better. She had looked totally dejected when he left. The thought of her crying and upset kept him awake. It had taken every bit of his willpower to wait until morning to return and try to get her to listen to reason. The least she could do was not shut him out while they worked out their problems. There was no sense in them being this miserable.

Daniel pulled into Madelyn's apartment complex with the firm belief she was in bed, bereft and heart-broken. Parking several doors down, he got out and started toward her apartment.

Madelyn's laughter, light and teasing, reached him first, then he saw her as she emerged from her apartment. Dressed in a hot pink linen suit, she looked beautiful and joyously happy. Shocked, he stopped in his tracks. A well-dressed Sid in a light gray tailored suit came out behind her. In a matter of seconds, they were leaving in Sid's car.

Daniel watched until the Lexus disappeared. Only then did he slowly make his way back to his truck. Madelyn wasn't crying and waiting for him, she was going on with her life. He was human enough to admit he wished it hadn't been so easy for her, but man enough to admit he was glad she had the resilience and courage to take control of her life, glad she had friends who cared. But he'd be damned if any other man was going to be her birthing partner when she delivered their child.

Madelyn might have gone on with her life, but Daniel was going to make sure there was a place in it for him. He paused and looked to where he had last seen Sid's car, then concluded silently that making his wish a reality might be the most difficult thing he had ever done.

Daniel was in trouble, and he knew it. Pacing the length of his bedroom long after midnight, he discarded one idea after the other. Three days had passed since he had seen Madelyn and Sid drive away from her apartment.

Of course he'd called. She was coolly polite and continued refusing to see him. Since he didn't want to upset her, he complied. But he wasn't sure how much longer he could take not seeing her. He missed her, worried about her.

His parents had called, and he had given them the good news/bad news. His proposal; her refusal. He hadn't gone into any other details. They were due back Saturday morning. If he was still clueless, he might have to ask his mother for advice.

Even as the idea came to him, he rejected it. Somehow he knew he had to come up with the answer himself. Obtaining help from an outside source would diminish whatever plan he put into action. The usual things that enticed a woman—flowers, candy, expensive gifts or trips—wouldn't work on Madelyn. But what would?

She kept on saying it had to come from his heart. So he was reasonably sure it had to be something just for her, but again what?

He tried to think of what his married friends did and drew a blank. He had made a point of staying away from weddings since he didn't believe ninety percent of them would last ten years. He sent his gift on the happy occasion and his condolences on learning of the divorce.

Staring down at the landscaped, lighted backyard, Daniel tried to think of something. His business was ideas. But at a time when one was the most important, he drew a blank.

The thought went through him like an electrical shock. His body tensed. It couldn't be. Yet he knew it was. He had been running from the idea since their first kiss.

It was important because he loved her.

He loved her: totally, irrevocably.

Daniel went to sleep thinking of Madelyn. He woke up thinking about her. She occupied most of his thoughts during the day. He worried, he wondered, he ached with a loneliness for her that nothing else could appease.

Usually, at this time of year, he was getting ready to begin his documentary on African-American and Native American history and contributions. This time he had assigned someone else to the project. The thought of leaving town and not being near Madelyn if she needed him made him physically ill.

She had become the most important thing in his life.

His parents were acting like lovesick teenagers, his wandering sister was due home soon, his business was flourishing, he had friends, he was in good health—yet he didn't remember ever being so . . . so melancholy and lonely.

Damn! It had to be true. He laughed with the sweet knowledge. "Look out, Madelyn, I'm coming after you. And I know the perfect day."

Chapter 19

"Happy birthday, Madelyn," yelled her family. All of them—her parents, Kane and Victoria and the twins, Matt and Shannon—were crowded in front of her door.

Surprised, pleased, and lonelier than she thought possible, Madelyn couldn't keep the sparkle of tears from her eyes. Her palms covered her mouth and nose. She had felt so sorry for herself lately, she hadn't remembered her birthday.

"I think she thought we forgot," said Kane, holding a huge boxed sheet cake in his hands.

"We've never forgotten one in the past," said her mother, her hands holding a beautiful gold-foil-wrapped package. "Are you going to ask us in, or are we going to have this party in the doorway?"

Stepping aside, Madelyn brushed back tears. Now she wouldn't have to spend a miserable Friday night by herself, thinking and aching for Daniel. It seemed an eternity instead of only six days since she had last seen him.

The twins came barreling through the door dressed in matching jumpers appliqued with apples and ABC's. "Happy birthday, Auntie," Chandler said, a beautiful replica of her mother. "I helped picked out the cake."

Not to be outdone, Kane Jr. said, "Me, too."

"Thank you both." Leaning down, she hugged them both. She thought of holding her own child one day. Her throat tightened.

"I picked out your gift by myself," Victoria said, handing her sister-in-law a box wrapped in lavender-colored paper with a silk orchid on top.

Another box was handed to Madelyn, then another and another until her arms were full. Although she knew tradition forbade her from opening the gifts until after they had dinner at some exclusive restaurant and cut the cake, the outpouring of her family's love caused her throat to constrict just a little more.

"Hurry up and go change," Shannon said, eyeing Madelyn's T-shirt and sweatpants. "I'm starving."

Matt threw his arms around his wife and hugged her to his side. "You always are these days."

Something clicked in Madelyn's brain. "You're pregnant?"

Her sister-in-law beamed. "Isn't it wonderful? We decided to wait and tell you in person."

"You're going to be an aunt again," Matt told her proudly.

Her parents looked at them lovingly. Kane pulled Victoria into his arms. That was how it should be. Her eyes closed in adjunct misery.

"Kitten, what's the matter?" her father asked, coming to her.

Tears flowed down her cheek. "I messed up, Daddy. I let all of you down."

"Kane Jr., Chandler. Why don't you go outside on Aunt Madelyn's patio and ride her stone elephant," asked Kane quietly.

"Me first."

"No, me."

Madelyn swallowed the knot in her throat. She didn't want to see the disappointment in the faces of those she loved. "I'm pregnant."

She expected the broken cry from her mother, the sizzling epithet from her brothers. The tears in the eyes of her father broke the last of her restraint. "I'm sorry. Please, please don't hate me or the baby."

"Oh, my baby," her mother cried, drawing her daughter into her arms. "We could never hate you or the baby."

"I'm going to kill him," Matt growled.

"Not if I get to him first," Kane said.

Madelyn heard the threats and lifted her head from her mother's shoulder. "Please, just stay out of this."

"I warned Daniel, and he didn't listen," Kane said.

"It . . . it was too late then," she confessed, her voice strained and embarrassed.

Her brothers' faces hardened. They turned as one toward the front door. Clearly they weren't going to listen. Dread swept through Madelyn. "Let it go. It's over between us."

"Are you defending him?" asked her father, his voice and gaze cutting.

"Beating up Daniel isn't going to solve anything," she said, dashing away tears. "He's their friend."

"Was," Kane said, opening the door. Matt followed. Their wives threw one sympathetic look at Madelyn and rushed after their husbands.

Madelyn covered her face with her hands. What a mess.

Daniel was in a good mood. Everything was set for his surprise. Whistling, he bounced down the stairs, heading for the garage. The pounding on his front door changed his direction.

The housekeeper reached the door first. In strode a

visibly irate Matt and Kane, their wives ineffectually trying to hold on to their arms.

In an instant Daniel knew. "I take full responsibility."

"You should have listened to me," Kane said, anger in every word he spit out.

"Kane, she cares about him," Victoria told her husband.

"She picked the wrong man to cry over," Matt stated, trying to shake off Shannon's hold without jarring her.

"Crying. What did you do to her?" Daniel asked, closing the distance separating them. "If you upset her, I'll tear you apart."

"Me? You're the one who got her pregnant and dumped her," Kane said, having just as much difficulty untangling Victoria's arms from around his neck as his brother was having with Shannon.

"I didn't dump Madelyn, she dumped me," Daniel said.

"I don't believe you, Daniel," Shannon said, hanging on to Matt's neck. "Madelyn loves you."

"That's why she dumped me," he explained. "She didn't believe I loved her in return."

"Was she right?" Victoria demanded.

"No!" Daniel said. "It just took me a little time to realize it. I was on my way over there now to ask her to marry me again."

Matt stopped struggling with his wife and almost smiled. "Daddy will be glad to see you."

Madelyn's eyes widened on seeing Daniel and her brothers and sisters-in-law enter her apartment. He didn't appear bruised or intimidated. Immediately his dark gaze locked on her. There was something softer, warmer in the way he looked at her.

"You've got some nerve coming here," greeted her father, advancing purposely toward Daniel.

Her father's angry expression caused Madelyn to spring up from the sofa, where she had been sitting with her mother, and place herself in his path. She dreaded doing so because she would have to look into his face again and see the disappointment and pain in his eyes and know she had put it there.

She didn't think it was a coincidence that he was the one to go and check on the twins after her brothers left. He hadn't returned until now. "Daddy, please—this will only make things worse."

With gentle but determined hands, Daniel moved Madelyn out of the way. "Stay out of this before you get hurt."

"Get away from him," her father ordered when Madelyn moved back in front of Daniel.

"Daddy, maybe you should know Daniel asked Madelyn to marry him, and she refused," Kane said.

"What?" Mrs. Taggart said, moving around the sofa to her daughter. "Is this true?"

Madelyn couldn't stand much more of this. She glanced from one to the other. "I know you mean well, but this is my life—and I'm going to live it the way I want."

"They're angry at me, not you." Daniel's fingers entwined with hers. "You can do your worst to me if you want, but leave Madelyn alone. She's been through enough."

"You caused it," her father shouted, his voice as sharp and biting as a whip.

"Yes, I did. I take full responsibility. I'm not proud of the way I behaved, but I'm proud of your daughter and our child she's carrying," Daniel said, tightening his hold on Madelyn's hand when she attempted to pull away. "I made a mistake. I won't make another one. If I can convince Madelyn to marry me, I'll cherish her always."

Her head fell. She bit her lip. "I won't marry you, Daniel."

"You said you would if I could prove to you I loved you," he reminded her, wanting to hold her so badly his arms ached.

Madelyn's head came up, heat flushed her face. No one seemed inclined to leave. "This isn't the time."

"I disagree." He glanced at his watch. "It should be arriving about now."

The doorbell rang. Kane opened the door. A man in a dark brown uniform stood there. "Delivery for Miss Madelyn June Taggart."

"There she is," supplied Shannon, nodding toward an unmoving Madelyn.

"Could you sign this while I start unloading?" he asked.

Kane took the clipboard, since his sister didn't appear inclined to move. "It'll be signed by the time you return."

His hand in hers, Daniel tugged her to the doorway. "I promise you'll like it."

She signed her name, then cautiously took a step forward. The man jumped out of the back of the truck, then reached in to pull out a large white box with a huge red bow on top. She looked at Daniel.

He smiled. "I'll hold it."

Trembling fingers untied the bow and removed the lid. She glanced from Daniel back to the dozens of colorful slips of paper inside. She picked up one, read it, then held it to her erratically beating heart, her gaze on Daniel.

Victoria and Shannon both rushed over, wanting to know what was written on the paper.

Madelyn swallowed before she could whisper an answer. "It's a promise from Daniel to fulfill whatever wish or fantasy I have that's just for me. Anytime, any-place."

Victoria and Shannon glanced at their husbands. They simply folded their arms and smiled. The women grinned.

The deliveryman returned and handed Madelyn a slightly smaller box with a red bow. Opening the top, she pulled back the white tissue paper to reveal a beau-tiful cherry chest.

Her heart rate going crazy, she lifted the lid. On a bed of red velvet lay a ring of keys. Lifting the heavy gold ring, she stared at Daniel.

"They're to all my properties, my safe-deposit boxes—everything I have. If you'll look, I had your initial engraved on all of them." He held up a small key to show her. "Of course your signature will be needed on file in some cases, but a representative can fly out so you won't have to take off work."

Her hand fisted over the keys. Sadness touched her eyes. "It wasn't about money."

"I know that. It's about love and trust." He nodded toward the keys in her hand. "You asked me to give you the heart of the falcon. You have it. Everything that I have—all that I've accumulated over the years—is in your hands. In the bottom of the case is the location and the access codes. All my life I've worked to be the best there was, but I realized nothing meant anything if I couldn't have you."

Pulling a flawless, five-carat pink, heart-shaped diamond from his pocket, he picked up her left hand

and slid the ring on her third finger. "I give you my heart, my love, my life. Please marry me."

A tear slipped past her lashes. For countless moments she gazed at him, then her head lowered. The fingers of her other hand closed over the ring and began slipping it from her hand. Panic assailed him.

"No—wait—please." He rushed out the door. Everyone in the room except Madelyn went to watch Daniel climb inside the delivery truck. Seeing him emerge moments later, they were even more puzzled.

Daniel was slightly winded from his dash. He knew time was running out, and this might be his last chance. More frightened than he had been in his entire life, he prayed every step of the way to Madelyn. He knew she loved him. He just had to find a way for her to know he loved her.

"You don't know how much trouble I had tracking this fellow down. I was so nervous, it took me three tries to win him in Brownsville."

He took a step closer, bringing with him the scruffy teddy bear from the carnival in San Antonio. "Everyone does need love. I was wrong. Don't shut me out. Nothing I have means anything without you."

He racked his brain to come up with something else when she remained unmoved, staring at the stuffed animal. "Madelyn, you have to believe me." Jamming his hand into his pocket, he pulled out the tattered remains of the targets. "I swear it's the same teddy bear—the mate to the one I won for you."

Her head remained bowed.

He looked around desperately as if seeking help from her family members. The sad expressions in Shannon and Victoria's eyes escalated his fear.

"Madelyn, please. I even tracked down Jerome and gave him a job because I knew you wanted to give him another chance." In rising frustration, he shoved his hand through his hair, dislodging the band. "I've resigned from half the boards I'm on so I can stay home with the baby since I know you want to work. Madelyn, I love you. I'll even learn how to cook if you want."

She finally lifted her head. In her teary eyes he saw love and hope and a lifetime shining back at him. With a cry of happiness, she launched herself into his arms . . . where she belonged. "Oh, Daniel, you really do love me. Give me a little time, and I'm going to cook you the best meals you've ever tasted."

"She must love him," Kane quipped.

"He must love her if he's going to eat her cooking," Matt said, not even grunting when his wife elbowed him in his side.

"Kitten?"

Madelyn briefly glanced at her father. "I love him, Daddy."

"I'll be watching," Mr. Taggart promised.

"I wouldn't have it any other way." Daniel smiled down into Madelyn's glowing face. "We can be in Nevada and married in three hours."

"There is not going to be another elopement," Mrs. Taggart said firmly.

"Mrs. Taggart, Madelyn deserves to have the wedding of her dreams, but I think it's more expedient if we are married as soon as possible, then leak the information to the press in a couple of weeks with an earlier date," he explained. "My mother can take care of the arrangements for the second wedding."

Mrs. Taggart humphed. "I have a few suggestions."

Everyone in the room groaned. Daniel didn't know or care why. The most important thing was Madelyn and the baby were going to belong to him and he to them. "Whatever you want—although I've never been to a wedding, I read a couple of books Rhona helped me pick out at Nia's, and I think I have everything planned for this one."

His future mother-in-law sent him a stern look. "I hope you don't think this absolves you."

"No, ma'am. I'm just glad you and Mr. Taggart will come to the wedding and give me another chance." His arm tightened around Madelyn's waist. "The wedding plans I made for tomorrow wouldn't mean very much to her if her family wouldn't be there and happy for her."

Grace Taggart unbent only slightly. "On that we agree. Just to make sure everything is in order, I'd like to go over those plans with you."

Again there was a chorus of groans. "Anything you say," Daniel agreed quickly.

Madelyn smiled up into her future husband's puzzled face. "Remember, you asked for it."

"And thank God I'm going to get it," he said, kissing her with tender restraint and love.

Epilogue

Daniel's plans for their Saturday afternoon began spectacularly. With surprise and delight, Madelyn used one of the keys on her gold ring to open the massive front door of a magnificent ten-thousand-square-foot, six-bedroom, seven-bath home outside Las Vegas. The turn-of-the-century Mexican colonial hacienda with its beautiful grounds on two private acres with lush greenery, koi ponds, tennis courts, swimming pools, and majestic mountain view was the perfect setting for a romantic wedding.

Daniel insisted the wedding be informal and that Madelyn wear the white gauzy sundress she had worn when they first met. Beneath the arched foyer, he had welcomed everyone to their home, but his gaze never left Madelyn's.

The passionate look in his eyes caused her to blush, and her parents to glare at their future son-in-law. But the tender way he placed the plastic-enclosed sundress in her arms, then kissed her lightly on the cheek, had her parents nodding in approval.

Moments later the housekeeper escorted Madelyn upstairs to a spacious suite, overlooking an enclosed garden, where she could dress and relax. Daniel watched until she disappeared, knowing that it was the last time he'd ever unwillingly be separated from her.

While the women fussed over Madelyn and helped her to get ready, Daniel listened to the advice of the men and kept his eyes on the magnificent black wrought-iron staircase for his bride. He couldn't stop smiling.

Somehow he had gotten his parents and their parents, Victoria Taggart's grandparents, Sid, and even Octavia Ralston and Cleve Redmon from Matt's ranch in Jackson Falls to his house for the wedding. Daniel was determined that Madelyn know she was loved and cherished, and enjoy their nuptials. He had checked and rechecked every detail. Interestingly enough, Mrs. Tagg—

His thoughts came to an abrupt halt when he saw Victoria and her daughter, hand in hand, coming down the stairs. They made a beautiful sight. He didn't have to look around to know Kane wore a proud expression on his face. Mother and child. Daniel's chest hurt. He couldn't wait for Madelyn to belong completely to him and to hold his own child.

"Daniel, you have to wait for Madelyn in the gazebo," Victoria instructed with a smile, then turned to Mr. Taggart. "If you'll come with me, Madelyn is waiting for you to escort her."

Mr. Taggart swallowed, placed the glass he was holding on the table, and started from the room. Daniel's voice stopped him. "Thank you."

The older man turned. Daniel's gaze was as steady as his extended hand.

Slowly Mr. Taggart lifted his hand. The handshake was sure and strong. "She'll always be my little girl."

"I know," Daniel said. "That's why I'm thanking you for trusting me to take care of her."

"Come on," Kane said, taking Daniel by the arm as his father started for the stairs again with Victoria and Chandler. "You don't want to keep baby sis waiting, do you?"

Daniel was the first one out the terrace door. He completely missed Kane and Matt's pleased smiles.

The initial sight of Madelyn literally stole Daniel's breath. She had always been beautiful to him, but today she glowed. He didn't know if it was her pregnancy, her happiness, or that in his eyes she could never be less than perfect. He didn't care.

Daniel noticed her glancing around as she slowly came toward him and silently went over his list again. She was carrying the water lilies bridal bouquet; all the women held a single water lily.

From his vantage point he could see the buffet table, the three-tiered wedding cake with small, gold-foil boxes nearby for their guests to take cake home as mementoes. A more lasting memento in the form of a Baccarat crystal heart paperweight was probably being placed in each guests's room at this very moment. He'd even slipped a blue garter to Madelyn while they were on the plane.

Finally she reached his side beneath the flower-draped gazebo. "What's the matter?" he asked anxiously.

"Where's Dominique?"

"Between here and the airport in Vegas, I hope," he said. "I have a helicopter standing by to bring her here as soon as her plane lands from New York."

"Could we please wait for her, Daniel?" Madelyn asked. "I'd like all of our immediate family to be here."

Pleased and unsurprised by her thoughtfulness, Daniel ignored everyone and everything and pulled Madelyn into his arms. "I'd like for her to be here, too.

As long as I don't have to let you out of my sight again, I don't see why not. Today is your day."

"And yours," Madelyn said, smiling up at him, their faces inches apart.

"Oh, no, I'm too late," proclaimed an out of breath female voice from behind them.

Everyone turned toward the sound. More than one might have thought it, but only Sid mumbled, "Goodness gracious."

The woman standing at the back of the small wedding party was absolutely stunning. A glorious mane of jet-black hair framed a sensually exotic face. The hot-pink Versace dress flowed flawlessly over a curvacious body and stopped midthigh to reveal long, sleek legs.

"You didn't miss the wedding, Dominique. Madelyn wanted to wait for you," Daniel told his sister. "Now be a good girl and be quiet while I marry the woman I love."

Instead of doing as he requested, Dominique's gaze flicked from Daniel to Madelyn. "I was thinking of kidnaping you until you came to your senses, but I can see that would take a lifetime."

There were shocked gasps from the Taggart side of the family and groans from the Falcon side.

"Be happy for me," Daniel said.

"I will because I see the same love shining in her eyes. I pray that the Master of Breath will bless your love for all of your lifetimes," Dominique proclaimed, then glanced around. "Hello, Mother, Daddy, and all the grands. Where's my flower?"

The double-ring ceremony proceeded without further interruptions. Madelyn took great pride and pleasure in sliding a heavily carved gold band engraved with their initials onto Daniel's finger. No one was surprised when Grace Taggart and Felicia Falcon began to weep softly during the exchange of vows.

After many toasts were made for their happiness, after dinner and dancing, it was time to toss the bouquet and the garter. The only single adults were Octavia, Dominique, Cleve, and Sid. When Madelyn tossed the bouquet, Dominique just happened to lean down to speak to the twins. The flowers landed at her feet. Chandler picked them up. Sid was watching Dominique, and the garter popped off his forehead. Kane Jr. nabbed that one.

Bidding their guests good night, the newlyweds retired to the guest house, leaving the main house to their still partying guests. As soon as Daniel carried Madelyn across the threshold, he kissed her. They were both breathing hard when he lifted his head.

"Thank you for believing in me," Daniel said fervently, "I won't let you down."

"I know. I love you, Daniel."

"I love you, too." He set her on her feet. "Why don't you get changed. I left something for you to put on in the bathroom."

Madelyn blushed, then laughed. "Did Victoria help you?"

He kissed her on the nose. "Nope, I did this all by myself."

Still smiling, Madelyn went into the bathroom. The smile slowly faded. Tears pricked her eyes as her hand touched the white bathrobe. Somehow she knew it was the same one from his hotel room in San Antonio. The entire day had been reminiscent of their first meeting. He couldn't have expressed his love more eloquently.

Dashing away tears, she quickly undressed and put on the robe. As before, Daniel was waiting for her.

"Daniel." It was the only word she could get past the constriction in her throat.

His large hands tenderly cupped her face. "I envisioned sliding this off you, envisioned making you mine. Even knowing it wasn't possible, I wasn't able to leave the robe behind."

"I'm glad you didn't."

"I love and need you so much."

Her hands palmed his cheeks. "I'm yours, now and forever. Make me yours again."

He needed no further urging. "Now and forever," he murmured just before his lips closed over hers.

A falcon had lost his heart and found his soul mate. He might soar in the clouds, but his mate would always be by his side. Love didn't bind, it freed.

The heart of Daniel Falcon was at peace.

His sister Dominique's was another story.

MORE TO LOVE

From the *New York Times* bestselling author

FRANCIS RAY

When it comes to contemporary romance, no one delivers the goods like Francis Ray. Look for these trade-sized editions of this acclaimed author's sophisticated, sensual, and sizzling novels of modern love…

**Available in trade paperback from
St. Martin's Griffin**

Don't miss this first-ever short-story collection
from *New York Times* bestselling author

FRANCIS RAY

TWICE THE
TEMPTATION

ISBN: 978-0-312-61430-0

Coming in June 2011, in trade paperback,
from St. Martin's Griffin